When Archie Met Rosie

Lynda Renham

About the Author

Lynda Renham is the author of the best-selling psychological thriller *Remember Me*. Lynda is also the author of a number of popular romantic comedy novels including *Croissants and Jam, Coconuts and Wonderbras, Confessions of a Chocoholic, Pink Wellies and Flat Caps, It Had To be You, Rory's Proposal, Fudge Berries and Frogs Knickers, Fifty Shades of Roxie Brown, Phoebe Smith's Private Blog, Perfect Weddings* and *The Dog's Bollocks*.

Lynda Renham

The right of Lynda Renham to be identified as the author of the work has been asserted by her in accordance with the Copyright, Designs and Patents Act 1988.

first edition

Apart from any use permitted under UK copyright law, this publication may only be reproduced, stored, or transmitted, in any form, or by any means, with prior permission in writing of the publishers or, in the case of reprographic production, in accordance with the terms of licences issued by the Copyright Licensing Agency.

All characters in this publication are fictitious and any resemblance to real persons, living or dead, is purely coincidental.

Copyright © Raucous Publishing 2018

www.raucouspublishing.co.uk

Chapter One
Rosie

Don't you just hate those people who win at everything without even trying? A flutter on the horses or a scratch card at the newsagent and they're laughing all the way to the bank. I don't think I've ever laughed all the way to the bank. I've cried maybe, but that's usually on the way back from the bank. I once considered robbing our local Barclays. I did seriously. That's what desperation does to you. I don't often think about robbing banks, just in case you think I do. It was only the once. Times can be hard sometimes, especially when Frank blows all our money on Millwall. The football club, that is, not the town. Not that anyone in their right mind would spend their money on Millwall, the town or the football club, but then I do sometimes wonder if Frank is in his right mind. Anyway, I digress. There's a lot of expense involved in robbing a bank, I discovered. I'm telling you this now, just in case you were thinking of robbing a bank yourself. You need a pair of tights for a start. Not just any old pair either. A decent pair costs you a fiver. Now, I don't know about you, but I can think of better things to spend a fiver on than a pair of nylons, that I'm just going to pull over my face. I did try an old laddered pair, but you could see my features. Not as good as you normally would, admittedly. It resembled a balaclava with one too many holes. Frank said I ought to wear it all the time.

'It's a great improvement,' he'd laughed.

Cheeky bugger.

And then there's the rucksack. You'll need one of those. All the best bank robbers have rucksacks. We have one, but the zip is broken. It would be just my kind of luck to have the newly stolen banknotes scattered through the streets of Essex. The expense of a new rucksack was a bit daunting too, especially as Frank only uses it when he trudges down to the off-licence. It nicely holds a six-pack, he's fond of telling me. It takes a lot of planning, does this bank robbery business. After all, you don't want to be bursting into Barclays brandishing your P'tit Clown 74560 automatic plastic gun at the wrong time of day, do you? Midday would be a perfect time for me because it's when I have my lunch break, but have you seen the queues? There's bound to be one pissed off customer wanting to be a hero, who'd think nothing of wrestling me and my P'tit Clown 74560 plastic gun to the ground, while I'd be yelling, 'Get your hands off my P'tit, you moron.'

I know what you're thinking. I have no idea why it's called P'tit. I imagine, because most of the people who buy it are tits, like me. Let's be honest, how many bank robbers buy their plastic guns from Amazon? Bank robbers like me, that's who. Anyway, last but not least, you need a getaway car. If you saw our old Fiesta you'd understand why it wouldn't have worked. For a start, there's no door on the driver's side. Actually, that's not strictly true. Obviously, there is a door. It would be a touch chilly without one and clearly illegal. It just doesn't open. No one is sure why. Sam offered to replace it with a spare yellow door he had lying around the garage. Our Fiesta's black and I didn't fancy driving around in a lookalike stripy tiger, so I said no and anyway, everyone would have recognised it on the *Crimewatch* reconstruction. It also takes forever to climb over onto the passenger seat. It's okay climbing over when you've got plenty of time. If your pantyhose got caught on the gearstick, you've got time to sort yourself out, haven't you? But when you've got a fleet of police cars after you it's a whole other ball game. I'm okay getting one leg over the gearstick but it's my dodgy hip in the other leg that's the problem. I've been known to get stuck in the Lidl car park before now, my crotch nestling nicely on the gears while some kind passer-by hoists my gammy leg over it. Frank says I only do it to pull the blokes. Huh, like I need another one. Although, I have to admit, it is often men who come to my rescue. I guess women are suspicious of a woman sitting on a gearstick. It's not something you see every day is it? They probably think I'm doing something sordid. I think the men just want a gander up my skirt. They certainly get that. Anyway, the point is, I don't imagine a kind passer-by is going to give me a leg over after I've just robbed Barclays bank, and quite right too.

Anyway, I never did rob the bank. I'm Rose Foster by the way, but everyone calls me Rosie. I like that. It makes me feel young. I live on the Tradmore Estate in Dagenham, Essex. It's quite well known. Ask anyone where it is, and they'll be able to tell you. They'll no doubt look at you with fear in their eyes and advise you to stay away. Tradmore Estate is a regular feature in our local paper. We're quite famous, although I suppose infamous is the correct word. We're well known for our raves and raids, usually in that order. We've been on Jeremy Kyle too. That is, a few of my neighbours have, not us. I really don't have the time to go on Jeremy Kyle. I'd love to live somewhere else, but Frank doesn't believe in mortgages, says they're a noose around your neck. We can't afford to rent a house, so I guess I'll stay on Tradmore Estate until they bring me out feet first. Although, knowing Frank, he'll bury me on the allotment if it means saving some money. It is expensive dying, isn't it? More expensive than living if you ask me. Frank works at the greyhound track in Walthamstow and I work three half days at Waitrose and two evenings at Cineworld in Romford. I like that job. They give us free popcorn on Saturdays. It's rare to get something for nothing these days isn't it?

Anyway, I've seriously digressed. Frank says I can talk the hind legs off a donkey. The reason I began talking about people who easily win things is because, I actually think, any minute now, I'm going to win something. Yes me, Rosie Foster, who never wins anything. I'm desperately wishing I'd had that glass of white wine that Shirl had offered earlier. It would calm my shaking hands. I'm at the Gala Bingo. That's a joke isn't it? After I've just rabbited on about how I don't bet. I only come once a fortnight. It's our girly night out. It's cheap, cheerful and a bit of a laugh. I've never won so much as a quid, until now ... right now. All I need is two fat ladies and number one. I can barely breathe. If I win this ... Oh God, if I win this, it will be five thousand quid. My head spins at the thought. What would I do with five thousand pounds? Apart from pay the back rent of course.

'Twenty-two,' shouts the caller. 'Two little ducks ...'

'Quackety quack,' yells Shirl beside me.

I feel sick. This is all I need. It would be just like me to throw up just as I'm about to shout *house* and win five thousand quid.

'On its own, number one,' shouts the caller.

That's me. Oh bejesus, I'm starting to think robbing the bank might have been easier. I'm likely to have a heart attack if this isn't over soon. I'll be carried out feet first from the Gala Bingo Hall instead of our flat. Oh well, at least the funeral directors will be pleased. There's no stairs at the

Gala Bingo. I hold my breath. I just know that someone is going to call 'house' any minute, and I feel sure it isn't going to be me. I'm Rosie Foster, from the Tradmore Estate. I don't win the bingo. I never win anything, not even a goldfish at the funfair, and everyone wins a goldfish, don't they?

'Eighty-eight ...'

'Two fat lad ...' Shirl begins but she doesn't get to finish because I almost knock her off her stool as I jump up.

'House,' I yell. 'House.'

'I've only gone and won,' I say turning to Shirl.

'You haven't,' she says, straightening up.

I'm shaking so much, I can barely speak.

'Let's see your card darling,' says the caller.

What if I got a number wrong? I wasn't concentrating properly at the start. What if ...?

'Congratulations darling, you've won five thousand pounds.'

'I have?' I stammer.

'Lucky cow,' says Shirl, squeezing my arm.

'Well done,' says Doris, draining her wine glass and struggling not to look jealous.

'I can't believe it,' I say finally. 'I never win anything.'

'Well, you have now.'

'Shall we quit while we're ahead,' suggests Doris.

I nod. I want to go home and tell Frank. Maybe we'll open that bottle of Prosecco that Waitrose gave me last Christmas. After all, five grand is something to celebrate isn't it? Not that I have any intention of telling Frank exactly how much I've won. I'm soft but I'm not that soft. Money burns a hole in Frank's trousers quicker than a firelighter. I'd like it to last us a bit longer than twenty-four hours.

'Shall we go up west on Saturday?' asks Shirl, 'Now that you're flush and all that.'

'I'm saving it,' I say.

Shirl and Doris look at me.

'Saving it for what?'

'I'd like to go to Paris,' I say without thinking.

The fact is, I've always wanted to go to Paris. I fancy climbing up the Eiffel Tower. The view from there must be amazing, I imagine.

'What do ya want to go there for? It stinks by all accounts.'

'That's Venice, you dopey mare,' laughs Doris, zipping up her fake Mulberry. 'Paris is romantic.'

'So, you won't be taking Frank then,' giggles Shirl.

I try Frank's mobile, but it goes to voicemail. He's probably got the tele up loud. You have to in our flat to cover the noise of the neighbour's shouting. If you like Jeremy Kyle, you should come to ours for the day. You'd love it.

We walk home arm in arm. We feel safer like that. I've got my five thousand quid tucked into the corner of my old *Top Shop* tote. The man at the Gala Bingo was reluctant to give me the cash at first.

'It's normally a cheque,' he'd said.

I didn't want a cheque. It would go straight into our bank account and straight out again to pay the overdraft. It was Frank's fault we had that. He'd wanted part ownership in a greyhound. So now, not only do we have an overdraft but also part of a dog. I don't know which part, the useless part probably, knowing our luck.

'We'll get our money back,' Frank had assured me.

But, of course, we hadn't and instead had accumulated interest on our overdraft. I've had this tote bag for donkey's years and I keep checking that there are no rips in it. That's sods law isn't it? You put five thousand quid in your bag thinking it's perfectly safe and don't realise you're dribbling tenners along Romford High Street. I'm not though. I know that, because I keep checking behind me. We arrive at the Tradmore Estate and I try to ignore the used condoms that litter the grass verge outside our block. A policeman hovers outside the main doors but I don't think anything of it. There are always police around the estate. It makes me feel safe to tell you the truth.

He straightens as we approach the doors.

'Mrs Foster?' he asks.

Doris and Shirl look at me anxiously.

'I'm Mrs Foster,' I say.

'What's 'appened?' asks Doris worriedly.

'I've got bad news I'm afraid,' he says removing his hat.

It's got to be bad hasn't it, if they take off their hat? I must have had a tear in my bag after all. They've no doubt been collecting ten-pound notes all over Romford.

'Oh,' I say, glancing into my bag.

'Your husband, Frank Foster, is dead I'm afraid.'

'Dead?' I repeat.

I sway, and Shirl supports me by the arm.

'You could 'ave waited until she was sitting down,' says Doris crossly.

How can Frank be dead? He was watching the tele.

'Sometimes it's best just to say it,' says the policeman.

'Are you sure?' I ask.

Oh dear, that didn't sound good, did it? It's as though I want to be sure he's well and truly brown bread.

'He fell into the road I'm afraid. He'd had a bit too much to drink and the Domino's Pizza van ...'

Frank was killed by a Domino's Pizza van?

'Domino's Pizza?' I repeat.

'He liked pizza,' says Doris.

That's wonderful isn't it? I win five thousand on the bingo and Frank decides to walk in front of a pizza delivery van. Now I'm most likely going to have to spend my winnings on Frank's funeral.

Chapter Two
Alfred

I can hear Moira breathing behind the door. How can I have a decent dump knowing she's there?

'Dad, is everything all right?'

It would be if I could just relieve myself and preferably without her outside the door. A good push and groan would do the trick but she'd no doubt call 999 and have firemen break the door down. It's no good. I need a good push. I try to fight back the groan, but it escapes and then she's banging on the door.

'Dad, Dad, are you okay?' She's verging on hysteria. I can hear it in her voice. All I'm trying to do is go to the loo.

I wish she wouldn't call me Dad. God knows she isn't the fruit of my loins. I'd have handed her over for adoption if she had been. A more self-centred, sour-faced woman I have yet to meet. Heaven knows what my son saw in her.

'Dad, you've not had an accident, have you?'

The truth is she couldn't care less about me. It's her precious bathroom, with its remote control and dual-action flush that she's worried about. I presume, when she says accident, she's alluding to me messing myself. Why does everyone presume that someone of a certain age must always have bowel problems? I'm only seventy-three and nowhere near ready for the knacker's yard yet. My bowel is in excellent condition, thank you very much. Well, apart from a bit of constipation and if you had to eat Moira's la-di-da cooking, you'd be bunged up too. It's all that garlic if you ask me. What I wouldn't do for a good old fry up. Cath used to make brilliant bacon and eggs. There's a definite knack to getting the eggs right and she had it down to a tee.

'Dad, can you open the door?' Moira calls anxiously.

Not while I've got my pants down I can't.

'In a second,' I say.

Can't a man go to the loo in peace? I open the door and Moira rushes in, a clean J-cloth in one hand and a bottle of Domestos in the other. I sometimes wonder if she came out of the womb brandishing a J-cloth. A tin of Pledge probably came with the afterbirth. She looks anxiously around the bathroom until her eyes focus on the slightly askew fluffy white towel. Damn, I keep forgetting they're not to be used.

'I gave you two towels, Dad,' she says, straightening the white fluffy one so it lines up with the others. 'You're not supposed to use these.'

'I keep forgetting,' I say.

Well, I can be forgiven, surely. After all, most people have towels in the bathroom that can be used, don't they?

'I don't know how you can forget,' she says, pouring a gallon of bleach down the loo.

'I'm sure you're not supposed to do that,' I say.

She looks closely at me.

'You're all right, aren't you?'

'Yes, I'm fine.'

'You look a bit pale.'

'I can't help my face.'

'I'll have to wash this now,' she sighs, yanking the fluffy white towel from its ornate brass ring holder. 'Why don't you go downstairs? I'll make a cup of tea.'

It's an order not a request. I fight back the urge to salute her and say instead,

'I can make the tea.'

A look of horror crosses her face.

'No,' she says sharply. 'You take it easy. *Countdown* is on soon.'

She's afraid I'll drop one of her china mugs. I hate *Countdown*. I can't think why she thinks I'd like it. The front door slams and I sigh with relief.

'Hello, only me,' calls Harry.

Moira's tense features relax.

'Harry's home,' she says with a smile.

Harry is my son and I'm temporarily living with him and his wife Moira in their three-bedroom semi in Gidea Park. It's a nice house. Moira likes to tell everyone that they live in the best part of Essex. I lost my wife six months ago and everyone seems to think I can't cope on my own. I'm not sure what they think I'll do. I miss my Cath, but she wouldn't want me to top myself.

'The house is far too big for you now,' Moira keeps telling me.

It's the same size now as it was when Cath and I lived there together. It hasn't grown in proportion since she died, but somehow my family think it has become too big for little old me. They want to put me in a home or as Moira referred to it, a retirement flat. Why would I want to live in a silly little flat when I've got a nice five-bedroom house? Besides, I'm too old to up sticks and move now and I've told them so.

'It's a family house,' Moira keeps saying. 'It's only fair that you sell it now. It's far too big for one person.'

I don't know what's fair about it. I worked blooming hard for that house, why should I hand it over to someone else just because they're younger. Both Cath and I worked hard. I put all the hours God sent into my building business. We went years without a holiday. Cath never complained, not like Moira. I don't see why I should sell my house to a family because it's only fair. If you want it, you've got to earn it, is my motto. I've lived there for fifty years. What Moira really means is, I should hand it over to her and Harry. That's what she's hoping.

'It needs a lot of work,' she's fond of saying.

A double flush and remote bog is what she means, and white fluffy towels all over the show. If she wants a nice five-bedroomed house, then

Harry should pull his socks up and stop fantasising that he's a modern-day Harold Pinter and knuckle down to his job. Everyone keeps climbing over him and getting promotions. He could have had his own accountancy business by now. I don't know what's wrong with my son letting a woman talk to him like Moira does. It's not natural. A man should be boss in his own home.

Harry's an accountant and I made the stupid mistake of letting him handle our finances. I thought I'd save a few bob. Never try and save a few bob, is my advice. Now, of course, he knows everything I'm worth and so does Moira and she's got her beady eyes on it. It wouldn't surprise me if she's already worked out what the inheritance will be after tax and whatnot.

'Hello son,' I say, reaching the bottom of the stairs.

'You okay Dad?'

I wish they'd stop asking me that. Of course I'm not okay. I only lost my wife six months ago.

'Yes, I'm fine.'

'You're early,' says Moira.

It sounds like a reprimand.

'I had a meeting in Ilford. It didn't seem worth going back.'

No, God forbid you may do an extra bit of work.

'He's going to watch *Countdown*,' says Moira following me; the strong aroma of Domestos trailing from her.

I wish she wouldn't talk about me as though I'm not here. As soon as you hit seventy, everyone treats you like you're deaf, blind and stupid. It's insulting.

'I didn't know you liked *Countdown*,' says Harry.

I don't but there's not much point saying anything. He hangs his coat neatly on the middle hook of the coat rack, while the Führer stands by to make sure he does. I watch in disgust, in disgust I tell you, as he removes his shiny shoes, places them neatly on a shelf in the hall cupboard and then pulls out a pair of blue mules. Well, he calls them mules. They're slippers, plain and simple. Slippers, I ask you? If you want my opinion, and of course, you may not, slippers are for wimps. I've never worn a pair of slippers in my life. Our Cath only tried that once. It was one of my Christmas presents. I soon put her straight.

'I'm not wearing slippers,' I told her. 'Real men don't wear slippers.'

'Okay Alf,' she'd said, and she never bought me another pair.

Harry now carefully places his wallet, loose change and iPhone onto the well-polished sideboard.

'Right,' says Moira, letting out a long breath. 'I'll make tea and then I have some paperwork to do.'

She shakes her head and sighs. 'No rest for the wicked.'

Huh. I fight back my scoff. Work, she calls it. Two days a week, she has, what she calls, 'her clients'. I call them 'people who need a kick up the backside'.

'People have issues Dad,' Harry told me. 'It affects their home life and their working week. There are people who struggle to get out of bed some days.'

That's where a good kick up the backside would come in useful if you ask me.

'Moira's a good counsellor, a good Christian counsellor,' he's fond of saying.

Oh yes, did I mention the God thing? I've got nothing against God myself. I just don't want to be mates with him, if you know what I mean? If you want him in your life, that's up to you but I prefer he steers clear of mine, thank you very much. But they're into it; church on a Sunday, Bible readings, sending shoeboxes to here there and everywhere, that kind of thing. And then there's this two days a week counselling job that Moira does. God inspired her apparently. I wish he'd inspire her to be a better daughter-in-law. Still it could be worse I suppose.

'I'll make tea,' says Harry.

'Oh, that would be lovely,' says Moira. 'I'll just pop these into the washing machine.'

She holds up the towels, looks at me and says under her breath, 'He used the white fluffy ones. I have given him his own towels.'

Harry shakes his head in sympathy. Moira thinks I'm deaf. That's why she's always shouting at me. I feigned deafness around her about ten years ago and after that she kept nagging Cath to get me some hearing aids.

'I'll go and watch *Countdown*,' I say, pretending I hadn't heard her comment.

'I'll have two sugars in mine and a couple of digestive biscuits,' I add with a smile.

'Dinner's in an hour and half,' Moira reminds me. It will be too. On the dot, I assure you.

'I'll be hungry then, won't I? You'd better make that four digestives, Harry.'

The lounge smells of leather and Pledge. I hate their leather sofas. They're so uncomfortable. The lounge reminds me of one of those showrooms at the Ideal Home exhibition. Cath and I went once. She wanted to go. I didn't, but I went for her. The showrooms were immaculate. All shiny and clean, just like Harry and Moira's. I reckon Moira copied the style from one of those house and garden magazines. Cath enjoyed the Ideal Home though and we came home with all sorts of strange gadgets. The only one we ever used was the can opener that you fixed to the wall. That was a handy little thing. It lasted us years. We must have been in our twenties then. We'd just had our Harry. He was normal then. I can't fathom what happened but he sure ain't normal now. I blame religion. It turns you funny if you want my opinion, but you probably don't. I mean, look at what religion has done. Take those …

The booming sound of the television breaks into my thoughts. It's too invasive this tele. It's huge too. It sits centre stage in their space-age living room, while the remotes stand like soldiers on the over-polished coffee table. I can't work them out. Cath and I had a normal tele. One remote and that was that, none of that 'catch up' malarkey. Who had the time? I was busy working my backside off to support my wife and son. You probably think I'm a crotchety old bugger and you're probably right. I've just lost my wife. She was only seventy. That was nice of Harry's God wasn't it?

'Need a pen and paper, Dad?' Harry asks.

'Oh, go on then,' I say.

He carefully places the tea mugs onto placemats that have photos printed on them from their skiing holiday in Austria last year. I can't imagine what they cost. Holly's pretty face is covered by a teacup ring but she still looks great. It's a shame she is so spoilt. I want to dip my digestive into the tea. I hope it's not that Earl Grey stuff. That's not blooming tea is it? I keep telling Moira I don't like it. I take the pen and play *Countdown* with my son. I've nothing else to do.

'I'll thrash you,' says Harry.

Life, it's a funny old game isn't it?

Chapter Three
Rosie

'We shouldn't have left that bacon frying,' whispers Doris, fidgeting beside me.

The letter box flap opens, and we duck down behind the couch.

'Your bum's in my face,' complains Doris.

'Hello, Mrs Foster. Are you there?' calls a voice.

'I can't believe I'm doing this,' I whisper.

'You can't believe it?' Doris sighs. 'I've never hidden behind a couch in my life and my knees really aren't up to it.'

It turns out that Frank didn't only owe fifty quid to Freemans catalogue, like he'd told me, but actually owed money to just about everyone in Romford, and now *everyone* wants me to cough up. I've never been so popular. I'm not letting on about my winnings. I've hidden that in a carrier bag under the bed. I know what you're thinking. That's not the safest place when you live on the Tradmore Estate.

As soon as the policeman had donned his hat and driven off in his Panda that night, Doris and Shirl had ushered me up the urine-scented stairs to my flat. They'd made me a hot sweet tea. Doris had said that's the best thing for shock, except I'd run out of normal sugar, so they used icing sugar instead, which was a bit weird. All the same, I drank the hot thick liquid and tried to take in the fact that Frank had gone.

'Will you get a bereavement allowance?' Doris had asked.

I couldn't even cry. I felt sad, but not distraught. The thing is Frank wasn't the love of my life. I don't even know why I married him. Well I do. It was because of Sam. I should have gone on the pill like all my mates had, but I hadn't, and Frank was likeable enough. Not a dreamboat or anything but we can't all have George Clooneys, can we? Anyway, once I got pregnant I didn't have much choice. Frank wasn't a great husband, but you just got on with things. Not like now, where everyone gets divorced at the drop of a hat. So, here I am, just past sixty and widowed. My husband cut down in his prime. Okay, Frank was sixty-five, but he always said he was in his prime. Not the way he'd have wanted to go, mind you, knocked down by a Domino's Pizza van because he was too shit-faced to see it coming. They tell me he wouldn't have felt anything. It was very quick. That's how I want to go. Not knocked down by a Domino's Pizza van, I don't mean, but quick. I don't want to know anything about it. I'd actually rather not even be there when it happens, but we're all in that queue aren't we? I only wish I was a bit nearer the back. I need to organise the funeral today. Not mine, obviously. I mean Frank's funeral. I bought myself a new holdall from the 99p shop so I could carry my five grand around with me. I'm starting to wish I'd taken a cheque now. But that would have meant putting into our bank account and then it would have gone on our, or I should say Frank's, outstanding debts immediately. No, it's best to have the cash, but I'm a woman alone now. Not that I was any safer when Frank was around. He was a bit of a wimp to tell you the truth. I know it's wrong to speak ill of the dead, but if I'm honest, I never had a good word for him when he was alive, so I'm not starting now. Frank won't come back and haunt me. He's too lazy for that.

'He's gone,' says Doris, helping me up from behind the sofa. 'Mind your hip.'

'I need to get an outfit for the funeral,' I say.

I have a vision of the five thousand quid slipping through my fingers. Honestly, Frank always gets my money, even when he's dead.

'You must have something black and dreary,' says Doris, hurrying to the frying bacon.

The only black outfit I have is the cocktail dress I bought for Sam's wedding. It's low cut and sequinned. Not quite the thing for your husband's funeral is it? I don't imagine people will expect me to be all tarted up. Not that there'll be many people there. Maybe I'll wear my black work trousers and buy a new top. I can't really wear my Waitrose blouse can I, although it is quite dark? No, Frank deserves better than that.

'I only have that dress I bought for Sam's wedding,' I say.

Doris wrinkles her nose.

'Mutton dressed as lamb that would be,' she mumbles while spreading HP sauce over our bacon butties. I don't like HP sauce. Frank chucks it over everything, or at least he did. He won't be chucking HP over anything now, will he? I feel a lump form in my throat. It's not for Frank if that's what you're thinking. I just don't know how I'll manage now. Frank didn't bring in much money, I'll grant you, but it was an income that I won't now have. I'll never cover the rent on my Waitrose salary and they won't accept a family-size bag of popcorn, will they? I'll have to ask for more hours at the store. They always have extra shifts going. Honestly, when my mum was my age she was drawing her pension. I don't feel sixty. Well you don't, do you? If I only looked as young as I feel, I'd be laughing. I'm not a bad-looking sixty-year old. I don't have too many wrinkles. Doris has loads. I keep myself nice. I'd like to buy one of those expensive face creams. I thought I might. It was one of the first things I thought of when I won the bingo. How vain was that? I've probably missed the boat, anyway. You can't repair the damage can you, but it would have been nice to try.

The doorbell rings making Doris and me jump.

'Oh no,' I mumble. 'Not again.'

Doris grabs my arm to pull me behind the sofa. She's clearly got the hang of this now. Unfortunately, we forgot to turn the cooker off and the smoke alarm is now shrieking like a banshee.

'Oh my gawd,' cries Doris.

'Mrs Foster? Is everything all right,' calls a voice through the letterbox.

I wade through the blue haze to the front door where a wiry man stands on the threshold. Thick black-rimmed glasses hover on his nose. He looks over them at me. Doris chokes in the background.

'Rose Foster?' he asks in an official voice.

'No, sorry, I can't help you there.'

'Rosie,' calls Doris. 'Pass us a tea towel duck, this pan is boiling hot.'

I sigh.

'I'm from Daniel's debt collection agency,' says the man. 'You owe Ladbrokes seven hundred pounds. How would you prefer to pay?'

'I'd prefer not to pay at all.'

'I can take a cheque.'

'You can,' I say. 'But they'll be nothing on it.'

'So, how do you intend to pay Mrs Foster?'

'I don't suppose you'll accept my body?'

He pushes the glasses further up his nose and frowns.

'I'll pretend I never heard that,' he says.

I watch the glasses slide down again.

'It was a joke,' I say. 'You're not my type.'

'Mrs Foster …'

'Precisely, I'm Mrs Foster. My husband isn't even cold yet.'

I imagine he must be. It's been three days now, but it sounds good doesn't it? 'And you're here demanding money,' I finish.

'I'm sorry for your loss,' he says, attempting a sympathetic expression. 'But debts have to be paid.'

'Oh sod off,' I say, slamming the door in his face.

'I'll be back,' he says, poking his nose through the letter box.

'Get a proper job,' I shout, 'Instead of harassing pensioners.'

What am I saying? I'm not even claiming my pension and the last thing I want to be thought of is as an OAP.

'You need a pit bull,' says Doris clicking the kettle on. 'That'll keep the vultures away. Our Becky's boyfriend's pit bull is having puppies. Shall I save one for you?'

When Archie Met Rosie

'No, thanks all the same Doris. You can't have a dog six floors up.'

'Huh, you've got Maureen Spiker next door.'

'I need another job,' I say.

'At your age?' says Doris, looking surprised.

I'm not that old. Sixty is the new forty isn't it? Well, that's what I'm telling myself anyway.

'But you've already got a job at Waitrose.'

'It's not going to be enough.'

'You can work for our Becky if you like. She's looking for cleaners. Did I tell you she got a contract with the Metropolitan Police to clean up murder scenes? She's got all the materials for clearing up the blood and getting stains out and ...'

'I don't think I should be doing that at my age. You know, cleaning up after a murder.'

Doris nods.

'No, it'll raise your blood pressure. She needs cleaners for normal jobs though. She provides all the cleaning materials. It pays alright as well.'

'Okay, I'll pop round and see her.'

Nothing shameful about cleaning is there? It's a pity I'll have to lug my five grand around with me. Shame about Paris too, that would have been nice.

Chapter Four
Rosie

'I wish I didn't have to do this,' I say, as we stand outside the funeral directors.

'You've got to do it. He can't stay here forever,' says Doris pulling me forward.

I wonder what happens to bodies that no one claims. That's daft isn't it? I'm sure there aren't unclaimed bodies. But what if there were? If I left Frank here, would they dispose of him?

'Come on,' says Doris, pushing me through the door.

It smells lovely inside; all flowery and calm. A smartly dressed man with a neatly trimmed beard seems to float towards us.

'Hello, you must be Mrs Foster,' he says. He speaks so quietly that I can barely hear him.

'Yes,' I say almost in a whisper. Are we afraid of waking the dead?

'I'm Graham,' he says, shaking my hand so slowly that it feels like everything is happening in slow motion. 'I'll be helping to arrange your funeral today.'

That's unfortunate wording isn't it? I've got no intention of arranging my funeral today, or any other day, come to that.

'And you must be?' he says, taking Doris's hand.

'Doris. Doris Smith.'

'My friend,' I say.

'Sorry?'

'My friend,' I say raising my voice.

'Come through,' he smiles.

There's a monotonous organ playing in the background. I'm sure if he turned that down and his voice up, I might be able to hear what he's saying.

'Please accept our sincerest condolences on the passing of your husband Frederick,' he says, pointing to two chairs.

Frederick? Who's Frederick when he's at home?

'Frank,' I correct. 'His name was Frank.'

Oh God, they do have Frank, don't they? I was sure I asked them to bring him here.

'What was that?' asks Doris.

I nudge her in the ribs and we both sit down. Graham looks at some paperwork on his desk.

'Ah yes, of course, Frank Foster. Domino's Pizza van wasn't it?'

Thank goodness. For one awful moment I thought Doris and I would have to spend the day trying to find Frank.

'Yes,' I say.

He nods sympathetically.

'We never know what's going to take us, do we?'

We don't expect it to be a Domino's Pizza van though, do we?

'Would you like a cup of tea, coffee or just a soft drink?' he asks.

'Tea for me,' says Doris. 'Two sugars, please.'

'I'll have tea too,' I say.

He nods and leaves the room.

'Crikey, that music's a bit much,' says Doris. 'I tell you what. It looks a bit pricey here.'

'Do you think they do budget funerals?' I ask, clutching my holdall.

'It won't sound nice you asking that will it? I don't somehow think the word budget is ever spoken here.'

I sigh.

When the police had asked me what funeral home they should take Frank to, I honestly hadn't a clue. So, I'd googled, and this was the first and the nearest. I wasn't thinking about cost then. Everything had been so quick, and I was in shock, both from my winnings and Frank's death. I didn't know if I was coming or going.

Graham returns with a tray of flowery china cups. He lays it on the table and spoons sugar in one cup and hands it to Doris. He says something and for the life of me I don't know what it was. He looks questioningly at us. Doris leans forward her forehead wrinkled in concentration.

'Can you say that again?' she asks.

'Do you already have something planned before we look at arrangements?'

'Oh, erm, not exactly,' I say. 'It was all a bit quick.'

Doris fiddles with her ear and whispers.

'I'm putting me 'earing aids in. God knows what you'll end up agreeing to if I don't.'

There's a high-pitched whistle and Graham glances around the room, a bewildered look on his face.

'Let me get some brochures,' he says.

He returns with a bunch of brochures in one hand and an iPad in the other.

When Archie Met Rosie

'We provide a comprehensive service with everything from the car to the flowers,' he says laying out the brochures.

'Right, erm ...'

'What's your cheapest funeral?' pipes up Doris.

I cringe.

'The cheapest plan do you mean?'

His voice has risen. Maybe cheap plan people don't get the soft voice treatment. I expect the music will be turned off next.

'Yeah,' says Doris, her hearing aid whistling each time she opens her mouth.

'Well ... we have a range of coffins. The cheapest are the cardboard stock,' he says pointing to a picture of a flowered coffin.

'A cardboard box?' questions Doris.

I can't put Frank in a cardboard box. What will people say?

'How many cars will you need?' he asks with a pained expression on his face.

'Oh,' I say, 'can't we drive there ourselves?'

'You and your family may not feel like driving to the funeral. It's a very difficult day.'

'We can always get a cab,' says Doris.

My head spins. This is going to take every penny of my winnings.

'I need to think about it. Is that alright?'

'What did you say?' asks Doris with another whistle.

'I said I need to think about it.'

'Yes, of course,' says Graham, handing me his card. 'We'll take care of Frank in the meantime.'

'Come on,' I say to Doris.

'Oh right, thanks,' says Doris standing up.

I turn at the door as a thought occurs to me.

'If I decide to use someone else ...' I say hesitantly.

'I'm sorry?' he says.

I'm not sure if he didn't hear me or if he was actually sorry I may go to another funeral director.

'If she finds somewhere cheaper,' clarifies Doris, with another whistle.

I groan.

'Can I take Frank out?' I say.

You'd think he was a child at school, wouldn't you?

'Of course,' he says forcing a smile.

'Thank you,' I smile.

Finally we're outside and I take a deep breath.

'I bet they don't give a monkey about old Frank now,' says Doris, whistling for all she's worth as she takes out the hearing aids. 'I hate these sodding things.'

I sigh.

'I don't know what I'm going to do.'

'Brian, who goes down the pub, has got a second-hand hearse. He uses it for his 'man and a van' business. He'll do it for fifty quid, I'm sure. The rest of us can follow in our cars. You don't need all that bowing and scraping at the front, do you? Tesco do nice flowers, we can get them on the day. You just need a vicar to say all the right stuff and you're sorted. You'll need a coffin of course, but there must be cheaper places than this one,' she says, nodding at the door of the funeral parlour. 'You should try eBay. You can get everything on eBay.'

'I can't buy a coffin on eBay. What will people think?'

'What people will know?'

I nod.

'I'll think about it.'

Sam had reminded me that Frank wanted a horse and cart to see him off. I don't know who he thought was going to pay for that. I don't think Freemans catalogue do that on the weekly.

'Do you think a couple of hundred will cover it? Only Frank said he wanted a horse and cart.'

'Did he?' scoffs Doris. 'Good job he won't know he ain't got it. Get one of those cheap coffins. Don't piss about with brass handles and all that malarkey. It's not like it's going to sit in your living room is it?'

'Do you think I should?' I say thoughtfully.

'What?'

'Have the coffin in the living room? Do people still do that?'

'Only the weird ones love. Besides how do you expect to get it up there? It's not going to go in the lift is it? And they'll never get it up six flights. Besides who's going to want to come and look at your dead Frank's face?'

She's quite right, of course. Oh dear, death is a real pain isn't it, especially for those of us still alive.

Chapter Five
Alfred

'They're lovely people, aren't they?'

'Who are?' I say, looking up from the *Daily Mail*.

'Moira and Harry, they're so good, aren't they?'

'They sure are,' I nod, lowering my head back into the newspaper.

'Moira's really helped me,' he persists.

I nod again.

'That's good.'

'I expect she's helped you too, hasn't she? You know, to get over your wife's death. That must have been hard.'

How does he know about Cath's death? I look up at the blond-haired lad in front of me.

'Not really,' I say roughly. 'She won't even let me use the fluffy towels in the bathroom.'

The lad blinks nervously and wrings his hands. I suppose no one has ever said anything bad about his Moira before.

'Oh,' he mumbles. 'Still, they let you live here. That's nice isn't it?'

I look at him. Don't get cross, I tell myself. He's an idiot. He probably can't help it.

'You what?' I say.

'They let you live with them, that's nice. I suppose they don't want you to be alone.'

'She wants my house, that's all she wants. She'd have me in a nursing home as quick as damn it and I'll have you know Cath and I paid the deposit on this house, so I have every right to live here if I want to.'

I don't know what I'm doing talking to this good for nothing. I need my head examined.

'Well, she's helped me anyway. I've got a little part-time job now and ...'

'Blimey, don't overdo it.'

'I'm sorry.'

I push the table back and stand up just as Moira walks in.

'Dad, what are you saying?' she snaps.

'Oh, it's okay. I expect he's upset about his wife,' says Blondie.

'Are you telling all your layabout friends that I just lost my wife?' I bark.

Stupidly I feel tears well up. How dare she discuss my business? Cath and I don't discuss our business with strangers.

'Dad, don't be rude. Luke is one of my clients,' she hisses.

'Don't call me Dad. I'm not your dad, thank goodness. He deserves a medal, he does. How dare you discuss my private life with these people.'

'What does he mean, 'these people'?' asks Blondie.

'Why don't you wait in my consulting room, Luke?' says Moira gently.

Consulting room, my backside. It's nothing but a spare bedroom with two tatty couches in it, and it stinks of lavender. I can't stand that stuff, it gives me a headache.

'Luke is very sensitive, Dad,' she says fiddling with the pearls around her neck.

'So am I, I don't like everyone knowing my business. What a bloody cheek.'

She winces.

'Please don't swear Dad. You know how it affects me. We're Evangelical Christians and ...'

'Oh for God's sake,' I say without thinking. She slaps a hand to her chest and takes a deep breath.

'I know you're suffering from grief and ...'

'I want to go home,' I say.

'Home?' she questions, looking bewildered.

'Yes, I do have one Moira. It is still mine.'

'It's far too big and we don't feel you can cope on your own. We were thinking ...'

'Were you?' I snap.

'We can discuss it tonight. Why don't you make yourself a cup of tea? You know where the everyday mugs are.'

Before I can shoot back a sarcastic reply she has strolled up the stairs to her layabout client. I know what the chat tonight will be about. I'm not stupid. Moira and Harry want my five-bedroom detached house. It's nice. It needs a good clean and a bit of decorating, but that's all. They know I'm not short of a bob or two. Take my advice and never tell your kids what you've got in the bank. They think they're entitled to it. What do I want to go into an old people's home for? I won't know anyone and most likely half of them will be in cloud cuckoo land. No, I'm not doing that. While I can still get myself to the loo and take a shower on my own I'm not going into a home, and Moira can stick that in her pipe and smoke it. I miss my Cath. I miss watching her while she does her knitting. I should wear some of those jumpers she made me. Problem is they're either too tight or too baggy. I do miss her. If only she were still here. She knew how to handle Moira. Cath was always sensitive but firm. I call a spade a spade and that's it. I'm seventy-three. I'm not going to change now. I'll stand my ground. I'll thank them tonight for all they've done, they've done bugger all, and tell them that I am going home. What's the worst that can happen? Moira is probably worried I'll burn her precious inheritance down. I can't picture my house with fluffy towels and dual-action flushes. Give me a good old standard bog. That's all you need. I hear Blondie crying upstairs and sigh. What's happened to the real men, that's what I want to know?

Chapter Six
Moira and Harry

'I'm trying to be really patient with him Harry.'

'I know you are. Let's keep our voices down though.'

'He's having a bath. He won't hear us down here.'

Moira picked up Harry's tie from the table and shook her head in irritation.

'Why is this here?' she asked with a sigh.

'You started talking to me when I came in so …'

'Ties don't live on the kitchen table, Harry.'

Harry picked up the tie and took it into the hall where he carefully laid it over his jacket in the hall cupboard. Moira stirred the bolognese sauce, her hand gripping the wooden spoon so tightly that her knuckles turned white.

'He doesn't need that house. He's just hanging onto it to spite us,' she said angrily.

'Of course he isn't,' sighed Harry.

'You've got to talk to him. He can't live in that house alone.'

Harry took plates from the Welsh dresser. He wasn't feeling too good. There were a lot of colds going around at the office. He'd most likely picked one up. He'd take a cold remedy. He wished Moira wouldn't go on so much about his dad's house. It really wasn't theirs to have, at least not yet anyway. There was nothing wrong with their three-bedroomed semi-detached, but Moira always seemed to want more.

'We can't tell him he has to leave his home,' he said.

Moira glared at him.

'But it is a complete waste for him to live in that huge house on his own. A family could live there. *We could live there.* Think what we could do with that house. It's huge. We could have some lovely barbecues there in the summer and ...'

The kitchen door opened, and Holly strode in. Moira stared in shock. Holly's face was caked in make-up and she was wearing a dress so short that you could see the top of her thighs. Her long brown hair had bright pink streaks in it.

'What's happened to your hair?' asked Harry.

'Will that wash out?' said Moira worriedly.

Holly took a selfie with her iPhone and uploaded it to her Instagram account.

'I'm off out,' she said.

Her phone bleeped, and she tapped at it again, while Moira looked on anxiously.

'Not dressed like that, surely?' she gasped.

'Dressed like what? We're off to Heartlands. It's Phoebe's birthday.'

'But I've made bolognese.'

'I did tell you,' Holly sighed, taking another selfie.

'Harry, do something,' pleaded Moira.

'What exactly do you want me to do?' asked Harry laying out the cutlery.

'She's asking for it, dressed like that.'

'A girl isn't asking for anything just because she wears a short skirt and make-up,' protested Holly. 'Where've you been?'

'Huh,' scoffed Moira. 'You look like a tart.'

'Mum,' squealed Holly.

'Hello Holly, alright?' said Alfred stepping into the kitchen. 'That scent's a bit strong.'

'It's perfume, not scent.'

Alfred nodded.

'Well, whatever it is, it's a bit strong.'

Holly sighed.

'On your phone for a change,' Alfred quipped.

'Harry,' exclaimed Moira. 'For goodness sake, do something.'

'You're not going out like that, are you?' asked Alfred, sitting down.

'Like what?' Holly demanded.

'Like a typical Essex girl. The boys will be asking you how much?'

'For goodness sake,' groaned Moira.

'I'm going,' said Holly. 'Can I have twenty quid? Only I've got no money.'

'I may have twenty in my wallet ...' began Harry.

'Are you insane Harry? She can't go out like that. She's only seventeen,' snapped Moira.

'All my friends are going,' shouted Holly. 'I'll be the only one not there. It's not fair.'

'Why haven't you got twenty quid?' asked Alfred. 'You only borrowed thirty off me yesterday.'

'What? Why did you give her thirty quid?' asked Moira.

'The sauce,' cried Harry.

Moira spun around and watched in horror as the sauce boiled over onto her shiny white hob.

'She lost her purse,' said Alfred.

'Grandad,' pleaded Holly with a pained look on her face. 'I said not to say anything.'

'Where did you lose your purse?' asked Harry.

'If I knew that then it wouldn't be lost would it, dumbass,' she retorted.

'Holly!' Moira exclaimed, while Alfred stifled a snigger.

'She does have a point though,' Alfred said.

'You shouldn't disrespect your father, Holly. Have you picked this behaviour up from your friends?' asked Moira.

Holly responded by putting her hand behind her back and secretly giving her mum the middle finger. Alfred raised his eyebrows.

'Don't be late then,' said Harry, as he handed Holly a twenty-pound note.

'You're not letting her go,' said Moira, surprised.

'If all her friends are going ...'

'For goodness sake,' Moira sighed.

'She's spoilt,' said Alfred.

'All right, Dad,' said Harry.

'I won't get any rest tonight for worrying,' Moira groaned.

'When will dinner be ready?' asked Alfred. 'I'm starving.'

Moira grabbed a pan of spaghetti from the hob and slung the contents into a colander.

'I want you home by ten,' she said firmly.

'You'll be lucky,' Holly said under her breath.

Harry sneezed loudly.

'I hope you haven't got a cold,' said Moira. 'That's the last thing we need.'

Harry fought back a sigh and sat at the table next to his dad.

'Kids,' he said. 'Who'd have them?'

'Too right,' said Alfred.

Harry felt too rough to realise what he meant.

Chapter Seven
Rosie

Some thieving rotter has only gone and nicked my car. Honestly, can you believe it? Of all the posh cars sitting around our estate, they have to choose mine. I'm not even sure if it's insured. I was going to ask Frank about that. He always took care of those things. I don't want to phone the police in case it isn't. I've got enough on my plate. I don't have much left but what I do have the rotters take. How I'm going to cope without the Fiesta, I'll never know. I don't have my bus pass yet. What's the point of getting older when you don't get anything for it? I've got to wait another seven years yet. I'll probably die the day before I'm due to get it. I suppose that's what the government are hoping.

'Alright Grandma?' yells a lad, as he passes me on his bike.

I'd throttle the little monkey if I could get hold of him. Surely I don't look sixty. Maybe I'll get my hair done. Properly that is, at the hairdressers. Maybe I'll have some highlights. After all, I can afford to spend a bit on myself now.

'I'm going to have to get the bus,' I tell Sam. 'Someone's nicked my car.'

'The little rotters. Look, don't go getting buses. I'll come and pick you up. Our Michael can keep an eye on dinner. It's only pie with mash. I'll be ten minutes.'

I pop the mobile back into my holdall and look around. You never know. I may have parked it somewhere different to where I thought I had. I do that sometimes, and that's when I don't have a lot on my plate. Let's face it my plate has been overflowing recently. I've had quite a few shocks and I don't just mean Frank's death. Just about everyone is claiming Frank owed them money. You can take bets on how long my five grand will last. It won't be long before everyone knows I've had a little windfall. Only this morning John, from the off-licence, sought me out in Waitrose. I did consider not going back to work so soon after Frank's death, but I figured staying at home wouldn't bring him back from the dead and it's much better to be with people isn't it? I like my job at the store, especially when I'm on the till. I get to meet all kinds of people that way. They're very good to their staff at our branch and did tell me to take the week off. What am I going to do with a whole week off work? I'd go mad. Mind you, if I'd known John was going to seek me out, I would at least have taken the day off. I know he only came in to see me, because he always does his shopping at Aldi. He's a tight sod, so I knew something must be up for him to be in Waitrose. He only bought a roll and then queued for ages at my till, even though there were others free.

"eard you had a win at the bingo,' he'd said the moment he reached me.

'Is that what people are saying? Liars aren't they?'

'A few thousand, I 'eard.'

'You need to get your hearing checked then. I won ten quid,' I'd said, deliberately scanning his roll twice.

'Two pound forty.'

'How much? They're 50p in Aldi.'

'This isn't Aldi is it?'

He'd fumbled in his jeans pocket and handed over the money.

'Well I 'eard it was a few thousand.'

'Well, you *'eard* wrong.'

'Your Frank owed me eight hundred.'

He'd been lying. Frank had owed him eighty quid. I knew that much because they'd found an IOU in Frank's jacket. It had been made out to John. Frank had obviously been taking it to John the night he was hit by the pizza van. What a pig trying to get eight hundred out of a defenceless old woman.

'He was going to pay me the night he popped his clogs.'

'Is that right?'

'They say you'll be getting something from Domino's too.'

He wasn't wrong there. Domino's had sent over ten large pizzas. Nice ones too. They had attached a lovely note.

We know this won't bring back your husband but we very much hope you enjoy.

They'll do nicely for the little do after the funeral. After all, he was run over by a Domino's Pizza, so it's kind of fitting isn't it? They also included a crate of coke and some garlic bread. You can't complain at that can you? They've already made it clear that I won't get any money from them. Frank was as pissed as a newt when he stepped into the road. He was probably hoping to stop the van for a ham and pineapple. We've got pizza coming out of our ears now. Frank always did like pizza. I'll say they're in memory of him. I won't admit I can't afford the food for the wake. I'll use the coke too. If Frank's cronies think they're going to get free beer, then they'll get a surprise, won't they?

'I'll be around after the funeral,' John had threatened.

'I'll be sure to be out then,' I'd retorted.

So, here I am. Widowed at sixty and sitting on a graffiti-decorated bench on the notorious Tradmore Estate. I look at the inscription on the bench. *In memory of Sid Johnson, Headmaster and long-term resident.* Except now it has been morphed by colourful graffiti to read *Sid Johnson, masturbator and long turd resident*. No respect. It was probably the same little rotters who took my car. Frank always said he wanted a bench with his name on it. I don't know what planet he was on when he said that. He must have thought we were rolling in it; first a horse and cart and then a bench. I'm surprised he didn't want a memorial at Millwall. I could ask if Domino's would name a pizza after him in his memory. It could be called 'Frank's Feast' or 'Frank's for the Memory.' Maybe I could get a job writing slogans. No, what I need is a proper job. Doris's daughter said she'd pay me cash in hand. I told her I didn't want to be cleaning up after murders though. Can you imagine? I'd never sleep at night. I never knew that there were that many murders in our area.

'You'd be surprised,' Becky had said. 'The more murders there are the more work for me.'

I couldn't be that mercenary myself. It occurs to me that maybe Frank was knocked off. He had a few enemies. Although, I don't suppose they'd use a Domino's Pizza van, would they? It attracts too much attention. I feel a hot tear on my cheek and quickly wipe it away. I don't want Sam to see I've been crying. I don't know what I've done with my life. Not really. I've never owned my own home or been abroad apart from a day trip to Calais to visit the hypermarkets. I should have gone to Paris while I was there. I should have done a lot of things. I always wanted to study, but we never had the money. I didn't think I'd still be stuck on the Tradmore Estate when I reached pensionable age. I don't know where I thought I would be, but I didn't think I'd still be here. I should have left Frank when I was younger. I did think about it, but it was difficult with a child. I know I can't blame anyone else for my mistakes. It was my fault for settling. But you do, don't you? You just keep thinking things will get better next year, but of course they never do, and before you know it, twenty years have passed and you're still in the same shit hole. I miss Frank. He was a difficult bugger but at least it had been company. I never realised how much company he was. They say you don't appreciate things until they've gone. It's lonely without someone to talk to in the evenings.

I check the time on my watch. Sam should be here soon. I don't want to sit here for too long. It's getting dark. The last thing I need is to get mugged and if word has got around that I won five thousand then there is bound to be some little rotter that'll chance it. They think nothing of beating up old ladies these days, do they? There I go again. I must stop it with the 'old'.

Sam's car roars around the corner and I sigh with relief.

'It needs a new exhaust,' he explains. He kisses me on the cheek. 'You okay, Mum?'

'Oh yes,' I say. 'Are you okay?'

'I'm alright,' he smiles.

He's good looking is my Sam. I like to think he takes after me. Mind you, Frank was a bit of a looker in his younger days. The booze took all his looks as time went on.

'It's only pie and mash. That's okay isn't it?'

'Lovely.'

'We can watch something on Netflix later if you like?'

'Doris asked me out tonight. There's a new pub opened in town, she thought it would do me good.'

He's relieved, I can tell.

'That'll be nice,' he says.

'You don't think it's too soon?'

'You and Dad weren't exactly Gavin and Stacey, were you? It'll do you good,' he says, tapping me on the knee. 'I'll sort you out a little car. I've got something at the garage.'

Sam owns a garage. It does okay. He'd be doing better if he didn't have to pay that nasty little cow he divorced. Still, I won't bore you with that sob story. I'd blather on all night if you gave me the chance. Frank always said I was a blatherer.

'I'll pay you. I don't want you out of pocket.'

'Don't be daft. Have you told the police?'

I shrug.

'I'm not sure if your dad had it insured.'

He sighs.

'I've just got to stop off and get some baked beans.'

That's how we handle things in our family. We just change the subject.

Chapter Eight
Alfred

Moira strolls into the living room carrying a silver tray. She places it carefully onto the coffee table and nods to Harry. He jumps up to get the holiday photo place mats. There's a decanter of sherry on the tray and three sherry glasses.

I turn my eyes back to the tele. I don't understand what my son is doing with a woman like Moira. I never brought my son up to be posh. Perhaps we had too much money. He didn't want for anything. He had a good education, we made sure of that. I didn't want him fighting tooth and nail for everything like I did. It didn't do me any harm, mind you. I worked hard for what we have. I stepped on a few toes, but you have to in business, don't you? There were times, at the beginning, when we only had newspaper to wipe our bums, but it makes a man of you, if you want my opinion. Not wiping your bum on newspaper, I don't mean, but struggling. Struggling doesn't do you any harm. My Harry isn't a man. He's a doormat. I'm disappointed in him. That's what a university education does for you. Bugger all, if you marry the wrong woman.

Moira raises her eyebrows at Harry and I fight back a sigh. Here we go.

'We thought we'd have a little chat, Dad,' says Harry, carefully pouring sherry into the glasses.

'Well, don't worry about me. You chat away. I'll watch the sport on the tele.'

Moira clicks her tongue in agitation.

'With you, Dad,' she says with a smile.

Two-faced whatsit, pretending she likes me.

'Would you like a sherry Dad?' Harry asks.

Huh, they're plying me with drink now.

'No ta. Have you got any whisky?'

'We've got a bottle of Bell's haven't we Moira?'

'I don't want that rubbish,' I scoff. 'I'll have a G and T.'

Moira flounces from the room and I turn to Harry.

'You don't drink Bell's, do you? That's not a proper whisky.'

Harry fidgets under his starched white collar.

'Maybe sometimes.'

'You want to buy decent malt.'

Moira bounces back into the room carrying another silver tray. I can't think where she keeps them.

'Just a little chat,' says Harry. 'Only I've got my theatre group tonight.'

'That play coming along okay is it?' I ask.

'We have a great cast …' begins Harry.

'Time,' says Moira, pointing to the clock on their mantelpiece. 'You don't want to be late.'

'Right, yes. It's about the future Dad,' says Harry.

'Not much you can do about that, son.'

Stop making it difficult for him, I tell myself. Let him spit it out and then we can all get some peace. I might even be able to watch something decent on this tele of theirs. I might as well put them out of their misery now as later.

'The thing is … well, Moira said you mentioned about going back home …'

'That's my plan.'

Moira nods eagerly at Harry. I look at him expectantly.

'Don't you think that house is a bit big for you now Dad?'

'You never thought it was too big when I was living there with your mother. It's only one less living there now.'

I take a large gulp of the G and T and thump the glass onto the tray.

'It was different when you were both there ...' splutters Harry.

I intimidate him. I should be softer with him. Cath was always telling me.

'You're far too hard on him Alf. He's more sensitive than you,' she would say.

'I'm not going into some residential home and I'm not selling my house either.'

'I'm not suggesting you sell it as such. What we thought was that Moira and I could move in and you could live with us.'

'We need a bigger house,' pipes up Moira.

'What for?'

They look at each other.

'Well, it would be nice to have a detached for a start,' she says. 'We have a lot of things and ...'

'So, you want me to give you my house?'

Harry looks at Moira, his cheeks reddening.

'It's not quite like that it's ...'

'You'll leave it to us anyway,' says Moira bluntly. 'Harry says that if you hand it over now then we won't have to pay the inheritance tax.'

There, she's said it, as bold as brass.

'Oh he did, did he? I say, giving Harry daggers. 'You've got a decent house here. It's got three bedrooms, a dual-flush loo, en suite and heaven knows what else. You've both got cars in the driveway. If you were homeless I might think about it.'

'You'll never keep it clean,' argues Moira. 'What about meals? You'll need to eat and you'll get lonely on your own.'

'If I go into a home I'll have to sell the house to pay for it.'

'That's not true,' Moira snaps. 'You've got plenty in the bank. You could buy a little retirement flat and still keep the house.'

'But you don't have to buy a retirement flat,' adds Harry. 'You could live with us.'

'He's just being difficult,' says Moira, her face reddening

'Keep calm Moira,' warns Harry.

'It's ridiculous,' she says, tears welling up in her eyes. 'He's deliberately making us wait and ...'

'What makes you think you're getting it anyway?' I say standing up.

My dodgy knee gives way and Harry jumps up to support me.

'Alright Dad, don't upset yourself.'

'Six months your mother's been dead and all you've been thinking about is that house. Well, you're not having it. If you want a detached house in Emerson Park, get a mortgage and buy one. That's if you can afford it. You need to get a promotion instead of letting every upstart jump over you for theirs. Show yourself to be a man,' I bark.

I limp to the door and curse my knee.

'I'm off to my bed. I'll go home tomorrow. My home,' I shout. 'Do you hear me, *my home*?'

I slam the door behind me. Kids! Sometimes I wish Cath and I hadn't bothered.

Chapter Nine
Rosie

Palliser's, the new pub, is noisy. They've got a Happy Hour. That's why Doris suggested it. I don't really like pubs. I'm not sure why I agreed to come. I must look a right tit carrying all my gubbins in a holdall. All the other women have sparkly clutch bags but not me, oh no. I have a nice holdall. Some guy at the opposite table keeps giving me funny looks. I hope he doesn't think I'm a terrorist. I must look a bit suspicious. It's a bit rough this pub. I can't help feeling a bit on edge. After all, I've got five thousand in cash on me. I know I keep saying it, but it's a fact isn't it? Well, I say five thousand. It's a bit less now. It's freezing tonight. I need to buy some new bras. Mine have had it. Every time someone opens the doors my tits turn blue. I'll get some tomorrow. Maybe I'll have one of those bra fittings. Although I'm not sure I want some strange woman feeling up my breasts. I know there's nothing sexual about it, but all the same.

'It's not bad 'ere is it?' Doris calls over the music.

'It's for youngsters,' groans Shirl.

'Everything is for youngsters,' I say.

'You're as young as you feel.'

'I haven't felt anything young for some time,' giggles Shirl.

I spot Johnny Crabbers sitting at the bar and cringe. I hope he doesn't see me. He's always fancied me, or at least that's what he's told people. I look terrible. Not that I care what Crabbers thinks of me, or any man come to that. But I don't want them saying, 'that Rosie Foster's let herself go.' I did make an effort and put on a bit of make-up, but I'm in mourning so it didn't seem right to put on too much. Sam said not to be daft.

'Go and enjoy yourself. God knows, you never do.'

I told Sam I'd won some money on the bingo.

'A few hundred,' I'd said.

I don't know why I wasn't truthful. My grandson Michael got a bit excited. I said I'd give him thirty quid. It's important not to spoil them isn't it? Not that I'm ever going to be in a position to do that. The thing is if I let on about the five thousand then it won't be long before everyone knows. I don't want the landlord knowing I'm flush. I'm surprised Doris and Shirl have managed to keep quiet about it.

'Who's getting the next round?' Doris asks, looking at me. 'We've got thirty minutes left of Happy Hour.'

'Oh, I will,' I say, even though I've been nursing a Pernod and orange for the past half an hour.

It feels wrong being here. I should really be at home writing a poem for Frank's funeral. Although, what makes me think I can write a poem, I don't know. I've never written a poem in my life. Sam said he'd read the eulogy. I can't think what he's going to say. Well, not if he speaks the truth anyway. He said he and Michael will carry the coffin in. I feel bad about the horse and cart. I wonder if I can hire one on the cheap from somewhere.

'Rosie Foster, what are you doing 'ere?'

I look up to see Crabbers lolling in front of me. He's rubbed gel in his hair. It looks greasy. He thinks he looks great. He tries to swagger but there are too many people around, so he just looks like he's dying for the loo.

'You're looking nice. Being widowed suits you.'

Crabbers is harmless enough, blind as a bat and with a club foot. It's never held him back though. He runs his own stall at Romford market. I've had some decent towels from him. People say women only go out with him for the free bedspreads and pillow shams. I've never had a bedspread or pillow shams, come to that. I'm sure they look lovely, but I wouldn't go out with Crabbers just to get a free one. Everything has a price is my philosophy. He's not wearing his glasses, so he's talking to me but looking at Doris.

'I'll have you know my old man is still alive and kicking, thank you very much,' says Doris.

'I'm over here,' I say.

'Anyway, that's not a nice thing to say no matter who you're talking to,' says Shirl wrinkling her nose in disgust.

He stinks of aftershave. It reminds me of the cheap air freshener I buy for the loo except the air freshener smells better.

'You and I should get together sometime?' he says, curling his lip, in what I imagine is supposed to be a sexy way.

'Me or her?' says Doris. 'You should wear your glasses. You'll go blind straining your eyes like that.'

He ignores her and turns so he's facing me.

'I got myself a new car,' he says.

'That's funny. I've just had mine nicked. It's not a Fiesta by any chance?'

'Give over,' he laughs, stepping forward and tripping over my holdall and almost landing in Shirl's lap.

'Blimey,' says Shirl. 'Mind where you're falling.'

'What's in there?' he asks, pointing at my holdall.

'All her worldly goods,' laughs Doris.

I pull my purse from the holdall and hand Doris a twenty-pound note.

'I'll have a Pernod and orange,' I say.

She's already had one too many. It will be just like her to open her gobby mouth and tell all about my winnings.

'Make mine a pint,' says Crabbers.

'You can buy your own,' Shirl says, shifting closer to me so Crabbers can't sit down.

'You'll be needing a man around the house,' he says.

'Why? She's never had one before,' says Shirl.

'Frank wasn't that bad,' I say.

'Depends what we're talking about?' he grins.

It's a shame about his hair. He's not bad looking if his hair wasn't so greasy.

'That's disgusting,' says Shirl. 'Saying things like that to a woman who's just lost her husband.'

'Fancy a little spin?' he asks.

He's got to be joking. I must look stupid. He's already had a tankful and can't see further than his nose.

'If I want a roller coaster ride, I'll go to a funfair,' I say, gripping the straps of the holdall. There's a bit of a ruckus at the bar and I'm afraid someone is going to grab it. They'll have to take me too. No way am I handing this over. This is my money and I'm damn well keeping it.

'Not now,' he laughs. 'Another time, you know, like during the day.'

'Let's go,' says Doris, pulling me up. 'There's a bloke at the bar with a knife. Who knows what he'll do with it.'

Slash through my holdall knowing my luck.

'We're too old for this malarkey,' agrees Shirl.

I couldn't agree more, although I'd never admit it.

'I'll see you girls home,' says Crabbers, swaying unsteadily.

'Oh give over, Crabbers,' Shirl says.

I throw back the last of my Pernod and follow them out. I'm relieved to be honest. I thought it would do me good to come out with the girls, but quite honestly, I'd much prefer a quiet night in the flat, although Saturday in the flat is far from quiet.

'Bill will be home from the footie by now,' says Shirl, 'so I ought to get back. I didn't tell him I was going out. I only came because he was at an away game.'

Doris spots our bus and we begin to run. It's as we pass the alley that I see them.

Chapter Ten
Rosie

Her soft whimper reaches my ears.

'Let go, please.'

I stop and peer into the alley. Doris and Shirl have already leapt onto the bus.

'Rosie, what are you doing? Come on, hurry up.'

I don't want to shout back and draw attention to myself.

'Oh, please help me,' calls the young voice.

I step into the alley and see the girl. One of her shoes lies nearby and on closer inspection I can see her breast is hanging out of her low-cut top.

'Are you okay?' I ask timidly.

Stupid question really.

'Piss off,' replies a gruff voice.

'Please,' calls the girl.

'What's going on?' I say venturing further in. Okay, you can call me daft, but I can't leave a young girl at the hands of a drunken yob, can I? It wouldn't be right. Besides, the bus has gone now. Some friends Doris and Shirl are. The man has the girl pushed against the wall. I pull my mobile from my holdall and switch on the torch. The girl's mascara-streaked face stares back at me. The bloke is only trying to push her hand onto his penis.

'You dirty little so and so. Let her go, you filthy paedophile,' I shout.

'You what?' he yells, turning to face me. 'I'm no paedophile.'

'Up to no good though.'

He's an ugly little so and so too.

'You're at least ten years older than her. Paedophile,' I shout again.

I've never seen an erect penis turn flaccid so quickly. Well, I have. Frank's often did but I'm not going to blather on about that.

He rushes past me.

'Old bitch.'

'Hey, less with the old.'

The girl sobs and throws herself into my arms.

'I didn't do anything,' she hiccups. 'I didn't, honest. He said he was going to show me his bike.'

'Is that what he called it?'

She's trembling so much that I can barely hold onto her.

'Where's your coat?'

'I don't have one.'

I'm surprised these girls don't get pneumonia. I thought my tits were suffering. Hers must be getting frostbite.

'Here, have mine,' I say somewhat reluctantly. I lead her out of the alley. To be honest, I'm glad to get out of there and back to where there are street lamps. There's no sign of Doris and Shirl. Just wait until I see them. I'm newly widowed. You'd think they'd have stayed with me, wouldn't you?

'Are you with your mates?' I ask, feeling inside my holdall. You never know. He could have pickpocketed it. No, it's all still there.

'They're in Heartlands. I don't want to go back in there.'

'There's a burger stall over there, let's get you a hot sweet cuppa and then we'll phone your mum. Is she able to come and get you?'

She nods.

'What's your name?'

'Holly. Can you phone my mum?'

'Sure.'

'Two teas, one with lots of sugar please,' I order.

'Hey Rosie girl, 'old up.'

I groan. It's Crabbers.

'What's 'appening?' he asks, staring at Holly.

'Some filthy whatsit tried to have it away with her in the alley.'

He fumbles for his glasses, puts them on and gapes at Holly.

'Blimey, how old are you?'

'Seventeen, but I'm almost eighteen.'

I hand her the hot plastic cup of tea and we walk to a nearby bench.

'Where is he now?' asks Crabbers.

'He legged it,' I say. 'What's your mum's phone number, Holly?'

Holly's face creases and fresh tears stream down her cheeks.

'She'll blame me,' she sobs.

'Of course she won't.'

'To cheer you up,' Crabbers says as he hands each of us a burger. Men have a funny idea of what will cheer you up, haven't they? Nevertheless, Holly wolfs hers down.

'I've had a lot of Prosecco,' she admits.

She hands me her phone.

'Press 1 and it will go straight to my mum.'

I sigh.

'What shall I say?'

'Don't you want your burger?' asks Crabbers, looking hungrily at it.

'You can have it,' I say, handing the burger over. It's most likely a bap full of salmonella anyway.

We're surrounded by teenagers guzzling cider out of cans and frantically puffing away on cigarettes as if their life depended on the next drag. If only they knew what I now know. The wisdom of age and no one wants to listen to you, do they? The phone at the other end rings once and then a high-pitched posh voice attacks my eardrum.

'Holly, what's wrong? Are you on your way home?'

'Hello,' I say, my voice quivering. I've never been so cold. It must be zero degrees and I'm sitting on a bench in a holey bra and skimpy cardigan. I dressed for a night in the pub. I figured my coat would be enough to keep me warm. I didn't for one minute think I'd be handing it over to a half-drunk seventeen-year-old.

'Hello,' I say again. Oh dear, do I sound common? How ridiculous. You can't sound common just saying hello, can you? I can't go putting on my posh phone voice with Crabbers watching me.

'Who's this? Oh heavens, what's happened to Holly?'

'I'm with her now. She's okay, a little shook up. She had a ...'

'Shook up? Oh heavens ... Dad!' She screeches down the phone and I feel sure there is no way my ear avoided being perforated.

'We're coming to get her right now. Put her on please.'

'Your mum wants to speak to you,' I say, handing the phone to Holly.

Holly's face drops. She takes the phone reluctantly. I hope they get here soon. I swear it's colder than the Antarctic. Even my hot flushes are doing nothing to heat me up. I see Crabbers looking at my erect nipples.

'And you can take those glasses off, you dirty bugger. You could at least offer me your jacket. Call yourself a gentleman?'

He drags his eyes away and rips off his jacket.

'Here you go Rosie.'

I wrap the jacket around me gratefully. Even the musty smell of his aftershave does nothing to mar my enjoyment of the warmth coming from it. Holly is trying to talk to her mum but all we can hear are the screams from the other end of the line.

'I am …' begins Holly. 'No, she isn't … I tried … she's lovely … I'm grateful to her. Mum, don't say that … Okay, see you soon.'

She clicks off the phone and turns to Crabbers.

'What's wrong with your foot?'

He looks down at his club foot as if he's never seen it before.

'Oh, it's an 'andicap. I 'ad it when I was born.'

She nods.

'I've got a handicap too. It's called *my mum*.'

I fight back a gasp. My phone trills and I fumble around in the holdall to find it.

'Why have you got such a big bag?' Holly asks.

She's full of questions this one.

'It's me Doris, are you okay? Why didn't you get the bus with us?' she asks.

'Why didn't you wait for me?'

'The bus only runs every half an hour, you know that?'

Oh well, as long as there was a good reason.

'I'm with someone. She was getting molested by some bloke in the alley.'

Doris gasps.

'Oh no, are you okay?'

'He was molesting her, not me. Crabbers is with us. Her mum's on her way.'

'Hang onto your holdall.'

'Don't worry I have every intention of doing so.'

What I wouldn't do to have my little Fiesta. It might have a wonky door, but the heater was A1.

'I'll get us another cuppa,' says Crabbers.

I smile but the truth is, I've already consumed too much liquid and I'm dying for a pee and let's be honest, when you get to sixty, holding it in is something of a mission. I only hope Holly's mum puts her foot down.

Chapter Eleven
Alfred

'His phone must be off,' I say.

The church hall is probably the only place Harry can get a break from Moira.

'Of all the times,' says Moira, swerving around a bus. 'That stupid play, it's taking him over. Why on earth would he turn his phone off? He's most likely got no signal in the church hall. Typical.'

I close my eyes and tense my shoulders. I don't like being in a car with Moira at the best of times but right now it feels like she's on a suicide mission.

'No need to rush,' I say calmly. 'Holly's quite safe.'

'Safe?' she yells, 'What are you talking about Dad? Some maniac almost had her.'

'Well fortunately, he didn't, did he?'

'Did you leave Harry a message?'

'No.'

'Text him then please, Dad.'

'I'm not good with that texting malarkey, Moira.'

She sighs heavily.

'You really must keep up with the times Dad. I hope Holly is alright. Who knows what kind of woman she's with? I feel so guilty. It's Harry's fault, he should have stopped her from going out.'

'Sounds like we've got a lot to be grateful for to this woman,' I say, gripping my seat as Moira narrowly misses a cyclist.

'She'll probably expect money. We don't give her anything Dad.'

'Not even a thank you? That light is red,' I say, pointing ahead.

Moira slams on the brakes and I'm thrown forward. Luckily I don't go through the windscreen. I miss my Cath, but I don't want to be joining her just yet. The light turns green and Moira shoots forward, grinding the gears. We finally arrive, much to my relief, and Moira parks on a double yellow line and leaps from the car before I've even got my seat belt off.

'Come on Dad,' she snaps.

'I've got to get me stick,' I say, reaching into the back of the car.

If there's one thing I hate, it's Romford on a Friday night. It's full of yobs and drunks. Why Harry and Moira let Holly come here is beyond me. If anyone starts on me they'll get a whack around the head with my walking stick. The place is full of scantily dressed giggling girls, swigging cider and taking selfies on their phones. No wonder our Holly got into a pickle, I mean, is it any wonder? Holly looks dead embarrassed to see us.

'Are you alright?' Moira asks anxiously, rushing to her. She roughly pushes past the woman standing beside Holly, knocking a steaming tea cup out of her hand.

'Oy careful,' says the man standing with her.

Moira is so unaware of them, it's embarrassing. I'm only glad she's my daughter-in-law as opposed to my daughter. Cath always wanted a girl but after Harry it never happened. So we just had our Harry.

'Still,' Cath used to say. 'We'll have a daughter-in-law one day. So that will be nice.'

Moira wasn't exactly what we'd envisaged.

'Let me buy you another,' I say to the woman.

She glares at me.

'No thanks,' she says briskly, wiping at her wet clothes. She's huddled up inside an oversized jacket. The bloke with her is almost blue from the cold.

'What on earth are you wearing?' Moira demands of Holly.

'It's the lady's coat,' Holly says, inclining her head. 'I was shaking a lot.'

Moira looks at it in disgust.

'Give it back now.'

I can't stand by and listen to this. This isn't how we brought up our Harry.

'Thank you so much for helping Holly,' I say, stepping forward. The woman pulls her holdall over her shoulder protectively.

'I'm Alfred,' I say, holding out my hand. 'And this is my daughter-in-law, Moira.'

I don't want anyone to think this rude upstart is my own flesh and blood. The woman looks at my hand and then puts hers into it,

'Nice to meet you Archie, I'm Rosie.'

'Alfred,' I correct, but Moira has pushed herself between us.

'Did you report it?' she demands of Rosie with an accusatory tone in her voice.

'Mum,' complains Holly.

'Your daughter ...' begins Rosie.

'She's seventeen. It's not for her to ...'

'Moira,' I warn.

'I'll handle this Dad.'

'I'm not her dad,' I quickly add.

'No, I didn't report it,' says Rosie, ignoring me. 'The little rascal ran off, so it didn't ...'

'Didn't you stop him?' Moira asks the bloke standing next to Rosie.

'I wasn't there,' he says.

'We didn't have to stay with your daughter,' says Rosie calmly but I can see she's trying to control her temper. 'But we'll accept your gratitude.'

Moira scoffs.

'What did I tell you?' she says turning to me.

'Okay, how much do you want?' she demands.

Rosie steps back in shock.

'You what?' she says.

I wince and lean heavily on my stick. I can't believe Moira is insinuating that the woman wants money.

'Let's get Holly home, shall we?' I say.

'It comes to something when people expect to be rewarded for helping someone. How insulting,' Moira scoffs.

'Now hang on a minute,' Rosie retorts with her hands on her hips. 'I'm the one being insulted here. I never asked for your money. Don't try and put your guilt on me, just because you're a bad parent.'

'How dare you,' spits Moira.

'Right,' I say, stepping between them. 'Moira, we're going home. We should be very grateful to Rosie and her chap ...'

'Johnny,' says the man, taking my hand. 'Johnny Crabtree.'

'He's not my chap, Archie,' says Rosie.

'Alfred,' I correct.

'Let's go,' says Moira, taking Holly by the arm.

'Can we offer you a lift home?' I ask.

Moira gives me a filthy look. Well, there's plenty of room in that car of hers. It's the least we can do.

'I really don't think ...' begins Moira.

'That'd be great, won't it Johnny?' says Rosie.

Johnny looks unsure.

'Well ... there's my car ...' he begins.

'You can collect it tomorrow,' I say.

'Yeah, sure I can,' he agrees.

'Thanks Grandad,' says Holly, slipping her arm through mine. Moira makes a huffing sound and strides off along the street. Where's my Harry when you need him, that's what I want to know.

Chapter Twelve
Harry

Eric Ledbetter, who had always considered himself Braintree's answer to Ryan Gosling, now saw his chance to tread the boards. He had as good a chance as anyone, if not better, he'd decided. After all, he'd attended an evening class in drama at the local school, that's more than could be said for most people. Okay, there had only been three of them on the course and one of those had been a bored OAP and the other a young lad on benefits who only came to keep warm on a Wednesday night, but that hadn't deterred Eric. He focused his eyes on a chair at the back of the village hall, took a deep breath and bellowed into the microphone.

'To be, or not to be, that is the question. Whether 'tis nobler in the mind to suffer the arrows and slings of righteous misfortune.'

Harry winced and shot his hand into the air.

'No, no, Eric,' he shouted.

Steph covered her ears as the speakers screeched.

'Too right,' she groaned. 'You're going to perforate me eardrums, mate.'

'It's the slings and arrows of outrageous fortune,' corrected Harry.

'You what?' asked Steph.

Eric stopped in the middle of his flow, his face contorting in confusion.

'That's what I said wasn't it?'

'No, I don't think so,' Harry said, struggling to hide his disgust.

'I'm sure I did,' said Eric indignantly, his apple red cheeks turning an even brighter red.

'I know what I heard,' snapped Harry.

Steph made a clicking noise with her tongue.

'Still it doesn't really matter, does it, Harry?' she said. 'After all, we're not doing Shakespeare, are we? I mean, who'd want to? The thing is we don't have a lot of choice. We need to replace Robin as soon as possible.'

Harry sniffed.

'I don't understand how Robin can have a perforated ulcer when he never even knew he had an ulcer to start with?' complained Harry.

'That's how it happens I suppose.'

Harry sighed, pushed his glasses onto his head and rubbed his eyes.

'You're looking rough, Harry, do you need an aspirin?'

'It's just a cold,' he shivered.

'You need someone to warm you up,' she said with a wink.

Eric shuffled on his feet.

'Do you want me to carry on or what? It was only a little mistake. I thought it sounded okay.'

Harry sighed heavily.

'Well, it wasn't okay. It's slings and arrows of outrageous fortune not arrows and slings of righteous fortune. It's Hamlet, for goodness' sake.'

'It was brill,' said Steph.

'I could kill Robin,' muttered Harry.

'Thanks for auditioning Eric. We'll let you know in a few minutes.'

Eric gave Harry a dirty look and shuffled out of the hall. Steph laid her hand on Harry's knee.

'You don't have to hurry back do you?'

'No,' he said laying his hand on hers.

'Oh,' said Eric, popping his head around the door. Harry quickly pulled away from Steph and ran his hand through his hair. 'I left my jacket.'

Harry sneezed, and Steph passed him a tissue.

'Harry and I were just talking about the part, weren't we Harry?' she said.

Harry nodded.

'We think you'd be great.'

'Wow really?' gasped Eric.

'Yes,' said Harry. He knew it was much too late to find anyone else. It was Eric or nothing.

'I'll see you out,' said Steph. 'I'll give you the script, so you can practise it. The next rehearsal is Wednesday at seven.'

'I'll know it off by heart by then,' said Eric.

Steph locked the church hall doors while Harry was dissolving the aspirin in water. She slid her arms around his waist and then lowered one hand to his crotch.

'Let's give Eric time to get in his car and then let's go back to my place.'

'I've got this awful cold,' he sniffed, feeling himself harden beneath her hand.

'I'll make you feel loads better,' she whispered. Her lips met his and he pushed her against the wall.

'I have to be back by ten. I might have to collect Holly from town.'

'That gives us plenty of time,' she smiled.

Harry pulled his phone from his pocket and turned it to silent. There's nothing more likely to dampen his erection than a phone call from Moira.

'Let's go,' he said.

Chapter Thirteen
Rosie

Frank always said I was as daft as a brush and I'm beginning to think he was right. I was daft tonight, alright. I should have stayed with Doris and Shirl and got on that bus. I'd be sitting at home now, lovely and warm, watching some rubbish on Netflix. Instead I'm accepting a lift from some posh tart's father and all because I don't want to be on my own with Crabbers. I wish Frank were still here. I'm really missing him. You wouldn't believe it would you? It's not like we were madly in love or anything. But he was always there. I kind of miss him telling me what an idiot I've been. I can almost hear him.

What were you thinking of helping out that girl? The bugger might have had a knife. You're daft you are.

He would be quite right of course.

'Mum's got a proper nice car,' Holly says proudly.

She's fully recovered now and no doubt snug as a bug in a rug with my coat wrapped around her. I'd given Crabbers back his jacket and I'm bitterly regretting it. Holly's right. Her mum has got a posh car. It's one of those four by four jobbies. Except right now it's in the process of being clamped. I mean, right now. The guy is in the process of doing it as we approach him.

'What are you doing?' calls Moira. 'You can't do that. I had to rush to my daughter's aid, she was being assaulted.'

'Is that right?' says the guy with a smirk.

'It's true mate,' says Crabbers.

'Yes it is,' says Archie. 'I'm her grandfather. I can vouch for what they're saying. I can't walk far without my stick, so I don't know how we'll get home if you do that. We had to park close by, so I could walk, and we had to get to my granddaughter quickly. It was a bit of an emergency.'

He's alright is Archie, unlike his daughter, or was it daughter-in-law? Yes, probably daughter-in-law. She's not much like him.

'Come on, don't be a dick,' I say to the guy who is still intent on clamping. 'Take it off and let us go home. We're all freezing, and she's had a horrible shock.' I nod towards Holly.

The truth is I don't want to lay out for a cab for me and Crabbers. He might get all sorts of ideas into his head. Anyway, they'll charge double on a Friday night.

'Okay, I'll let you off this once.'

'Thanks mate,' says Crabbers, handing him a fiver.

'What are you doing?' I say snatching it out of his hand.

'I thought ...'

'I don't think it is a good idea you thinking. You'll get us done you will.'

Archie opens the back door and Holly, Crabbers and I climb in. It smells of new leather and fancy perfume. It's warm too, but I still can't stop shivering.

'Thanks so much, Rosie,' Holly says as she hands me my coat. Moira slams the car door with such force that I jump out of my skin.

'I'm really not happy about this, Dad,' she grumbles. 'Will you please try Harry again?'

'Harry's my dad,' Holly explains.

'In a minute Moira,' says Archie. 'There's no urgency now.

'I WhatsApped him,' says Holly.

'You what?' asks Archie.

'Never mind,' smiles Holly.

'Where shall we drop you?' Archie asks craning his neck around to look at us.

Now, put yourself in my shoes. Posh car, posh family, and they're no doubt from the top end of Romford. The mother already thinks I'm the scum of the earth. She probably thinks I'm some kind of bag lady the way I'm strutting around with this holdall. I wonder what they'd think if they knew what was inside it. It would be interesting to see their faces. All the same, the minute I say *Tradmore Estate* I'll be labelled. After all, what decent person lives on the Tradmore Estate? A decent poor person, that's what. I open my mouth to say *Princes Street*, which is at the bottom of our estate, when Crabbers says,

'Tradmore Estate for Rosie, and I can walk from there.'

Great. Thanks a lot Crabbers. There's silence for a moment. Holly turns to look at me and I feel myself shrink in my seat.

'Is that where you live?' she asks. 'I've got mates there.'

'You never told me you had friends that live on Tradmore Estate,' Moira says, not hiding her disapproval.

'Destiny lives there. Number 103b. Do you know her?' Holly asks turning to me.

'Can't say I do.'

'She's all right is Destiny.'

'What a ridiculous name,' Moira snaps. 'Dad can you please try Harry again.'

'Bolton Builders, that's you ain't it?' says Crabbers suddenly. 'I knew you looked familiar. You did my mum's roof. You knocked off a fair bit because we'd just lost our dad.'

Archie smiles.

'Ah yes, I remember that. Bet Crabtree, that's your mum isn't it?

'Good memory,' says Crabbers.

'You can drop us in Princes Street,' I say. 'It's just before.'

I don't want them driving into the estate. Heaven knows what's going down on a Friday night.

'No, we'll drop you at your place,' says Archie. 'It's late. You don't want to be walking home.'

He clearly thinks Crabbers is no knight in shining armour.

'There's no need,' I say. 'Honestly, Princes Street is fine.'

'Don't be daft,' says Archie.

I wish he'd stop arguing with me. It looks like I've little to say in the matter. I know you shouldn't be ashamed of where you live but I am and that's that. If I have one dream, it's to get off the Tradmore Estate.

'I'll drop you here,' Moira says stopping the car some way from the flats.

'For goodness' sake,' says Archie.

This is getting painful. I think Moira has made it very clear I live in a dump. I'd much rather get out now while I still have an ounce of self-respect left. No doubt she's just waiting for Johnny and me to pull out knives and mug her of her four by four.

'Right,' I say, pushing Crabbers. 'Thanks very much.'

'See you Rosie,' Holly says.

'Moira, we can take Rosie to her flat,' says Archie firmly.

It's very nice of him but I do wish he would let up going on about it.

'Dad, I don't think that's ...'

'Right, I'll walk her home myself then,' he says, swinging open the door. I slide out of the car and button up my coat before nodding to Crabbers.

'Thanks Johnny, I'll see you around then?'

'Oh,' he says uncertainly. 'Yeah course. I'll see you at the funeral, won't I?'

'Dad, I don't think you should,' calls Moira. 'It's very rough in these parts and ...'

'I'll be five minutes,' he says, firmly taking my arm.

'She makes me feel like Bruce Willis,' he whispers. 'You lead the way.'

'What about your stick,' Moira shouts.

He ignores her.

'This is very kind of you, but you really don't need to escort me. She's quite right, your daughter, it is a bit rough here.'

'I'm not afraid of anyone, girl,' he smiles. 'Anyway, you rescued our Holly. I'm grateful if no one else seems to be.'

I can feel Moira's eyes stabbing into my back. If looks could kill I'd be on the floor by now. The estate is quiet and I'm grateful for that. I feel stupidly ashamed that I live here, especially at my age. Here I go again. But it's true isn't it? Most decent women of my age live in a nice house on a nice estate, don't they? I'm grateful it's dark. Archie won't be able to see the discarded condoms and syringes.

'Thanks,' I say at the entrance.

'Are you on the ground floor?' asks Archie.

'Sixth floor, but I'm used to it.'

Oh dear. I hope he doesn't offer to walk me up. Moira will have my guts for garters if he has a heart attack on the way.

'Can you see your flat from here?' he asks looking up. 'You can wave from the window. I'll know you're home safe then.'

'Your daughter will be waiting.'

'Daughter-in-law,' he corrects. 'And she can wait.'

She'll have to wait an awful long time too. It takes me a while to get up those stairs now with this dodgy hip of mine.

'Right,' I say.

I desperately want to go to the loo. I swear I don't know how I've held it back for so long. Now I've got to hold it back a bit longer, so I can wave from the window. My bladder will burst. It's going to be freezing in the flat too. I can't afford to leave the heating on when I'm not here and it will take forever to warm up. I hurry up the stairs as quickly as I can, my hip not thanking me in the least for this overexertion. My toes are numb from the cold. I can't make him wait too long. He must be seventy years old if he's a day. The last thing I need is for him to be mugged. Moira would never forgive me. I push my key into the lock and hurry to the window to wave to Archie. He waves back, and I watch him limp back to the car. How silly is this? I only want to rush back downstairs and escort him back to Moira. Life's mad isn't it?

Chapter Fourteen
Alfred

'Here we are,' says Harry, before sneezing loudly.

'Do cover your mouth, Harry,' says Moira distastefully. 'We don't all want to catch it.'

The car tyres scrunch on the gravel. I look up at my house and feel a small pang of loneliness. The front door remains closed and no matter how much I will it, Cath doesn't open the door to welcome us. I can't think of a single time when I've pulled up on the driveway and she hasn't run out to greet me. It's going to be a miserable Christmas without her. My Peugeot 205 sits in the driveway. It needs a good clean.

'I'll get your case,' says Harry.

Moira, meanwhile, strides to the door and waits while I hobble behind her. My arthritic knee is playing up something chronic in this cold weather. I'll be glad to take my pills. I hadn't liked to mention I'd forgotten them. I didn't want Moira going on about something else. I push the key into the lock and the door swings open. A foul odour hits us. I pretend to ignore it. Harry with his cold, mercifully, can't smell anything. Moira wrinkles her nose.

'What's that terrible smell?' she grimaces.

'I can't smell anything,' I say.

'It's freezing in here. Didn't you leave the heating on?'

'No,' I snap. 'I'm not throwing money away.'

Moira sniffs the air. At that moment Cleo, the cat, rushes towards us, meowing for all she's worth. Harry almost trips over her as she runs under his feet. Moira is quite right though. It is freezing in here. I really should have left the heating on.

Lynda Renham

'Just leave the case in the hall,' I say. 'I'll sort it later.'

'Is your bed made?' Moira asks running a finger along the sideboard. She'd never have done that if our Cath was here. There was never a speck of dust when my Cath was alive.

'It'll be fine,' I say.

'I'll put the heating on,' says Harry, shivering.

'You need a Beechams,' I tell him.

The kitchen's a mess. I'll grant you that.

'Oh my goodness,' says Moira peeking in.

Molly from next door has been feeding Cleo. It was very kind of her. She's not all the ticket, is Molly. She's lovely and everything but she's one of those bohemian types, head in the clouds and all that. She does palm readings. Cath tried to get me to have mine read. She'd go to Molly's regularly to get hers done. It's all a load of rubbish if you ask me. How can you read someone's future from looking at their hand? Still, it was lovely of her to feed Cleo. It's just a shame she put the empty tins in the kitchen bin instead of the dustbin outside. The room stinks of gone off *Sheba*. Cleo wanders under Moira's feet and she utters a curse, Moira that is, not Cleo the cat. The sink is full of the dirty dishes I'd left. I'm not sure why I'm surprised to see them. Molly barely washes up her own stuff, so it was pretty clear she wasn't going to do mine.

'I'll put the kettle on and empty these bins,' sniffs Harry.

'We're not having a cup of tea, Harry, until I've done something with this kitchen,' says Moira. 'It stinks in here.'

'It's not that bad,' I say, sitting at the kitchen table.

'We'll never get this smell out,' she complains.

Harry sniffs again.

'I can't smell anything,' he says.

God bless colds.

When Archie Met Rosie

'Check the bedroom,' instructs Moira. 'I'll make a start on the kitchen.'

'I'd rather you didn't,' I say.

I don't want her fiddling around in Cath's kitchen. Come to that, I don't want her fiddling about in any part of the house.

'At least let me wash up. Why you haven't got a dishwasher, I'll never know. I was always telling Cath ...'

'Please leave it,' I say sharply, but she ignores me and begins to clear away the sympathy cards that sit on the kitchen dresser.

'For pity's sake, just leave my things alone, will you?' I bark.

I'm harsher than I mean to be and when I see tears well up in her eyes, I feel suddenly guilty. But it is my home, damn it. I just wish she'd respect that.

'We should leave,' says Harry.

He's angry with me, I can tell. Moira rushes from the kitchen. Harry looks at me, blows his nose viciously on a tissue and says, 'you can be a bit sharp sometimes.'

I nod.

'Yes, sorry but she does push it.'

'We'll get a cleaner for you. I think that's probably the best thing.'

'It probably is,' I agree.

He looks at the photos on the dresser, blows his nose again, and turns to leave.

'You know where we are if you need anything. I'll pop in at the end of the week.'

'I'll be alright,' I say. 'Holly showed me how to do internet shopping.'

He nods and turns to leave. I wait until I hear the car scrunch on the driveway and then fill the kettle. It's good to be home where a loo is a loo and the towels are there to be used.

Chapter Fifteen
Rosie

Domino's said they don't name pizzas after people, not even if they killed them. I thought that was a bit unreasonable and told them so.

'If you hadn't knocked him down with your pizza van I wouldn't need to be asking for a pizza to be named after him, would I?'

They couldn't really argue with that and offered me three more pizzas and five hundred pounds. I had to accept, didn't I?

'Are you ready?' Sam calls.

I check my hair one last time and reluctantly follow Sam out. We're leaving for the funeral from Sam's house. I didn't want to leave from the Tradmore Estate with all those gaping eyes and twitching net curtains. Brian stands by the hearse, smoking a Marlborough Light. He quickly stubs it out at the sight of me.

'Alright then Rosie? A sad day,' he says nodding solemnly.

'Yes,' I say, glancing at the battered hearse.

It's only a dent in the side, but you just don't see dents in hearses, do you?

'You want me to walk in front for a bit?' he asks.

I shake my head. I don't think Brian walking in front of the hearse puffing on a Marlborough Light is quite what people expect to see.

'Take it slowly though,' says Sam ushering a tearful Michael into the car.

I don't think Michael is crying for his grandad. He hardly had anything to do with him. It's the coffin that sets you off, isn't it? I'd got some flowers from Marks in the end. They're better quality aren't they, and likely to last a bit longer. I sit in the back with Michael and Sam gets in the front with Brian. Michael puts his hand on my knee.

'Are you alright Nan?'

'Yes I'm fine.'

Doris and Bert follow behind in their car with Shirl and Bill. I stare through the window at the coffin. I can't believe Frank's in there. Well, I hope it's Frank. You can't really be sure, can you? I certainly wasn't going to go checking. It seems to take forever to get to the crematorium. I have visions of the hearse breaking down. Can you imagine that, everyone getting out and pushing the hearse into the crematorium? That would be a first wouldn't it? We finally get there, and I let out a sigh of relief.

As I watch Frank's coffin being carried in, I can't help feeling that I've let him down. I'd got a cardboard coffin in the end. It's nice enough. It has poppies around the bottom. A few people asked if it was because he'd been in the forces. I had to laugh. Frank didn't get out of bed until eleven. I can't imagine the army contending with that, can you? It was hard choosing the right coffin. I did ask about a Millwall one, but it cost a lot more to have it personalised. As it was, the poppy one was over four hundred pounds. I ask you, four hundred quid for a cardboard box. I can't imagine what a horse and cart would have cost. I did look on eBay as Doris had suggested, but it seemed all wrong somehow. They did have cheap coffins. I just wasn't sure how they would deliver it. It's not the sort of thing you want left outside your door if you're not in when they deliver. How can people afford to die these days? The cost of living is bad enough. You'd think the government would make dying more affordable, wouldn't you?

Several of Frank's mates are standing outside the crematorium smoking roll-ups. I pat down my new skirt and with Sam beside me, follow the coffin in. I'd bought a new top and skirt from Primark. I've still got £4,800 left from my win. I'd had to transfer it from the holdall to a little black clutch that Doris had lent me for the funeral. It barely closes with all the notes inside it. I'd rolled them up and secured them in an elastic band but still the damn thing wouldn't shut. I had to squeeze it with all my might to get the clip to catch. The thing is bursting and the only other things in it are a comb and tissues. Doris waves from her seat at the front and dabs at her eyes. Doris always weeps at funerals. Doesn't matter whose funeral it is. Often, she won't even know the person. Shirl smiles encouragingly.

The funeral was cheaper than I thought it would be. Sam had paid half. He's a good sort, my Sam. He isn't a bit like his dad, thank goodness. That and Domino's Pizza's five hundred softened the blow considerably. There are more people here than I imagined there would be. They're probably hoping for a free booze-up later. They'll get a surprise. It'll be pizza and coke.

I still can't believe Frank's gone. It's harder to come to terms with a loss when it's sudden isn't it? The service is lovely though. Frank couldn't have asked for better. I didn't know what music to suggest and eventually chose the Millwall anthem for when they bring in the coffin. It's a bit dramatic and takes everyone by surprise but I think Frank would have liked it. He wasn't big on music. He always said classical music was for toffs. I quite like it myself and chose a piece from Mozart's requiem for the committal. Frank's mates don't know what to make of it all. I'd chosen a poem by Keats too. Well, you've got to have some culture, haven't you? I sniff and Michael hands me a tissue. I don't like to tell him it's a flower allergy.

'Thanks Mike.'

He puts my arm through his.

'It's okay Nan,' he whispers.

I do want to cry for Frank, but nothing seems forthcoming. Doris is looking earnestly at me and nodding her head to the other side of the church. I follow her nod and see a blonde woman with over-backcombed hair sobbing into a tissue. She's wearing a fancy black fur stole over her shoulders. I don't recognise her at all. I look back at Doris and shrug my shoulders, but my stomach does a little somersault. If that little sod was having it away with some backcombed dolly bird, then I'll … Well, I can't kill him, can I? He's already dead. Her shoulders shake with her sobs.

'Who's that?' Sam asks.

'I don't know,' I say honestly.

But whoever it is, she's sobbing for England.

The coffin disappears through the curtain and she sobs even more. She's beginning to get on my tits now. The service ends and I'm relieved to get outside.

'He was a good bloke,' says his mate Billy. 'Heart of gold. You were a lucky woman.'

'Nice words your Sam said,' says Pete.

I can't take my eyes off the blonde. Her mascara-streaked eyes meet mine and she hurriedly turns away. I don't believe it. What a two-timing little sod. Here am I spending a fortune on his funeral. Okay, so it wasn't a fortune, but it could have been if I had forked out for a horse and cart. Huh, I should have thrown him on a pyre and saved myself even more money. I don't believe it. Well, I do, if I'm being honest. All those late nights when he was supposedly having a pint with the boys, and to think I believed him. I can see now that the so-called boys knew all about it too. They're all looking shamefaced. Am I glad I didn't get booze for the little toerags?

'Shall we look at the flowers?' Sam asks.

'You go on ahead. I'm just going to talk to some of your dad's mates.'

'Back to yours is it?' asks Billy. 'Laid on a spread, have you?'

'Oh yes,' I smile.

'That was a nice service,' says Crabbers.

'Thanks,' I say.

At least he's wearing his glasses. I'd hate him to give his condolences to the wrong woman.

'Got home okay then on Friday night?'

'Yes, Archie walked me to the flats.'

'That was good of him.'

I look past him to the blonde woman. He follows my gaze.

'Do you know her?' I ask Crabbers.

'No, she doesn't look familiar to me.'

Doris takes my arm.

'Don't do anything stupid,' she whispers.

'He was having it away with some tart,' I say angrily.

'Well he's gone now.'

'That doesn't make it better Doris. I wonder how much money he spent on her.'

'You don't think …' begins Crabbers.

From the look of the fur around her shoulders I imagine Frank spent a fair bit.

I march over to her. Her tear-filled eyes widen in horror.

'Thanks for coming,' I say coldly.

'Oh … I …' she stammers.

'Knew our Frank intimately, did you?'

My eyes lock onto her tear-filled ones. She's more distressed than I am.

'We knew each other from the dogs. We were friends.'

'Yeah, I can believe he met you at the dogs,' I say scathingly.

'I …'

'How dare you come to the funeral? Do you think I'm stupid?'

She dabs at her eyes.

'He would have wanted me here.'

'Well I don't so you can bugger off.'

I turn on my heel and collide with Doris.

'Don't show yourself up,' she says.

'Huh,' I scoff. 'There was me feeling guilty that I'd put him in a cardboard box.'

'Still it was lovely.'

'He didn't damn well deserve it.'

'Still, you don't have to get a headstone.'

'Doris, you're not helping.'

'Sorry.'

Shirl joins us, grabs me by the arm and says,

'What a pig. She must be thirty-five if that.'

That's what hurts. I suddenly feel very old. That's me finished with men. They're nothing but trouble and heartache. Frank didn't even have life insurance. That's consideration for you.

Sam puts an arm around my shoulder.

'Who is that?' he asks, following my eyes to the blonde woman who is now tearfully making her way to the gates.

'Oh some trollop your dad used to chat to in the pub.'

'She's very upset.'

'Crocodile tears. He spent a lot of money in the pub. Let's get home and tuck into those pizzas. Your dad would have approved.'

As if I give a toss what Frank did or didn't approve of, the shagging little so and so. I don't feel guilty about the horse and cart now. No not in the least.

Chapter Sixteen
Rosie

I wasn't going to do murders. That's what I said wasn't it? I don't mean I wasn't going to murder people. Although I could quite easily murder my Frank if he wasn't already dead. I can't believe he was getting his leg over with some peroxide bimbo. It has been on my mind for days. I barely ate any of the pizza at Frank's wake. Mind you, they went so quickly I don't imagine I would have got much of a look in, anyway.

'Do you think you should have some tests?' Doris had asked.

'What kind of tests?'

'You know, for sexually transmitted diseases.'

I'd fallen into my chair.

'I can't go to the doctors at my age and ask to be tested for that kind of thing. They'll wonder what I've been up to.'

'You just tell them,' said Shirl.

'What? Tell the doctor my dead husband had been dipping his wick? I can't do that.'

'You don't know what she had,' said Doris soberly.

'You could go to one of those sex clinics. At least they wouldn't know you there.'

'You did do it with Frank didn't you?' asked Doris.

'Of course, well not much. But we did it.'

Frank wasn't a fantastic lover. Not that I've had many. Well, I've had one apart from Frank. Guy was his name. Good looking he was too. I can't remember why I chucked him. I sometimes think I've lost out. I've no real idea if Frank was good in bed or not. I've got nothing to compare it with, have I? Apart from Guy all those years ago and quite honestly, I can't remember what that was like. Anyway, that's why I'm now sitting in the waiting room of the sexual health clinic. I've got one hour before I meet Becky. I'm going to help her clean up after a murder in a maisonette in Ilford. I wasn't going to do murders, like I said, but one of her girls is off sick and as it's my first day as a regular cleaner, she wanted me to shadow her. So it seems I don't have any choice in the matter. I think this is going to be a very traumatic day in more ways than one. Yesterday I agreed to go for training. Well, I had nothing else to do. Let me tell you, cleaning up after a crime scene isn't just mopping up blood. I was there a whole day. I was knackered by the end of it. It was embarrassing as I must have been the only over-sixty there. Most of them were youngsters. I did think of asking if they did concessions, but in the end changed my mind. After all, I don't want the whole world knowing I'm sixty, and it would have been a bit demoralising if they'd sent me home because they were concerned about my blood pressure. I learnt a lot about bodily fluids. It was interesting. But I'm not sure about cleaning up after the real thing. I felt quite ill during the mock-up session. I can't begin to tell you how much skin and body fluids get scattered around the room. I came over all faint during the training and a lovely young woman called Lucy took me for a cuppa. She didn't seem in the least fazed by all that blood and gore.

The thing is I need a job. I know I've got just under five grand, but I don't want it trickling through my fingers. You don't spend that kind of winnings on the rent, do you? You need to think through what you're going to spend it on. If our Frank had got his hands on it, it would all be gone by now. No, now I'm on my own, I need to earn more.

You don't half have to dress up for this cleaning malarkey too. You can't just throw on a pinny. You have to get a biohazard suit, full facemasks and loads of gloves. I look like something out of *Star Wars*. I only wish I'd had this getup when I wanted to rob Lloyds. There's no way anyone would have recognised me. It would have been difficult making my getaway though, but I don't think anyone would have tried to stop me. Oh well, maybe I'll hang onto one for when times get hard again.

'Hello,' says a kind-looking nurse. 'Come this way please.'

I walk past several girls who look younger than our Michael. They're tapping away on their mobile phones. They're here for the morning after pill, I suppose. Shirl says they do it all the time. It seems wrong to me. I never put it about when I was their age. It's a whole other world now isn't it? They have it too easy these days, if you ask me. Listen to me, blathering like an old woman. Here I go again. Ever since Frank died I've really felt my age. I follow the nurse into a small consulting room.

'How can I help you?'

I'd been rehearsing this for the past two days and still it comes out all wrong.

'My husband is dead. It was sudden, but it looks like he may have been, you know, with some other woman. Not while he was dead, obviously, but you know, before, and I'm worried I've caught something.'

She doesn't bat an eyelid.

'Right, shall we take some swabs and put your mind at ease.'

'Yes, let's do that,' I say while really not wanting to open my legs to anyone.

Honestly, who'd have thought, me, Rosie Foster, would be having tests for syphilis and all sorts, at sixty. It's not decent is it? Not at sixty. I suppose it's fashionable when you're thirty but I'm not thirty am I?

'We'll let you know the results in a week. I wouldn't worry. It's pretty unlikely.'

I pull my headscarf back on and don my oversize sunglasses. I could be mistaken for Victoria Beckham with these monsters. Well, you don't know who you might see do you? If I'm here, who knows who else might be? I reach the bus stop just as the bus turns the corner.

Becky is waiting outside the maisonette. It's not what I expected. I thought there would at least be a police cordon. I'd pictured us walking through a row of policemen too. I watch too much rubbish on Netflix, that's my problem.

'Hiya Rosie, how are you doing?' Becky asks.

'I'm fine.'

'My mum said the funeral went well. You know as well as can be expected.'

I nod. The last person I want to talk about is Frank.

'So, what happened here?' I ask looking up at the flat.

'Jealous boyfriend. He left her in the bath tub apparently, so the bathroom is where we have to focus. There's no one living here now which is good.'

'Right,' I say feeling my stomach churn. 'What about the other rooms?'

'Yeah, we have to clean the whole flat. I'll get your stuff. Haven't you got your car?' she says looking around.

'It was nicked.'

'It's a bit heavy to carry on the bus.'

'My Sam is bringing a car round tonight.'

'Oh good,' she sighs. 'I like my girls to have their own supplies. After this I'll take you to the house that will be your regular.'

I help carry the boxes of cleaning chemicals from the car and follow her up the stairs.

'We can get our gear on here' says Becky when we reach the landing of the flat. I pull on my biohazard suit with trembling hands.

'I'll clean the other rooms if you like,' I say.

What am I doing in a flat where a murder was committed? I cling onto my holdall tightly.

'You can leave your things in the hallway,' says Becky eyeing up the bag.

'Oh right,' I say.

She dons her facemask and gloves.

Lynda Renham

'I always wear two pairs,' she says. 'We don't want to have an aids test.'

Blimey, no. First the sexual health clinic and then an aids test, crikey, the NHS will think I'm a one-woman brothel.

'No, that's right,' I agree.

'We'll work on the bathroom first. It will take us a while.'

'Right,' I say, trying to disguise the tremble in my voice.

'I've got a new shower curtain and stuff. They've got someone moving in next week, so we'll need to change the nets too. Apparently the blood went everywhere.'

I'm seriously going to gag. Becky throws open the bathroom door.

'It's not too bad,' she says.

I reel back in shock. Not too bad? Not too bad? It looks like an abattoir.

'Oh,' is all I can muster.

'I know what you're thinking,' Becky says. 'I thought the same the first time. The key is not to think about the murder. I tell myself it's no worse than when the kids spill tomato ketchup. So as I'm cleaning up, I think, blooming kids and their mess.'

Heaven, if I had kids that made this mess with tomato ketchup I'd throttle them.

'I don't know,' I mumble, feeling faint.

'It would be brilliant if you could,' says Becky encouragingly. 'I'd pay you forty pounds an hour for these jobs. I can't get anyone you see. I can only pay fifteen for the normal cleaning.'

It's very tempting. I'd worked out the finances last night. We owed the bank a thousand. They said I could pay it off each month. Then there are Frank's debts. Five thousand so far and those are just the ones I know about. There's the rent and bills and of course I've got to eat. If I take the murders, along with Waitrose and the cinema, I should get the debts paid

When Archie Met Rosie

off and still hang onto my winnings. If I get five murders a week that would be good wouldn't it? I'm talking rubbish, aren't I? There aren't five murders a week in Essex are there?

'How many murders could I do a week?' I ask.

Becky laughs.

'I hope no one can hear us,' she says. 'It varies from week to week. I get offered some jobs in East London and sometimes even further out. It depends. If you don't mind travelling I could probably get you a few. It'll help me a lot.'

'I'll see how this one goes.'

If I get enough money I could take myself off to Paris. It's about time I lived my life for me. Frank would never go, said it was pointless.

'There's nothing to see that you can't see on the tele,' he'd said. But who wants to see it on the tele. I want to be there, feel the atmosphere and the breeze in my hair. I've done enough for others and look what's happened. I've got nothing, been nowhere, and now I'm all alone. I went to the library the other day. Frank used to moan about that too.

'What you reading posh books for? You'll forget your place if you go on like that.'

Well, I'm coming out of my place. I like the library and I like my books. I'm reading *Far from the Madding Crowd*. It's so inspirational. Frank would have ridiculed it, but Frank isn't here is he? Frank's dead and you know what, I'm going to Paris.

Chapter Seventeen
Rosie

I'm knackered by the time we finish. It's hard work cleaning up after a murder. So much blood, I can't begin to tell you. But Becky was quite right. You soon get used to it and once you stop thinking about the murder, it's fine.

Apparently the teachers are on strike. It's about pay. They want more money. Everyone wants more these days, don't they?

'It's great,' says Becky. 'No school runs.'

We're on our way to what will be my regular job. It's just after three and Becky warns me it won't always be like this.

'When the kids are at school it's awful,' she moans. 'The local school is just up the road and it's a nightmare when they collect the little darlings.'

We're in Emerson Park. It's a million miles from the Tradmore Estate, I can tell you. The houses are lovely here. I always wanted a house. Nothing big, just a little terrace would have done me. A two-up two-down would have been lovely. I think Frank was mad to keep paying rent when we could have had a place of our own. Sam says we'd be paying a lot less now if we'd had a mortgage. Still, I've got a roof over my head and I'm grateful for that.

Becky said she'd pay me cash in hand if that's what I wanted.

'The blooming tax man gets enough if you ask me,' she'd said.

'If you don't mind, it would help.'

'Nah, course not.'

She turns into a tree-lined street.

When Archie Met Rosie

'It's nice here,' she says wistfully. 'I'm saving for a house. That's why I do the murders.'

It really does sound like we kill people doesn't it? She steers the car onto a gravelled driveway and I look up at the huge double-fronted house.

'He lives alone, this bloke,' she says climbing from the car. 'He lost his wife a few months back. He's lovely. I said we'd come weekly but if he needed any shopping or whatnot we'd help out. He's loaded I reckon.'

'Okay,' I say helping her lift the cleaning materials from the boot.

'His name's Alfred. He likes to be called Alf. He did all the work on the house himself.'

'Right,' I say, admiring the bay windows.

She lifts the door knocker and knocks several times. It seems an age before we hear movement on the other side.

'Who is it?' calls a voice. 'If you're selling something, I don't want it, and if you're peddling religion you can bugger off now. We don't do God in this house.'

I look at Becky.

'Is he expecting us?'

'Oh yes,' she laughs.

'Alf,' she shouts. She turns to me. 'His daughter-in-law says he's deaf.'

'It's me, Becky. Come to do the cleaning,' she shouts.

'Oh right,' he says. 'Hold on and I'll unlock the door.'

We wait while he fiddles with a key in the lock. The door swings open and I step back in surprise. It's Archie.

'Hello Rosie,' he says. 'What are you doing here?'

*

'Fancy you two knowing each other,' says Becky.

'Yes, who'd have thought it,' says Archie, smiling. 'Small world isn't it?'

I feel stupidly embarrassed. He now knows that not only do I live on the dreaded Tradmore Estate but that I'm also a cleaner. I really could die of shame. He must think I'm a right loser. Well, he wouldn't be wrong, would he? For one awful embarrassing moment I find myself having to hold back tears.

'Can I use your loo?' I ask.

I suppose that's common too isn't it? I expect he and Moira call it the lavatory. Becky shows me to the downstairs loo and would you believe, as soon as I'm inside, I have a little cry. It's grief, that's what it is. Who am I kidding? It's not grief. It's me, suddenly realising who I actually am. I should never have married so young. I could have got myself an education. I wipe my tears on the soft toilet tissue. I haven't got time for this. I look around the nicely decorated loo. Archie probably doesn't realise that there are still poor people out in the world and that we have to work our backsides off. I suppose Archie's worked hard for this, though. What did Becky say? Something about he'd done all the work on the house himself. His wife was lucky. I wipe my tears away. I'm knackered, that's what it is. I've got to go back to the cinema tomorrow. I've had a week off, that's enough. It'll be nice to get some popcorn. I wash my face and find Becky in the kitchen talking to Archie.

'So you're going to be my cleaner then, girl,' he says when I walk in.

'I thought your name was Archie,' I say blushing.

'No, it's Alfred,' he laughs. 'I did keep telling you.'

'I've got Archie in my head now.'

'How did you two meet?' asks Becky.

'It's a long story,' I say, pulling dusters out of a box.

'She rescued my granddaughter from a sexual predator,' Archie says.

'Crikey,' exclaims Becky. 'When was that?'

'Last Friday,' I say. 'Where do you want me to start?'

When Archie Met Rosie

'Do you have a list, Alf?' asks Becky.

'Nah, I forgot,' he smiles. 'But my bed needs changing if you don't mind.'

'I'll show Rosie around and then we'll get on,' says Becky.

'You can hang that bag up in the hallway,' says Archie pointing to my holdall.

'Oh right, thanks,' I say, with absolutely no intention of letting it out of my sight. Don't get me wrong, I don't imagine Archie is going to steal my winnings. He's got plenty already by the look of things. But I like to be able to see it. Just to be on the safe side.

'You girls want a cuppa?'

'Ooh lovely,' says Becky. 'I'm parched.'

I follow Becky out of the kitchen and along the hallway.

'I'll quickly show you the place,' she says.

The house is gorgeous. It's huge compared to my little flat. It's a mess though.

'I'll show you where the bed linen is kept. If you could change the bed once a week that would be great,' says Becky opening an airing cupboard on the landing.

'The house is so big,' I say, amazed at the number of rooms.

'Yes, I know. It's got five bedrooms. His daughter-in-law wants him to go into a retirement flat. He's having none of it.'

'I met her,' I grimace.

'Yeah, she's a bit toffee-nosed. She hired me.'

Archie has a pile of books on the bedside cabinet and I quickly glance through them. Maybe he can recommend some books for me to read. Huh, he most likely thinks I can't read.

'Tea's made,' he shouts.

'Thanks Alf,' calls Becky.

I must stop thinking of him as Archie. But he looks like an Archie if you know what I mean, more of an Archie than an Alf anyway.

'What you doing later?' asks Becky.

'Later?' I repeat.

'Mum's coming over and we're getting fish and chips. You're welcome to join us.'

'That'll be nice, thanks.'

I've only got a Fray Bentos pie and some oven chips. I really must start cooking myself some decent dinners. This widow malarkey is no fun.

'Great. Come over about seven. Johnny Crabtree is coming too.'

Oh no. It's too late now to back out isn't it?

Chapter Eighteen
Alfred

How odd to see Rosie. Oddly enough, I'd been thinking about her just last night. I'd been thinking I should have apologised for how Moira had behaved. Sticking her nose up in the air the way she had. It had been embarrassing.

'I'm off,' Becky calls up the stairs to Rosie. 'Are you sure you'll be okay on the bus with your stuff. It's a lot to carry.'

'I'll be fine,' shouts Rosie.

'I can take her home,' I hear myself saying.

Becky turns in surprise.

'Are you sure? Rosie lives on the Tradmore Estate. It's not like 'ere?'

'I've been there. I dropped her off that Friday. I don't think anyone is going to bother an old bloke like me.'

'Huh,' scoffs Becky. 'Don't hold your breath is all I can say. Think it over. You don't have to mention it to Rosie until she leaves.'

The front door slams and I sigh with relief. She's a nice enough girl, is Becky, but she does rabbit on a bit. I don't think Rosie will blather on like that somehow. I make another pot of tea and carry a mug upstairs to Rosie. I peer around the bedroom door. She's changed my bed and is looking through one of my books.

'That was a good one,' I say. 'I brought you a cuppa.'

She drops the book in surprise

'Oh, I didn't mean to ...'

'You can borrow it if you like.'

'I couldn't,' she says, her cheeks turning pink.

'Why not?'

'I can get it from the library.'

'Don't be daft. You can borrow it off me. You're coming back, aren't you?'

'Well yes …'

'Take it then. I'm in a book club so I've got loads to read on the shelf downstairs.'

She picks up the copy of *Rebecca* and slips into her overall pocket.

'It was a film,' I say, 'Have you seen it?'

'No,' she says.

'Here's your tea.'

'I'll be forever in the loo,' she says, taking it from me.

'Bed looks nice,' I say and then feel awkward.

She blushes again and says, 'I'd better get on.'

'I'm really sorry about the other night Rosie. My daughter-in-law was quite rude. I'm really sorry. She's a bit toffee-nosed at times.'

She looks flustered.

'Oh, it's okay. I didn't notice.'

She's a good liar.

'I'll let you get on. I don't want to make you late. You've probably got your husband's tea to do.'

'He died,' she says flatly. 'A few weeks ago, Domino's Pizza killed him with their van.'

My mouth widens, and I quickly close it.

'Oh, I'm so sorry.'

'It's okay. He liked pizza. Anyway, turns out he was knocking off some blonde behind my back. So …'

'Angel cake?' I say.

'What?' she questions looking at me blankly.

'Angel Cake. It goes great with a cuppa. I'll go and cut some. Pop down when you're ready.'

Hell's bells, knocked down by a Domino Pizza van, who'd have thought it?

Chapter Nineteen
Rosie

He probably thinks I'm light-fingered now. Oh dear, I hope he doesn't say anything to Becky. I really don't want to lose these cleaning jobs. I gingerly walk into the kitchen clutching my mug of tea.

'Ah great,' says Archie, pulling out a chair. 'Everyone should have a break.'

'I really shouldn't ...'

'Of course you should. I employed people and I know how important it is to have breaks.'

I sit at the table and wrap my hands around the hot mug. He passes me a slice of angel cake.

'This is the best. Cath, my wife, used to make her own. This isn't a patch on hers but it's better than nothing.'

'When did you lose your wife?'

'Aw, six months ago now. I've been staying with our Harry and Moira, but it's hard work there. She's got a dual flush with a remote control in her best loo. It's got white fluffy towels too, but you're not supposed to use those.'

I gape at him. He's pulling my leg, surely.

'Dual flush?' I repeat.

What's a dual flush when it's at home?

Archie laughs.

'You don't want one.'

'I can't afford one,' I say without thinking.

I bite into my slice of angel cake. I'm starving as it happens. I didn't think to bring lunch. How stupid was that?

'So how long have you been cleaning for Becky?' Archie asks.

He's not bad looking. I reckon he was quite handsome when he was younger. His hair is grey now. Frank used to dye his. I thought that was pointless at the time but now I'm beginning to understand why he was so obsessed with his appearance, the shagging little toad.

'This is my first day,' I say.

There's a tap at the back door and I jump. I look down to see a tabby cat.

'She's always in and out of her cat flap,' explains Archie. 'Her name's Cleo, we named her after Cleo Laine, the singer. Cleo is one of the reasons I came home. I couldn't leave her at the mercy of my neighbour, Molly, for too long.'

Cleo rubs herself against my leg and I stroke her

'I really should get on,' I say, getting up.

'How did your husband manage to get hit by a Domino's Pizza van?' he asks as I reach the door.

I sigh. I might as well tell the truth. He's probably already formed his opinion of us Tradmore Estate residents. That's if Moira hasn't already filled him in.

'He was drunk,' I say. 'He didn't see the van coming. I don't suppose in his state he saw much at all. They don't usually pay out when it was the victim's fault, but they gave me lots of pizza and five hundred pounds. I used the pizza for the wake. I've only got two left.'

I could have one of those tonight, couldn't I? At least then I won't have to see Crabbers. But I hate letting people down and I did say I'd go. I wonder what time Sam is bringing the car over. I'd better text him. It would be good not to have to get the bus to Becky's.

'I'm sorry for your loss,' he says.

'And yours,' I say.

'I'll let you get on,' Archie says, picking up a newspaper.

'Yes,' I say. 'I'll finish upstairs.'

Cleo follows me up and jumps onto the newly made bed. I stroke her and then switch the hoover on. It's lovely cleaning a house like this. Each room is interesting. It must have been lovely bringing up a family here. I bet his son had the best, not like our Sam who always got second-hand. There's a picture of Archie's son in the hallway. It's his graduation photo. I wish Sam had gone to university. I did try to encourage it. Frank just went on about how much it would cost and kept telling Sam to get a trade.

'Education's no good,' he'd said. 'A trade is what you need.'

Not that Frank ever had a trade. He was pig ignorant was Frank. I was stupid to have stayed with him. But when you're young and naïve you don't know any better do you? I wish I'd got an education. It's too late now, I suppose. But then again ... I read about this woman who got a PhD when she was a hundred. I can't see the point in that myself, but sixty isn't that old is it? I could do it now. I'll have a look when I get home. There are courses you can do at home aren't there? I read about them once. Now I've got a little bit of money maybe I could do it. I yawn and rub my eyes. That's if I'm not too tired of course. I'm going to be cream crackered with this cleaning and Waitrose. Not to mention the cinema at the weekend. Still, it's best to stay busy isn't it?

Chapter Twenty
Alfred

'It looks lovely,' says Moira, wiping her finger along the dresser. 'A good cleaner is worth their weight in gold.'

'Dad, are you ordering the takeaway or what? I'm starving,' complains Holly.

'It's flipping expensive,' I grumble.

'No it's not,' argues Holly. 'It's a lot cheaper than that posh pub you go to.'

'I'm talking about the cleaning company your mother recommended.'

'At least you know they can be trusted,' says Moira.

'Can we eat soon?' Holly groans, swiping at her phone.

'I wish you'd put that down for just once,' snaps Moira before turning to me and saying, 'Well, we have told you more than once that the house is too big. It would cost a lot less to clean something smaller.'

Here we go.

Harry pulls out his phone.

'Where's that list Moira? Does anyone want to change their mind before I place the order?'

We're all silent and then Holly's phone begins to bleep incessantly. Honestly, I can't think what these youngsters find to talk about. Harry phones our order through and then his phone starts bleeping too.

'Honestly,' I say. 'How did you lot cope before mobile phones were invented?'

Harry's face pales as he looks at his message.

'Everything all right, son?' I ask.

He looks up.

'Yes, it's just the play. There's so much to do,' he says, his voice shaking.

'It is only a play,' I say, surprised at his white face.

'It's ridiculous the hours he puts into it,' complains Moira.

'I've got my Christmas list,' says Holly, finally looking up from her phone. She pushes a crumpled piece of paper towards her mum.

'We need to get things organised for Christmas,' says Moira. 'You're welcome to come to us for the whole of Christmas, Dad, but we will be going to church and …'

'I'm not,' interrupts Holly.

'Yes, you are,' snaps Moira.

'I'm seventeen now and …'

Harry slams his hand down on the table and we all jump.

'That's enough Holly,' he says. 'You'll do what your mother tells you.'

'We always go to church together,' says Moira.

'My mates don't go and besides, I don't believe in God any more so it's hypocritical.'

'Holly!' gasps Moira.

'Destiny is having a do at her place on Christmas Eve. Her parents say it's okay and I'm going to that …'

'You're not,' says Moira heatedly. 'I won't have you going to that dump on Christmas Eve …'

'Destiny doesn't live in a dump,' protests Holly. 'Anyway, I'm almost eighteen so I can do what I like.'

'You're not eighteen yet,' says Harry firmly.

Holly looks at him and then rushes from the room in tears.

'For goodness' sake,' says Moira.

At that moment Harry's phone rings and I'm sure I see his hands shake.

'I've got to take this,' he says, also leaving the kitchen.

'Just you and me, girl,' I say to Moira.

I've never had such bad feelings in the house. Cath and I argued sometimes but it was pretty rare for either one of us to leave the room in a huff. These youngsters have far too much if you ask me. Why Holly isn't going to university, I don't know. I don't say anything. What's the point?

'I'd better go after her,' says Moira.

'That's probably not a good idea,' I say. 'Let me go.'

Honestly, what a crowd my lot are. I take a quick look at Holly's Christmas list and sigh. 'iPhone 10. Video camera. Chanel make-up. New boots.' Does she think we're made of money? I can hear her crying in the bedroom that she has claimed for her own. Not that she ever comes to stay. This is what I mean about religion. It's nothing but trouble. I'm about to go in when I overhear Harry talking in the bathroom. Call me a nosy old bugger but a couple of words catch my ears and it doesn't sound like he's talking about his play to me. He's trying to keep his voice low. Something's up. You don't come upstairs and shut yourself in the bathroom to talk about a silly play, do you? I go as close to the door as I can, avoiding the creaking floorboard. I don't want to give myself away.

'I told you I couldn't come over. What are you talking about? We're having a takeaway with my dad.'

I widen my eyes.

'I did tell you. Don't you dare Steph? I'm warning you.'

Steph, who the hell is Steph? I start to back away quietly.

'I'll give you a ring later, okay. Of course I still fancy you. Don't be so ridiculous.'

'Grandad, what are you doing?'

I spin round, twisting my bad knee in the process.

'Looking for you,' I say limping forward.

'I've been in my room,' says Holly.

The bathroom door clicks, and Harry emerges, slightly red-faced and with his hair askew.

'What's going on?' he asks.

I could ask the same question.

'I came to see if Holly was okay. Come on, let's go downstairs. Let's try and have our dinner without any arguments, shall we?'

Holly wipes away her tears.

'Dad, do I have to go to church?' she hiccups. 'I hate it.'

'Not now Holly,' he says.

'It's not fair,' she cries before storming down the stairs.

'Sorry Dad.'

'No worries,' I say.

He checks his phone and then wanders down the stairs.

'I'll go and get the food,' he says.

I rub my eyes and sigh. What's the stupid lad up to? I know Moira's not easy but surely another woman isn't the answer. I wouldn't like to be in his shoes when Moira finds out.

'Stupid idiot,' I mutter and then follow him. This is going to be a great Christmas if tonight is anything to go by.

Chapter Twenty-One
Rosie

'Who was the chicken and chips?' asks Bert.

'Did you get the curry sauce?' chorus Becky's twins.

'It's here somewhere,' says Bert.

'Do you want a beer?' asks Doris.

'No, I came in my new car. Sam brought it round this evening.'

'What is it?' asks Bert.

Men are always interested in cars, aren't they? I can't stand the things myself. They're nothing but hassle.

'It's a Vauxhall Astra,' I say.

The twins burst out laughing.

'You're in no danger of getting that nicked on the estate,' one says.

Becky whacks him around the head.

'Don't be cheeky. How did it go at Alf's?'

'Who?' I ask.

'Alf, you know, you cleaned for him today.'

'Oh Archie,' I say. 'It went well, he drove me home.'

'Who did?' asks Crabbers.

It's so noisy I can barely hear myself think. Everyone seems to be talking at once.

'Who's got the ketchup?'

'Pass a fork will you,'

'Do you want a pickled onion?' Crabbers asks.

'Oh yes, ta.'

'Who's Alf?' he asks again, dropping a pickled onion onto my plate.

'He's the bloke I'm cleaning for. You know him. He did your mum's roof.'

'What are you doing over Christmas?' asks Doris, handing me a plate of bread and butter.

I can't say I'm thinking of going to Paris, can I? They'll think I've lost my marbles.

'I'll be going to Sam's, I expect.'

'You can come to us Boxing Day if you like.'

'Thanks Doris.'

'No one wants to be alone over Christmas.'

'I'm going to a party on Christmas Eve, I was going to ask if you'd like to come,' says Crabbers shyly.

'I don't think I'll be feeling like going to a party,' I say.

I've made up my mind. I'm going to Paris for Christmas. I've not checked out the cost yet, but it can't be that much, can it? I'm not keen about going on my own but I'm sure I'll find an organised trip and it won't take me long to make friends will it? I'll look on the internet when I get home. Not that our computer works that well. I think Frank must have been looking at some dodgy sites because I feel sure we've got one of those viruses. I'd ask our Michael to take a look at it, but God knows what he'd find. He already doesn't have a great opinion of Frank. I wouldn't want to make it worse. It can take fifteen minutes to get into Google and that can't be right can it? By the time I get into the Paris Breaks page, it will time for bed.

When Archie Met Rosie

'It was a nice funeral, Rosie,' says Bert, making a chip butty.

'Thanks.'

'What are you doing with the ashes?'

'Maybe you can scatter them,' suggests Crabbers.

The way I feel about Frank at the moment I may well flush them down the loo. Oh, that's an awful thing to think isn't it? I wouldn't really flush them down the toilet. Anyway, how can I be sure they are even Frank's ashes? I know they're unlikely to be someone else's but you just don't know do you? They could get them muddled up, couldn't they? You can't help wondering, can you?

'What about Southend?' suggests Crabbers. 'He liked Southend, didn't he?'

'Yeah, we could all go for a day trip,' says Doris.

'The kids love Southend,' says Becky.

'In this weather,' I say with a shiver.

'We can wait until the summer, can't we?' says Doris. 'It's not like they're going to go off is it? We could go for a boat trip or something.'

I haven't collected the ashes yet. I suppose I should. It might look a bit uncaring if I leave it much longer.

'I ought to get them,' I say thinking aloud.

'Well, it's not always easy,' says Bert, tapping me on the shoulder.

I'm worried about going home later. Frank always used to meet me at the main doors. I'm a bit of a wreck going up the stairs on my own at night. I won't use the lift, just in case some bugger plays around with the buttons while I'm in it. I hate the Tradmore Estate and I've got it in my head that people know about my winnings. It's a lot of money to be carrying around. I'm scared when I'm out of the flat and scared when I'm in it. I don't know half the people Frank owed money to.

Bert looks at me and then says,

'I saw Matt Fisher at the funeral.'

'I thought that was him,' says Crabbers tensing beside me.

After spotting Miss Peroxide Blonde, I hadn't really noticed anyone else. My stomach somersaults at the name.

'Matt Fisher?' I repeat.

There were a few strange faces at the funeral, but Frank knew a lot of people at the dogs.

'Matt Fisher, the loan shark?'

My heart begins to race. Doris looks angrily at Bert.

'What did you have to go and frighten her for? Hasn't she got enough on her plate?'

'Did Frank owe him money?' I ask.

Bert sighs and puts down his butty.

'Word's going around that you won some money on the bingo.'

'I haven't told anyone,' says Doris quickly.

'I never knew you won some money,' says Becky.

'See, I never even told me own daughter,' says Doris, clearly vindicated.

'How much did you win?' asks Crabbers eagerly.

'She's not saying,' says Doris.

I push my plate away.

'What are people saying?' I ask.

'Just that you had a win at the bingo,' says Bert.

I sigh. How many people did Frank owe money to?

'Do you know how much he borrowed?'

'Matt's putting it around that it was about five thousand, plus the interest of course.'

'How much?' I gasp.

What on earth did Frank spend five grand on?

'You've upset her,' scolds Doris.

'No, it's okay,' I say.

'Well, he and Crabbers can follow you home and see you safely into your flat,' she says. 'Right Bert?'

Bert nods.

'Yeah, sure, of course.'

'Happy to,' says Crabbers.

This is great isn't it? I'll be spending the rest of my winnings on bodyguards. Who'd have thought you'd get up one day with nothing and then that same night have five grand and half of London after you? I'd heard of Matt Fisher, of course. It's one of those names that sends shivers through you. I've never had dealings with him and why should I? What I never had I couldn't spend, and I'd never take out loans. Our Sam would have a hundred canary fits if he knew about this. What was my silly-arse husband thinking of?

'I don't know how much longer you can keep your winnings a secret,' says Doris.

'How much did you win?' asks Crabbers again.

'I'd rather not say.'

'No, best not,' says Becky. 'That's why a lot of lottery winners don't go public isn't it?'

'It wasn't that much,' I say quickly.

'What was Frank doing borrowing five grand?' says Doris, licking vinegar from her fingers.

'Well, it didn't go on rent,' I say, standing up.

'It's okay borrowing money,' says Bert. 'But just not from loan sharks.'

I'll need to get new locks put on the front door. Triple locks I reckon. Maybe I'll get one for the bedroom door too. I'll also open a new bank account. I'll go to Halifax. I should have done it earlier really. It's dim of me to carry all this dosh around. The Halifax doesn't know me. They won't know about Frank's debts, will they?

I kiss Doris goodbye and thank Becky for the fish and chips. I'm grateful to have Bert and Crabbers to see me home. If I wasn't so scared, I could have enjoyed it and imagined myself a celebrity. Huh, that's a laugh. The only celebrity status I'll get is when I'm featured on the front page of the *Daily Mirror* after Matt and his cronies try to get what they're owed. I can almost see the headlines, *'Grandma beaten up in her own home by loan sharks.'*

I so hate being sixty.

Chapter Twenty-Two
Holly

'I don't think we should,' said Holly nervously, grappling with her tights. It was freezing in Bradley's bedroom. You'd think the heating would be on. 'Your mum might come home.'

'No she won't. She's at work until eight. I told you. Don't be a prick-teaser Hol,' said Bradley, fumbling at her blouse.

'I don't know,' said Holly, pushing her skirt down. 'My mum will kill me if she finds out.'

'She ain't gonna find out is she, unless you tell her?'

Holly sighed.

'Aw, come on Hol. You did promise. We don't have to go all the way.'

She'd been all prepared earlier and he was right, she had promised. All her mates had done it. She must be the only one left. She didn't want to be a virgin forever. It was embarrassing. Besides Bradley was real fit and all the girls fancied him. She was lucky he liked her. She knew if she didn't give in soon he would chuck her and go out with someone else and then she'd look a right idiot. It was bad enough that he kept calling her 'a little nun' in front of her friends.

'Is it because of God?' he kept asking her.

She hated her parents for the whole God thing. It made her look right prim. She didn't believe in God so why did she have to go to church with them. Grandad had the right idea. She supposed she'd have to go to that stupid play of her dad's. Honestly, anyone would think he was Martin Scorsese. The whole thing was embarrassing. It was only a local theatre group for goodness' sake. Anyway, she hated that church hall, it was always freezing in there.

'Don't you have the heating on?' she asked.

Bradley was busy trying to get her bra off.

'What?' he said.

'It's really cold in here.'

'You could always get in the bed,' he whispered into her ear. 'Come on Holly.'

He stuck his tongue into her mouth and Holly thought she would choke. His hand slid down her knickers and she tensed. She ought to get it over with. Lianne said it wasn't that bad, just a bit of pain at the start and that was that.

'You're a bit sore after but it gets better,' she'd told everyone. Holly didn't think she'd be boasting about it.

'Aw Hol,' Bradley groaned into her ear.

'Have you got something?' she asked.

That's what she'd seen the girls say in the TV programmes she watched. She looked down at his penis and grimaced. She'd never seen anything so big in her life. That would never get inside her.

'I thought you were on the pill?' he mumbled.

She pushed at his chest.

'No, I'm not ...'

'I'll use something,' he grunted, pushing her back onto the bed. She felt her knickers pulled down and before she could protest he had pushed the monstrous thing inside her.

'Bugger,' she moaned.

It hurt like hell. No one said it would hurt this much. When did he put the thing on?

'Brad, Brad, you did put something on, didn't you?'

'Yeah, course,' he said huskily.

She couldn't believe this. There must be something wrong with her. It surely shouldn't hurt like this. People wouldn't keep doing it if it was this painful. Suddenly he grunted and rolled off her. She felt the wetness between her legs and panic overwhelmed her. She must be bleeding. If she went to the hospital they'd phone her mum and she'd go insane when she found out.

'Here,' said Brad, handing her a tissue and lighting a Benson and Hedges. He jumped up to open the window.

'You were great,' he said.

She dabbed at herself with the tissue and peeked nervously at it. There was no blood. Maybe she was okay after all. She was so sore it was hard to sit up without wincing.

'Should you smoke in your bedroom?' she asked.

'Yeah, I do what I like. Shall we get something to eat? I think there's some pizza in the fridge.'

'No, I should get home,' said Holly.

She just wanted to get out of her clothes and into a warm bath. Maybe she'd feel better after that. She wished she could ask someone if this was okay and if it was alright to be so sore afterwards. Maybe she'd text Destiny later. Destiny had slept with loads. She would know, and she wouldn't breathe a word. She was alright was Destiny.

'Please yourself,' said Bradley. 'I'm having some.'

Holly buttoned her blouse and picked up her coat. She was waiting for him to kiss and cuddle her. She'd just given him her virginity after all. But he didn't. He checked his phone, laughed, sent a message and then jumped off the bed.

'Come on then,' he said and left the bedroom.

Holly fought back tears and followed him downstairs. The house was a tip. She hated coming to Brad's. It smelt of fried bacon and tobacco smoke. There were always piles of dirty dishes in the sink and cat litter trays in the hallway. The smell now made her feel sick and she hurried to the front door.

'See you,' called Brad from the kitchen.

Holly wiped away her tears and left the house. It hadn't been at all what she'd imagined. She'd thought that Brad would at least have given her a big hug. She hoped he wouldn't tell his mates. She would tell Destiny but no one else. She couldn't imagine ever doing it again. Not ever.

Chapter Twenty-Three
Sam

Sam looked down at his cholesterol-laden lunch. He really ought to make himself a packed lunch, but it was so easy to pop to the chippy for sausage roll and chips. The sausage roll had a curry taste about it. Sam grimaced and put it to one side and opened a tube of Pringles.

'Alright if I get off?' asked Joe, wiping his oily hands on a duster. 'I'm taking Rita for lunch at Wetherspoons. I'll be back in an hour.'

'Yeah, no worries,' said Sam, pouring coffee from his thermos flask. It was cold in the workshop and for the hundredth time Sam considered buying another heater.

'I hear your mum had a big win at the bingo a few weeks back,' said Joe.

Sam shrugged.

'It weren't much.'

'Really,' said Joe. 'I 'eard it was about ten grand.'

Sam widened his eyes and laughed.

'Ten grand? Where did you hear that?'

'Tom down the pub said. His missus was there that night apparently. It was the night your dad got knocked down weren't it?'

'Yeah, well it was about five hundred, not ten grand.'

Joe studied himself in the workshop's cracked mirror and drew a comb through his hair.

'I said to Rita it couldn't have been that much. She'd be well away from Tradmore if it had been. How's she coping?'

'She's alright,' Sam said and considered whether she really was.

'Everyone likes your mum. She's a good sort. It would have been nice if she had won a fair bit …'

'Well, she didn't,' said Sam, the words coming out more sharply than he meant them to.

'Okay, no need to snap my head off. I'm only saying what I heard.'

He gestured with his head.

'Oh, hold up, looks like someone else has heard too. Here's your ex.'

Sam followed Joe's nod to see Maureen standing at the entrance to the workshop, a look of distaste on her face. Sam stifled a groan.

'I've got me new Debenhams coat on,' she said. 'I'm not coming in. I don't want oil all over it, so you'd better come out.'

'Best of luck mate,' said Joe quietly. 'See you later.'

'Alright Maureen,' he said as he passed.

The radio blared out Queen's Bohemian Rhapsody and Sam switched it off.

'I'm really busy, Maureen,' he said.

He looked at Maureen's over-made-up face and raised his eyebrows. She pulled up her coat collar, flashing bright red fingernails at him.

'Jeff and I are going to Spain for Christmas.'

'That's nice for you both,' he said.

'We offered to take Michael, but he doesn't want to come.'

'I don't blame him. Costa del Sol isn't his thing.'

She wrinkled her nose and then pulled on a pair of furry mitts.

'It's going to take you forever to pay me that ten thousand pounds,' she said, eyeing him for his reaction. 'You've got to pay it, the court said so.'

'You're getting your payment every month.'

She sniffed.

'I heard your mum had a big win on the bingo.'

He laughed.

'Oh, so that's why you're here. Well, you heard wrong. It was five hundred and it went on my dad's funeral. Thanks for coming by the way.'

'No one wanted me there.'

'You could have sent some flowers. Michael would have liked it.'

'Anyway, I heard it was a few grand she won.'

'Like I said, it was five hundred.'

'Well, all I'm saying is, if she did, you could give me my ten thousand and cancel those monthly payments.'

'I've got to get back,' he said, throwing the last of his coffee into the street, narrowly missing her shiny shoes.

'It's only fair. The court decided,' she said, checking her shoes.

He turned on her.

'You left me for some smarmy computer engineer. He's alright for money. It's just greed with you. You don't need that new coat and all that make-up. That perfume you're wearing smells like cat's piss by the way.'

'It's Hermes, not that you'd know.'

'Who gives a toss if it's Herpes?'

'Hermes,' she corrected through gritted teeth.

'If Mum won some money, then it's hers not mine.'

'She could help you out.'

'Go off back to your poncy boyfriend, Maureen.'

He took a closer look at her.

'Or are things not working out? Is that why you're worried?'

She tossed her hair back.

'I'm not the one on my own,' she said.

She turned, and he watched her walk along the street, her hips swinging.

Chapter Twenty-Four
Alfred

I had to mess the house up a bit today, otherwise there wouldn't have been anything for Rosie to do. I only live in the two rooms. Maybe Moira's right. Perhaps I should give the place up. But I'm not giving it to her and Harry and that's that. I'm a stubborn mule. The more you poke me the worse I am. I don't want Rosie to stop coming. I can tell she needs the money and I'm enjoying the company. I bought another angel cake as she seems to like that. It's been nice talking to someone about books and programmes on the tele, that aren't silly soap operas. She's intelligent is Rosie. I don't know why she's cleaning houses. I want to ask her about her husband, but I don't want to pry too much.

There's the sound of a key in the lock and then her cheery voice.

'It's only me Archie.'

It's no good me telling her my name is Alfred. She's got it in her head that I'm Archie and that's that.

She walks into the kitchen and I feel my spirits rise.

'It's freezing out,' she says. 'It's lovely and warm in here though.'

'I've turned the heating up,' I say. 'Do you want a cuppa before you start?'

'Lovely, I'll take it with me as I work.'

She pulls on her apron and smiles.

'Shall I start downstairs?'

'Honestly Rosie, there isn't much to do upstairs but if you could clean out the fridge that would be great.'

The truth is Moira came and cleaned that out at the weekend. She had her usual moan about what was in it and said she'd bring some dinners round. She hasn't, but then I'm pleased as I can't stand her fancy cooking. I'll only be constipated for a week.

'Ooh that reminds me,' says Rosie suddenly. 'I left something in the car. I won't be a minute.'

She dons her coat again and hurries outside, returning a few minutes later with a casserole dish in one hand and the paperback I'd lent her in the other.

'I made you a shepherd's pie,' she says placing it on the kitchen table. The savoury fragrance wafts up towards me and I feel my stomach rumble.

'That's nice of you Rosie,' I say.

I'm chuffed.

'Well, I keep seeing all those TV dinners of yours and as I was cooking anyway I thought I'd make one for you too. It's not good eating that processed rubbish every day. My Sam does too and I'm always telling him ...'

She trails off and her face darkens.

'Anyway, it's only mince but there are plenty of carrots and mushrooms in there.'

'There's loads here,' I say. 'That'll do me several dinners.'

'Good,' she says but she seems distant now.

'Everything alright?' I ask, clicking the kettle on.

'Oh yes,' she says but I can tell it isn't.

She busies herself cleaning the kitchen and then says suddenly,

'He's a bit cross with me.'

'Who is?' I ask.

'My Sam.'

She sprays cleaning liquid into the sink.

'I won some money. It was a few weeks back and I told my Sam it was only a few hundred, but it was a few thousand actually.'

'It's your money,' I say angrily, thinking of Harry and Moira. 'Flipping kids; they expect far too much ...'

'Oh no,' she says looking taken aback. 'It isn't that he wants it. He just didn't understand why I told him it was less than it was. I didn't deliberately do it. It's just I didn't want it getting around and I suppose I got so used to telling everyone that it was less and ...'

I pop teabags into the mugs.

'I hope you won't stop cleaning,' I laugh.

She sighs, and I realise it isn't a joke for her.

'The day I stop work will be the day I pop my clogs.'

'Here, have your cuppa,' I say putting the steaming mugs onto the table.

'I'll drink it as I work,' she says leaning forward to take it.

'No, take five minutes,' I say.

I touch her arm and we both start. I'm taken aback at the effect touching her has on me. How stupid. I'm seventy-three and recently widowed. It's not possible to have a connection with someone so soon is it? But then again, Jack down at the bowls club was married again within the year after his wife, Barbara, died.

'If you've been with someone half your life, it's hard to be alone,' he'd said. 'Anyway, Barbara always said she didn't want me to be alone.'

Cath had said the very same thing.

'Don't go being all maudlin if I go before you. If I'm not here to keep you company, don't go being lonely.'

I was lonely. I miss having someone to chat to in the evenings, or simply to watch the tele with. I got one of those Saga brochures come through the door the other day. Cath and I used to laugh at those. But I've been really tempted to go on one of their group holidays. I just want to get away. But who wants to holiday on their own? Ridiculous that is. If I'm going to be on my own, then I might as well be on my own in my own country and in my own house.

Rosie's cheeks turn pink.

'Just five minutes,' she says.

'I'll cut some angel cake,' I say, mostly for the want of anything better to say.

'I finished *Rebecca*,' she says, pushing the book across the table.

'Did you enjoy it?'

'Oh yes I did.'

'There's a film of the book, you know. I've got it on DVD. You can borrow it if you like.'

She looks embarrassed again and wipes her hand on her apron.

'I don't have a DVD player.'

'Oh,' I say surprised.

Who doesn't have a DVD player these days? Even I've managed to keep up with those, although our Holly keeps telling me no one uses them now.

'Everyone streams these days,' she says. 'Anyway, haven't you heard of Netflix?'

I've not heard of streams or Netflix. Everyone can stream if they want. I'm happy with me DVDs thanks very much.

'We did have one,' explains Rosie, looking uncomfortable. 'But Frank, that was my husband, he broke it and we never bothered to get another.'

'That's a shame. You'd enjoy it.'

She smiles and gets up.

'I'll start on the living room,' she says.

She wants to get away from me. I hope she doesn't think I'm a dirty old man.

'Yeah, great,' I say, opening my newspaper.

She grabs her cleaning materials and disappears out of the room.

'Stupid idiot,' I mutter. 'You've scared her.'

Chapter Twenty-Five
Rosie

I like going to Archie's. Emerson Park is a lovely part of Essex. It's a million miles from Tradmore. You don't get women standing outside their houses puffing on roll-ups and cursing like fishwives here. I bet kids named Paris and Romeo don't live around here either. I've been looking at some flats in the area. There are some for rent. I asked at the estate agents. What a fool I am. I actually thought maybe I could move now that I have some money behind me and plenty of work. But the truth is I won't be able to do all these jobs, not now I'm sixty. My hip is creating and I'm so knackered at the end of the day that I barely have the energy to make myself dinner. I'm not sleeping well either. Some idiot's car alarm keeps going off in the early hours and someone in the flat upstairs keeps playing rap music at gone midnight. The rent is high in Emerson Park, and then of course I'd have to find the deposit. I need to hang onto Waitrose, just in case the murders dry up. Well, let's face it there aren't murders every day and thank goodness for that. This is Essex, not the Bronx. I saw a lovely place in Hornchurch. It's a converted house. An elderly lady lives on the ground floor. She's not going to be playing rap music at midnight, is she? But then again, who knows? I said I'd go back and take another look at the weekend. I've got the deposit and I should just be able to make the rent and bills if I keep Archie's cleaning job, Waitrose and the cinema. I've paid the back rent on the Tradmore flat and there are Frank's debts to pay each month but that won't last forever. It might be hard the first few months but I'm seriously thinking I could do it. Sam will always take care of the car if I have problems.

I like this job. I especially like cleaning the living room where all the books are. I don't want Archie thinking I'm being too familiar. I won't have any more tea or angel cake with him. Maybe I shouldn't borrow any more books from him either. After all, I can get them from the library. I'll just make a note of the titles that are on his bookshelf.

'Rosie.'

I spin round at the sound of his voice.

'Is everything okay?' I ask.

He fidgets uncomfortably.

'I didn't mean to offend you in the kitchen. It's just my way.'

'Oh, I know,' I say quickly.

'It's just I see us as friends, you know.'

I bow my head. Oh dear, this is awkward. I don't think Becky wants me being best mates with the clients. But he is lovely, is Archie.

'I … I just don't want Becky getting cross …' I trail off.

He looks confused.

'Why should she get cross?'

'She might think I'm not doing my job properly.'

He scoffs.

'You do a brilliant job. Even Moira admires it.'

I raise my eyebrows.

'She does?'

'Anyway,' he continues. 'It doesn't matter what she thinks. I'm happy with what you do, and I look forward to you coming. I don't talk to no one these days, so I enjoy our little chats, what's wrong with that? It's nice to talk to someone who knows a good book from a trashy one.'

'I enjoy the books,' I say with a smile.

'Right, that's settled,' he grins. 'So, you won't take this the wrong way then, will you? Why don't you pop back this evening and have some of that shepherd's pie with me? There's far too much there for one and then we can watch *Rebecca*. I'll see you back home. All proper and above board, after all, you've only recently lost your husband and me my wife.'

I'm taken aback, I don't mind admitting.

'People might talk,' I say stupidly.

'Huh, let them. I've never worried about other people and I'm not going to start now,' says Archie, looking me in the eye. 'What do you say?'

'I would like to see *Rebecca*,' I say.

I'm all timid. How ridiculous for a woman my age. I wonder if Archie has guessed my age. I hope not. It will be nice to sit somewhere quiet and eat my dinner for a change.

'So, we're on. Great,' he says slapping his thigh.

'I can bring popcorn,' I say. 'I work at the cinema and I get loads.'

'I haven't had popcorn in years. Yes, bring some.'

I turn back to the vacuum cleaner.

'I'll leave you to it,' says Archie, leaving the room and closing the door.

Who'd have thought it, me, having shepherd's pie and watching a DVD in a fancy house in Emerson Park? I won't know myself.

Chapter Twenty-Six
Rosie

'We're all going to the bingo,' says Doris over the phone. 'Do you want to come? You're our lucky mascot now.'

'I can't,' I say. 'I'm going out.'

'Oh,' she says surprised. 'Out where?'

'I'm going to a friend's house to watch a DVD.'

There's a few seconds of silence.

'You going to Crabbers then?'

'No, I'm not.'

'Oh, you're a dark horse.'

'No I'm not,' I protest.

'Alright, don't do anything I wouldn't do. Wish us luck.'

'Good luck,' I say.

I click off the phone and check my hair in the mirror. The flat reverberates with the shouting from next door. They haven't been in the flat very long and all they do is scream blue murder at each other. My nerves are in shreds. Twice there's been a thud against my wall. I don't imagine they've got much crockery left in that flat. I pull my hair up and then let it down again. I look older with it up. I study my reflection and sigh. I look knackered and no amount of make-up seems to cover it. I wonder if I should take the make-up off. I don't want Archie knowing I made a big effort. He'll think I'm after him and then Moira will think I'm after his money. I reckon he's got a lot. You don't have a house like that unless you've got a bit. He's got a nice car in the driveway too. Not brand new but newer than mine. Mind you, everyone's car is newer than mine. I bet his wife never had to work when she was past sixty. I smother my face in Ponds cold cream and remove the war paint. I then pinch my cheeks to give them some colour. Finally, I grab my handbag. It's a relief not to have that huge tote bag any more. I'd finally gone to the Halifax and opened an account. I'd been a quivering wreck convinced that when I told them my name they would say 'Oh no, we can't take that. You need to pay off your debts with that money.' But, of course, they had no idea about the debts or Frank's accident.

I take the veg from the fridge. I'd bought it especially, but I won't tell Archie that. There's another crash and a scream from my neighbours. I sigh and open my front door. I'll be glad to get away for an evening. I'm so taken aback at the sight of the two men standing outside my flat that I let out a little scream myself and promptly drop the veg. Not that anyone takes any notice of screams here. You could be murdered in your bed and no one would take any notice. It's a small landing and the men seem to fill all of it.

'Alright?' says one.

He's big and burly. I can see his rippling muscles through his open jacket. You can tell he's the type that spends hours in the gym. His blond hair is cut close to his scalp. An earring in the shape of a skull hangs from his earlobe and a large medallion dangles around his neck. I've seen him around the estate and I have no doubt he is Matt Fisher. He looks a Matt if you know what I mean.

'Yes, thanks,' I say nervously, locking my door and picking up the veg.

'You're Rosie Foster, aren't you?'

'No, you've got the wrong person,' I say, heading for the stairs.

My heart thumps in my chest. The other bloke is small and puny next to this burly one. He narrows his eyes and says, 'I don't think we 'ave.'

'Got time for a quick word,' says Burly. 'It's about your old man, Frank.'

'He's brown bread,' I say, taking another step down the stairs but Puny hurries down them ahead of me and is now blocking my way. 'He walked in front of a Domino's Pizza van.'

'The daft cockwomble,' says Puny.

I'm full of tricks but defending Frank isn't one of them. Let's face it, he doesn't deserve it.

'Yeah okay Rick,' says Burly, who I now feel certain is Matt Fisher. I'm so relieved I don't have the holdall any more.

'He owed me money, a fair bit as it 'appens.'

'Shame for you he's dead then,' I say.

'Yeah, that piece of crap twat waffle owed us a nice little sum when he got squashed,' says Puny. He's certainly got a way with words.

'Okay Rick,' says Burly with a sigh.

'I'm going to be late,' I say, attempting to side step Rick.

'We won't keep you a minute. Matt Fisher's the name. Everyone knows me on the estate. Frank was banging some bird from the dogs. Did you know that?'

'I do know,' I say.

If my heart thumps much harder I'll pass out.

'He liked to spend money on 'er. Fuck knows why. She was a right little slapper. He was a festering little scrote was Frank,' says Rick with venom.

Just as well I had those tests done. Turns out they were all clear, but you can't take any chances, can you? What was wrong with Frank putting it about with an old slapper?

'If you were a flower I'd spray weedkiller on you,' I snap at Puny.

'Sorry about Rick,' says Matt. 'He has no idea how to be around a woman. All I want is me money. I know you had a nice little win on the bingo.'

I should have known.

'Frank owed you the money, not me,' I say.

The door to the flat next door bursts open, and a screaming girl runs out in her nightie.

'Get away from me you mad sod,' she cries, running straight into Matt.

The mad sod appears at the door, takes one look at Matt and widens his eyes. He tries to close the door, but Matt is there before he has the chance.

'Darren, I was gonna give you a knock,' Matt smiles.

Rick moves up the stairs and I take the opportunity to dash past him.

'Oy,' yells Matt. 'I ain't finished talking to you.'

I'm out of the front entrance and in to my car before Rick has made it down the stairs. I can hardly get my breath mind you, and if hips could speak mine would be screaming blue murder. I'm only glad it isn't my old Fiesta otherwise I'd still be sitting on the gearstick. Luckily the car starts right away, and I skid out of Tradmore without a glance behind me. I know I haven't seen the last of Matt Fisher. I can't give them my five thousand, can I? Well, the fact is, I don't have five thousand any more. If I give them my winnings I won't be able to get my new flat or go to Paris. No, I'm damned if Frank is going to do me out of that. Why can't his slapper girlfriend sell her furs and pay Matt? I'll chase her up. I don't see why she should get off scot-free. I look in my rear-view mirror. No one is following me. I don't really fancy a *Bourne Identity* car chase, but if needs must.

By the time I reach Archie's I've calmed down a bit. I'm ten minutes late though. I grab the popcorn and veg from the back of the car and hurry to the front door. It opens before I have a chance to knock.

'Sorry I'm late,' I say.

He looks relieved.

'No worries,' he says casually. 'I didn't even notice. Come on in.'

Chapter Twenty-Seven
Alfred

I'm just starting to think that Rosie isn't coming when I hear her car pull into the driveway. She looks a bit flustered.

'Sorry I'm late,' she says.

'No worries,' I say. 'I didn't even notice.'

She pulls off her coat and takes the veg she'd brought into the kitchen.

'It looks different at night,' she says and then blushes.

'I suppose it does,' I say. 'I've lit the fire in the living room. It's bitter tonight. You've got antifreeze in your car, haven't you?'

'I think so. I imagine Sam would have done that.'

'Yeah, I think he would have. The pie's in the oven.'

She hands me the popcorn shyly.

'I'll do the veg,' I say, 'unless you want to.'

'Oh,' she says uncertainly.

'You'll probably make a better job of it than me.'

'Okay,' she says looking around.

'The pans are in here,' I say, opening a cupboard. She looks out of the kitchen window.

'You've got fairy lights in the garden.'

I laugh.

'Yeah, Cath wanted them, so I put them up. I used to tinker in the workshop out there. Wood carving, but I haven't done it since Cath got sick. She used to bring me a cuppa and complain she couldn't find her way, not even with the garden light. So she bought these fairy lights from Ikea. She liked Ikea.'

Rosie smiles at me.

'I went to Ikea once,' she says. 'I liked it too.'

She takes a pan from the cupboard, fills it with water and takes it to the Aga.

'Your house is huge,' she says. 'My whole flat must be the size of your living room and kitchen combined.'

I take some wine from the fridge. I don't know why. I don't normally drink wine, at least not on my own. A nice whisky after dinner does me.

'Shall I open this?' I ask.

'Oh no, I'm driving,' she says.

'Yeah, you're right,' I agree. 'I'll lay the table. You don't mind eating in the kitchen, do you?'

'It'll make a nice change from sitting with it on my lap,' she smiles.

I shake out the tablecloth and am about to put it on the table when there's a knock at the door. Rosie turns and looks at me nervously.

'No one else is coming, are they?'

'Not by my invitation,' I say.

I open the door to my neighbour, Celia. She flashes an orange card at me.

'They left my parcel with you. I had to go to the hospital. I'm usually home. I did give them a safe place to leave it, but you know what they're like.'

'Oh yes, I'll get it,' I say. 'It's in the kitchen cupboard.'

When Archie Met Rosie

I'd put it in the kitchen out of the way. I didn't want Cleo clawing at it. Rosie is laying the table. I turn to go back to the hall and stop when I see Celia standing in the kitchen doorway.

'It's a bit cold standing at your front door,' she says, looking past me to Rosie.

'Hello, you're Alf's cleaner, aren't you? He's keeping you late.'

'I ...' begins Rosie.

'Here it is,' I say handing her the parcel.

'Right,' she says looking from me to Rosie.

'I'll see you out, shall I?' I say giving her a little push.

Nosy old biddy. What a cheek walking straight into my kitchen without an invitation.

'Enjoy your evening,' she says smirking.

'I intend to.'

Before she can reply I close the front door. Rosie looks up as I walk back in.

'I didn't think about pudding,' she says.

'I've got some ice cream in the freezer,' I grin, pulling out a chair.

'Have a pew.'

'Thanks,' she says, sitting down nervously.

'Have you spoken to Sam yet?'

'No, I will though.'

She looks around the kitchen and says.

'It's so quiet here.'

'Is it?'

She nods.

'I'm thinking of getting myself a little flat in Hornchurch. I've got the deposit. I'm going to look at it again at the weekend.'

'You should,' I say nodding.

I don't like to think of her in that run-down estate. They'd think nothing of stabbing you for a few bob. She's better off out of there.

'I'll do the dinner,' she says jumping up.

I hope she calms down a bit by the time we watch the film. She seems much edgier than she did this morning.

'Anything I can do?' I ask.

'Oh no,' she smiles.

It's grand having a woman cook dinner. I hadn't realised how much I'd missed it.

Chapter Twenty-Eight
Rosie

It's lovely at Archie's, all quiet and peaceful. Even my shepherd's pie seems to taste better. How daft is that? But I swear it does. The trouble is I can't really enjoy it for thinking about Matt Fisher and the fact that I have to go home later. What if he's lurking around the flats? There are a lot of rumours about Matt Fisher and what he does to people who don't pay their debts. Della Gregory, who lives in the flat underneath mine, told everyone it was Matt Fisher who did her son's knees and not a scaffolding accident like he told everyone. I can believe it too. I can't imagine what possessed Frank to borrow five grand. What on earth did he do with it? If I pay the debt I'll have nothing left, and I'll be back where I started. I'll be worse off, in fact. I'll be stuck on the Tradmore Estate with no way out whatsoever. It's so unfair. It's not even my debt. I can't tell Sam. I don't want him worrying. Life sucks, it really does. Why are there some people like Archie, who have everything, and then people like me who have sod all? It's not like I haven't worked hard. I just seem to be forever climbing Mount Everest and not getting anywhere, whereas people like Archie reach the top and still have energy to carry on climbing. I'm rubbish, that's what I am. I can't even have a win at the bingo and enjoy it. This is no good is it? Self-pity? Where does that ever get you?

'Ice cream?' asks Archie.

'Matt Fisher, the loan shark, is after me,' I blurt out.

Where did that come from? I opened my mouth to say yes to ice cream and that came out instead. Poor Archie, he must think I'm a walking disaster area. He stops with his hand on the freezer door.

'Matt Fisher?' he questions.

Of course, Archie wouldn't know who Matt Fisher was. He's most likely never taken out a loan in his life. I wish I'd married someone like Archie instead of a spineless wimp.

'He's a loan shark. He's well known on the Tradmore Estate,' I say, blushing profusely at the shame of it all. 'He did Drew's kneecaps and Freda Morris, who lives in the block opposite me, well, her husband just disappeared. He went out one evening for a pint and never came home. They say he owed Matt Fisher a fortune. He gives you so many weeks and if you don't pay up ...' I hesitate, my throat turning dry. 'You could ... you could ... find yourself at the bottom of the Thames or something even worse.'

Although, there are not many things worse than ending up at the bottom of the Thames are there?

Archie stares at me. He's most likely thinking what a twat I am and wondering what on earth he was thinking of, inviting me here for dinner. He must be dead embarrassed that his neighbour saw me; some common piece from the worst part of Essex, in his house preparing dinner. He's probably trying to work out how to get rid of me. I ought to leave. I'm getting above myself, that's what I'm doing. I stand up in such a rush that Cleo runs to the cat flap.

'I should be going,' I say looking around for my bag.

'You what?' says Archie, looking flummoxed. 'We haven't seen the film.'

The cat flap slams shut, and I envy Cleo her escape.

'I know,' I say stupidly. 'It's just ...'

Tears rush to my eyes and I could die. I really could. I wish I'd been mowed down by a Domino's Pizza van. I wish I'd never won at the bingo. It's been nothing but a curse that money. I hurry into the hallway and look for my coat, but I can't see clearly for the tears blurring my eyes.

'Hold up Rosie. Hold up,' says Archie following me. 'What's happened? All I did was ask if you wanted ice cream.'

'It's not you Archie, it's me. I'm all ...'

Hormonal is what I am. Stupid menopause, I hate it.

'In a tither is what you are,' he says taking my arm.

'Let's have some ice cream and then I'll make a nice pot of tea and we can talk about Matt Fisher. I assure you that I won't let anyone throw you in the Thames.'

I sniff, and he hands me a nicely laundered hanky. A real hanky too, with the initial A embroidered into the corner.

'This is a nice hanky,' I say.

'Cath bought them for me one Christmas. She never knew what else to buy. I've got that many socks you'd think I was Jake the Peg.'

I laugh.

'Come on, girl. Let's put the kettle on.'

My whole life is putting the kettle on it seems and things still don't improve. What I need is a large glass of wine. But I settle for a strong mug of Tetley and Waitrose's chocolate chip ice cream.

'I expect you're used to this, what with you working there and everything,' smiles Archie, piling more into my dish. 'Tell me what Matt Fisher's been up to.'

So I do. I tell him all about our Frank too and the new locks on the doors, about regrets and getting older and finally Paris. I'm like a faulty tap. You just can't turn me off. Archie is silent the whole time and I'm not sure if it is because he's shocked or if he's just being polite. Finally I run out of things to say and sip my tea, which is now cold. Archie says nothing, gets up from the table, rummages in the dresser opposite and places a brochure in front of me.

'Saga,' he says. 'I wouldn't normally give them the time of day, but I can't be arsed to organise things these days. Paris, seven days, tours and everything, why don't we go together for Christmas, what do you say?'

Chapter Twenty-Nine
Rosie

Her name's Pat. I got it out of Pete, one of Frank's mates. I told him Frank had left her a bit of money.

'She'll be glad of that,' he'd said.

She'd be glad of it? I'd be glad of it too, except Frank had no money to leave anyone. She lives in a little house in Poplar. It's a slummy street, almost as bad as the Tradmore Estate. Flowery curtains are drawn across grubby windows. I bang on the front door, but no one answers.

'Are you looking for Pat?' calls a woman from the upstairs window of the house next door.

'Yes.'

'She'll be sleeping. She never gets up until about two. She's a lazy cow.'

'Is that right,' I say, hammering harder on the door. 'I've come from Essex so I'm not going until I've seen her.'

She closes her window and a few minutes later she has joined me at Pat's front door.

'Are you a debt collector?' she asks.

'No.'

The two of us stand on the porch. It's freezing. Down the street a couple of other women have come out to watch.

'They think you're a social worker,' says the neighbour, waving to the women.

'I'm not a social worker,' I say.

'I'm Joy,' she says, offering me her packet of cigarettes.

'I don't smoke.'

'You're sensible,' she says, lighting up.

I bang again on the door.

'You must be desperate to see her,' says Joy, peeking through a gap in the curtains.

'I just saw her poke her head through the upstairs curtain,' calls one of the women.

I open the letterbox.

'Pat, it's Rosie Foster. Open the door. I'm mad enough to kick it down if you don't.'

'Crikey,' says Joy. 'Are you the police?'

'No I'm not.'

'What's she done?' calls one of the other women.

It's not a bit like the Tradmore Estate now I come to think about it. A whiff of trouble and everyone makes out like nothing is happening. Not here. A bit of a commotion and the whole street comes out, it seems.

There's movement behind the door and then it opens slightly.

'You're making a scene,' says a hoarse voice.

'Let me in then.'

'Pete said you had some money for me,' says Pat.

I push at the door almost sending her flying. Joy tries to follow me in, but I slam the door shut. The house stinks of cats and stale beer. I wrinkle my nose.

'I'd have cleaned up, but I didn't know you were coming,' she says.

She's wearing a silk kimono. Her dyed blonde hair is askew, and she smells of stale cigarettes. What was Frank thinking? There's a bit of rough and a bit of rubbish. Frank always did get things mixed up.

'Frank owed money. No doubt borrowed so he could buy you lots of lovely things,' I say, looking around her living room. 'I imagine that kimono was one of them.'

The living room is lit by a single lamp. The room's a tip.

'Do you want something to drink?' she asks.

There's a loud squeal as I step on one of her numerous cats.

'Careful,' she snaps.

'I need all the things of value that Frank gave you. I have to pay his debts,' I say firmly.

My eyes land on a sparkling diamond on her finger.

'Oh no,' she says, backing away. 'Frank gave me that. It's special. It's my engagement ring.'

'He was married to me, you stupid mare. He couldn't get engaged to you.'

'He was going to divorce you.'

I roll my eyes.

'Hand it over.'

'No way.'

'Frank never had any money so that ring was bought with money he borrowed, and it has to go back. I'll have that fur coat you were wearing at the funeral, too.'

She hurries to the front door.

'You haven't got anything for me at all, have you? You lied. You can leave now.'

'I'm not going until I have that ring and coat,' I say, without any clear idea of how I'm going to get them.

'Fuck off,' she says.

That was it really. I'm mild mannered as a rule but things are really starting to get me down. Let's face it, everyone has walked over Rosie Foster. Frank walked over me every single day and look what he was doing behind my back.

'Right, fine,' I say determinedly. 'I'll send Matt Fisher around. He's the one owed the money. I'll tell him about that ring. Be prepared, he won't be as nice as me. Most likely he'll kick your door down without knocking.'

Her eyes widen.

'He'll cut your finger off too, if necessary but I want him off my back so he's all yours.'

I stroll to the front door where Joy and her neighbours are waiting outside amidst a cloud of cigarette smoke.

'Hold on,' calls Pat nervously. 'I don't want Matt Fisher here. I'll give you the coat.'

'I want the ring,' I say.

'Frank will be turning in his grave.'

'He would if he was in one. Didn't you notice he was cremated?'

'Can I have his ashes?' she asks tearfully.

'You're too late. I flushed them down the loo.'

The women gasp.

'Oh my godfathers,' says Joy, shocked.

'How could you?' cries Pat.

I shrug.

'I couldn't actually, you're quite right. Anyway, I'll give Matt your address. Good luck.'

I'm almost out of the door when she grabs my arm.

'Alright.'

She pulls the ring off and hands it to me.

'Can I keep the coat? It's the only one I've got.'

I nod and tuck the ring into my bag. The coat wouldn't fetch much anyway.

'I don't really want the ashes,' she says quietly. 'He was a selfish arse.'

I can't disagree with that.

'Don't tell Matt Fisher where I live.'

I give a nod and see myself out. The door closes behind me and I wade through the cigarette haze.

'All sorted then?' asks Joy.

'Yes, thank you.'

I walk to the bus stop with my head held high.

Chapter Thirty
Rosie

'It was a gangland killing,' says Becky. 'Apparently the husband and …'

'I don't want to know,' I interrupt.

'It was Russians that did it,' she says, like knowing it was Russian thugs would somehow make me feel loads better.

I wonder if Becky will clean my little flat after Matt Fisher has finished with me. She won't thank me. Those stairs are heart attack inducing. It's all I can do to get up them these days. I've been tempted to get into the lift, but the thought of Matt Fisher diving in after me has sent me trudging up the stairs. It's slow progress when you keep stopping to look over the stairwell. I hate these early nights when it's dark by four o'clock. I'm not quick enough for the timer these days. I'm always three steps away when it clicks off. I almost wet myself going up those three steps, I don't mind telling you. I fully expect a knife in my back. I'm sweating buckets by the time I switch the timer back on. I swear these stairs have taken ten years off my life. It was a total waste of money buying a jar of La Prairie face cream. I keep looking for a difference, but I can't see any. It takes time I imagine. I suppose it took a hell of a time for me to look like this in the first place, so it'll take a hell of a lot longer to repair won't it? There's not been any sign of Matt Fisher since that night. I imagine he's just biding his time. Meanwhile I'm aging by the second. Still, I have the ring to barter with. I've no idea what it is worth. But the diamond looks real, so it must be worth a bit. To think Frank couldn't be bothered to buy me a new wedding ring. I sigh. I really should collect the ashes.

'Are you okay?' asks Becky.

'I'm tired,' I admit.

'You'll get a nice break over Christmas,' she smiles.

That's the other thing. It's been over a week since Archie mentioned Paris and I just don't know what to do. I'm supposed to be thinking it over. He must think I've got sawdust for brains if it takes me this long. I daren't tell Becky. If she knew of my friendship with Archie she might get someone else to clean Archie's house. As it is we're conducting our friendship in such a clandestine fashion that you'd think we were having an affair. Archie doesn't want his Harry to find out.

'They'll get it all out of proportion,' he'd said.

I haven't mentioned anything to Sam either. Although I did tell the truth about the bingo win.

'Ah, that explains it then,' he'd said.

'Explains what?' I'd asked.

'Why Maureen was on my doorstep going on about it.'

'Maureen?' I'd said aghast.

That little cow, honestly. Where there's money, there's Maureen. I tell you, it's a true saying that *money is the root of all evil*. If Frank hadn't spent so much on that brassy blonde of his he may not have got into such terrible debt. Mind you, Frank was always broke. Frank and money just never went well together. If they had, we could have taken out a mortgage. I blame myself really. I was too accepting of my lot. I should have expected more but for some reason I didn't. I had this stupid mentality that people like us don't have fancy houses or money in a savings account. Now look at me. I have almost five thousand in the bank and I'm having the devil's own job hanging onto it. I should spend it. Spend the whole lot. No one can have it if I've spent it, can they?

I follow Becky into the cordoned off flat.

'Is there somewhere we can change?' she asks the police officer at the entrance.

This is only our second murder. I rather think Becky and I had a morbid view on life in Essex if we really thought there'd be one a week. Of course there wouldn't. Becky said we could do others, but we'd need to travel. I don't want to travel miles just to clean. Becky said she might, but she's got a family to feed.

'I'll show you,' says the police officer with a comforting smile.

I really don't know what I'm doing cleaning up murder scenes. The things we do for money huh? It always comes back to that doesn't it?

My phone bleeps and I pull it from my pocket. It's a message from Archie. *Are you doing a murder?*

Oh dear. I'd better delete that message once I've replied to it. It looks pretty odd otherwise. I'll probably need to delete my reply too.

Yes, just starting one. Is everything okay?

Archie has never texted me before. I gave him my number weeks ago when I first started cleaning his house, but I never imagined he would use it. It's been several minutes now and still he hasn't answered. Becky has tapped away numerous messages while I've been waiting.

'Let's go,' she says.

I look down at my phone. I wonder if I should phone him.

'I'll be there in a sec,' I say.

'Okey-dokey,' she says, pulling on her protective face mask.

'Latest fashion?' laughs the police officer.

It's odd how people can easily laugh at others misfortune isn't it? I stare at my phone, willing Archie to message me. It's been ages. Right, that's it. I'd better phone him.

'Sorry. I can't do this texting malarkey. Are you free later?' he asks.

'I'm doing a late shift at Waitrose.'

'You'll kill yourself you will. I want to show you something. We can get some lunch.'

I can't have lunch out with Archie. What if people see us?

'I ...'

'What time will you finish the murder?'

'About twelve I imagine.'

'Great. Do you know The George in Gidea Park?'

'I've seen it.'

'See you there sometime after twelve?'

'Rosie?' calls Becky.

'I'd better go,' I say.

'See you later.'

I push my phone into my pocket and don my outfit. What am I doing? I can't meet Archie. What would Becky say? It's unprofessional isn't it?

'Don't be a tit,' whispers a voice in my head. 'It's only lunch.'

I'm being silly, aren't I? It's okay to meet for lunch isn't it? I'm not planning on going back to a hotel with him, am I? Can you imagine, at my age? I can just picture Moira's face. She'd be mortified. It's probably worth it just to see her reaction. I smile to myself and then hurry up the stairs to the flat.

Chapter Thirty-One
Moira

Moira examined her newly painted finger nails.

'All ready for Christmas?' asked Amanda, packing away her manicure gear. She looked back at Moira's nails and nodded with approval.

'Not many women can carry off that colour, but you do it marvellously,' she said.

'It's perfect,' purred Moira.

'Are you at home for Christmas?' asked Amanda.

'Yes, but we're always busy at Christmas,' Moira sighed. 'Of course we've got Harry's play. I thought I'd do a little party afterwards, you know, for all the cast.'

Amanda felt her face grow hot at the sound of Harry's name.

'Sounds lovely,' she said.

Moira climbed carefully onto Amanda's couch.

'Just half a leg today,' said Moira.

'Of course,' said Amanda carefully taking her waxing materials from her bag.

The mention of Harry had thrown her into a bit of a tither. She wondered if she should tell Moira what she'd seen. It was difficult to find the words though and she didn't want to start poking a hornets nest. After all, Moira was only a client. If she'd been a close friend it might have been different. All the same, even telling a close friend that you'd seen her husband at a hotel with another woman would be difficult. What if it hadn't been Harry Bolton? She didn't want to stir up trouble when there wasn't any. She had only met Harry the once and she was doing Moira's underarms at the time, so she could easily be mistaken. All the same, she felt sure the man she'd seen at the Park Hotel in Thurrock was Harry. She'd said hello, but he'd not heard her. He'd walked straight past her and into the arms of a very attractive brunette. Amanda had quickly dived through the doors. She couldn't believe she had seen Moira's husband with another woman and at a hotel too. It could only mean one thing. He obviously hadn't expected to see anyone he knew. No doubt that was why they were in Thurrock. Amanda wouldn't have been there herself if it hadn't have been for the wedding. She'd been pretty knackered after doing all those bridesmaids' nails, so there was every chance she could have been mistaken and it hadn't been Harry Bolton at all. It was best not to say anything, she decided. Don't rock the boat, her mother always said.

'Don't forget to put the towel on the table,' said Moira breaking into Amanda's thoughts.

'Yes,' said Amanda, carefully placing her things on the towel that Moira had provided. It really wasn't big enough for everything but she daren't put her stuff on the floor. Amanda wasn't at all comfortable in Moira's house. It wasn't natural to have a house so immaculate. The floors were so well polished that her socks slid on them. Moira always had vases of perfectly arranged roses. There wasn't one wilted petal amongst them. Not like Amanda's flat where there were vases of dead carnations. Even the flowers were afraid to die in Moira's house. Amanda thought it was no surprise that Harry's eyes had wandered. Poor bloke was probably stifled, thought Amanda.

The doorbell rang, and Amanda jumped, dropping the wax strip she was holding. She dived after it, catching it in the nick of time.

'It didn't go on the carpet did it?' asked Moira alarmed.

'No, I caught it in time,' said Amanda shakily. 'Shall I get the door for you?'

'Thanks Amanda. I can't think who it could be,' Moira sighed, irritation evident in her voice. 'I didn't arrange anything because I knew you were coming. It's the perils of being a counsellor.'

Amanda rolled her eyes and hurried to the front door, relieved to be out of the stuffy lounge. Celia Richardson stood on the doorstep.

'I've come to see Moira,' she said briskly.

'I'm in the lounge Celia,' called Moira. 'Is everything okay with Dad?'

Celia pushed past Amanda and strode into the lounge.

'I think there's something you should know about Alfred,' declared Celia.

Chapter Thirty-Two
Rosie

I'm knackered. The thought of dragging my tired body to Waitrose for a late shift sends my head into a spin.

'Thanks Rosie,' says Becky helping me with my stuff. We shove it into the boot and I let out a little sigh.

'It was a tiring one, wasn't it?' she says, brushing stray hairs from her face.

I look back at the flat.

'You're not still worried about Matt Fisher, are you?' she asks.

'Just a touch,' I say forcing a laugh. 'I bet he knew the thugs that did that,' I say nodding towards the flat.

'Don't be daft. You looked knackered.'

'Well, like you say, I'll get a break over Christmas.'

Who knows, maybe Christmas in Paris?

'I'll be in touch,' waves Becky.

I wave back and climb into my car to drive to The George. Except when I arrive at the pub it isn't The George at all but The Swan. How could I have got those two mixed up? I tell you, the menopause has got a lot to answer for. Now, I have no idea where to go. I'm already late and I feel myself getting tearful again. Honestly, it's ridiculous. I'm crying about everything these days. I even shed a few tears this morning because the milk was off. I mean, seriously, that's surely telling you it's time to get a grip, isn't it? I try to message Archie to ask where the pub is, but I don't have enough reception on my phone.

'Damn it,' I say bursting into tears.

When Archie Met Rosie

In the rear-view mirror I see a police car pull up behind me and realise I'm on a double yellow line. I roughly wipe away my tears and open the window.

'Everything alright?' asks the policeman peering in through the window.

'I'm a bit lost,' I answer, trying not to let my lips quiver.

A bit lost is an understatement isn't it?

'You do realise that you can't park here?'

'I … yes …'

'Where do you want to go?'

I mumble the name of the pub.

'Alright love, you're not far away. Follow me.'

Great, I'll arrive to meet Archie with a police escort. He'll wonder what on earth has happened. I only hope if Matt Fisher is on my tail, it will well and truly put him off.

*

Archie is pacing up and down outside The George. He looks quite anxious. He's warmly dressed though so at least I don't have to worry about him catching pneumonia. He's wearing a nice thick overcoat. I bet that cost a few bob. I'm in a real quandary about lunch. I remember the pub now. I came here once with the Waitrose Christmas do. It's pricey and I really should offer to pay my half. Men don't pay for women these days do they, and rightly so too. I don't want Archie thinking I'm a gold-digger. The truth is I'd never spend more than a tenner on a meal out. I suppose I can afford to spend more but it doesn't seem right to me to spend a lot of money on food when other people are starving. I suppose that's daft really. After all, not eating isn't going to help the starving is it? If I really wanted to help them I'd give them my five thousand, or at least what's left of it. It's just, I can think of better things to spend money on than a meal out in a fancy restaurant.

Archie waves on seeing me and then frowns at the sight of the police car.

'What's happened?' he asks, looking at the policeman.

'I got lost,' I say. 'Stupid really. I went to the wrong pub.'

'The wrong pub?' he echoes.

'The car park is through there,' says the policeman, pointing. 'No parking on double yellows.'

'Thank you.'

'I'd better park,' I say, turning to Archie.

'Blimey, Rosie, you gave me the shock of my life.'

He looks quite handsome in his overcoat and striped scarf. He has a distinguished, intellectual look about him. I wish I'd had a chance to change. I'm wearing a pair of white slacks with a maroon jumper that I bought from Marks, but my boots are scuffed, and my coat has a button missing. I'll undo them all and then no one will notice. Archie meets me in the car park and I see his shoes are shiny where he'd polished them. I look a right scruff next to him.

'I booked a table,' he says, hooking my arm through his.

'Oh,' I say.

He opens the door for me and smiles.

'For a moment I thought you were going to stand me up.'

He has no idea how close I came.

'Hello Mr Bolton, how are you?' says a waitress approaching us.

Oh no, the staff know him here.

'Hello Rachel, how are you?' asks Archie and then turning to me, 'This is Rosie.'

'Hello Rosie, this way.'

When Archie Met Rosie

She leads us to a table and I feel myself blushing. It's lovelier than I remembered from the Waitrose do. Beautiful paintings of Japanese women adorn the walls and on the far side of the room is a wall-to-wall bookcase.

'Can I get you drinks?' she asks, handing us menus.

'I'll have a beer. My usual,' says Archie.

He looks at me.

'Would you like a glass of wine?'

'Oh no,' I say quickly, although I can't think of anything better. 'I've got to work tonight.'

'Ah yes,' he says. 'I'm forgetting.'

I look down at the menu. I wasn't wrong. It's dead pricey. Even the fish and chips are overpriced.

'Can I have a cup of tea?' I ask.

The waitress smiles.

'What tea would you like?'

'You don't like that Earl Grey rubbish, do you?' asks Archie.

'I don't mind it,' I say. 'But I'll have normal tea please.'

She must think I'm so common. I'm so relieved when she goes.

'When I saw that police car I thought that you'd had a run in with Matt Fisher,' Archie says, relaxing in his seat.

'It was stupid of me to go to the wrong pub,' I say shyly.

'Easily done, now what are you having? I can vouch for the ribs.'

'I only normally have a sandwich for lunch.'

'Let your hair down for once then.'

'I'll have the gammon,' I say.

I used to cook gammon for Frank. It would do us a dinner and then sandwiches the next day and maybe even a salad the day after that. Our Sam likes a good gammon too. I should make it one night and have him and Michael over for dinner.

'Heard any more from that thug Matt Fisher?' Archie asks, after our drinks have been brought over.

'No,' I say worriedly. 'But I have an awful feeling I will.'

'You need to get off that estate.'

People like Archie think it's that easy, don't they? Like I can just up and leave. I can now, because I've had a win at the bingo. But if I hadn't had that win, I'd be stuck, wouldn't I? Matt Fisher would no doubt still be chasing his money. The only difference is that it would be Frank running scared instead of me.

'That's what I want to talk to you about,' adds Archie leaning forward. I can smell his beer. It smells wonderful. I'd love one myself.

'You wanted to talk about Matt Fisher?' I say surprised.

I feel a little let down and quickly squash my feelings of disappointment. I shouldn't be feeling like this should I? I've only just lost my Frank. Of course, there is the little matter of his brassy blonde. It does rather colour everything. What in heaven's name did she see in Frank, with his smelly armpits and pimply back? I know older men can be appealing, I mean just look at Richard Gere. Although the only thing Richard Gere and Frank had in common is their grey hair. I suppose she liked the fact he spent money on her; borrowed money at that.

'Not Matt Fisher exactly, but the little flat you're going to look at.'

'What about it?'

'I want to show you another property that I think you might like more.'

I'm taken aback.

'I thought we could look at it after lunch,' he finishes.

'I have to be at work by six.'

'It's only one now,' he grins looking at his watch. 'There's plenty of time.'

I only hope Archie's kind gesture doesn't involve a flat with a price way over my budget.

Chapter Thirty-Three
Moira

Moira paced nervously as she waited for the kettle to boil.

'You'll wear out that lovely lino of yours if you carry on like this,' said Celia.

'It's not lino,' said Moira, insulted.

'Oh,' said Celia and quickly popped on her glasses.

'They're real flagstones,' said Moira.

'Oh,' repeated Celia. 'I thought it was that imitation lino that looks like flagstones. Of course I can see it isn't now.'

She made a big show of studying the floor. The kettle clicked, and Moira poured water into the teapot.

'Are you absolutely sure it was the cleaning woman?' she asked, taking coasters from a drawer.

'I'd seen her before. She works at Waitrose too. Rosie's her name.'

'Rosie?' said Moira. The memory of that Friday night when Holly was attacked came back to her.

Wasn't her name Rosie? Surely it wasn't the same woman. What was Dad thinking of?

'She was actually cooking dinner?'

'Yes. Alf was a bit cagey too. He can be a bit sharp can Alf. Rude almost.'

'Oh I know,' agreed Moira.

Moira sighed. What on earth was Dad up to now? The last thing she ever imagined was another woman on the scene. She'd fully expected Dad to wither away from a broken heart, not dive into another woman's arms and most certainly not that of the cleaner. Celia must have misunderstood, surely? There must be a reasonable explanation.

'I'm sure it's all very innocent,' said Moira.

'I'm sure,' agreed Celia and then added dubiously, 'all the same ...'

'Perhaps she'd forgotten something from earlier,' said Moira.

'It took her a long time to find it then. Her car was still there at ten o'clock.'

'Ten o'clock?' exclaimed Moira.

Celia nodded.

'Billy hadn't come back so I kept popping out to look for him.'

'Billy?' questioned Moira.

'My cat.'

'Oh, so what time did she leave?'

'It must have been about quarter past ten. It was the break during *News at Ten*. I remember that, so it must have been about quarter past ten when I looked again. Her car had gone then.'

Moira shook her head.

'There's nothing in it. He's still grieving for Cath.'

'That's when they get them though isn't it?' said Celia. 'Gold-diggers know when to strike. They go for the men when they're vulnerable. It wouldn't happen to us women but men ... they're so taken in. He was probably flattered and all that ...'

'Do you think?' said Moira doubtfully, 'No, I don't think Alfie would be taken in by a gold-digger. He's too tight with his money.'

Celia dunked her digestive into her tea.

'All the same, it's best you're aware of it. He's vulnerable. Why don't you phone the cleaning company she works for?'

'I don't know,' said Moira thoughtfully. 'I'll talk to Harry.'

Celia shook her head.

'The more time goes on,' she said in a warning voice. 'He's got that big house. Martha Sell's husband was married within six months of her passing. Nothing the family could do.'

Moira felt her heart lurch.

'I was worried about him getting lonely. We tried to get him to go into a retirement place. Lovely little flat it was. He was adamant he wanted to stay in that huge house on his own. I said if we had the house he could live with us.'

'He doesn't look lonely to me,' scoffed Celia.

Moira put her cup down and began pacing the room again.

'Well if he does marry again it can't be to his cleaner.'

'I couldn't agree more,' said Celia. 'I like your nails by the way. I couldn't get away with that colour.'

Moira glanced at her nails with disinterest.

'It's the perfect colour for Christmas,' said Celia.

What if he wanted to bring her for Christmas, thought Moira. It would be too unbearable for words. She must speak to Harry. They had to stop this madness before it got out of hand.

Chapter Thirty-Four
Rosie

'It's lovely,' I say. 'But it will be way out of my price range.'

Way, way out of my price range, I'd say. It's the sort of place I dream of. A nice two-up two-down little house on a new development. Archie must think my idea of a reasonably priced home matches his. We couldn't be more different. Archie doesn't seem to be listening and opens the front door.

'How did you get the key?' I ask, surprised.

'Ah,' he says tapping his nose.

It's lovely inside and I let out a little gasp. I thought the little flat I looked at in Hornchurch was nicely decorated but everything here is perfect. I can smell the newness of the cream shag pile carpets.

'I'll take my boots off,' I say.

We both pull off our shoes and wander through the lounge in our socks. I'm surprised to see Archie's has a hole in them. I wonder if it would be alright to buy him a pair for Christmas. No, that's a daft idea isn't it? Didn't he say he had hundreds of socks? What do you buy a man for Christmas when he seems to have everything? Anyway, cleaners don't buy Christmas presents for the people they work for. I'm as daft as a brush me, I really am.

'This is the kitchen,' says Archie.

It's lovely and bright with new fitted units.

'They built these last year,' he says, opening the back door. 'There's a little garden. It's not much but ...'

'Oh,' I say, a sigh of appreciation escaping me.

The flat in Hornchurch doesn't have a garden but I hadn't minded. After all, I've never had a garden my whole life. I did have an allotment once, but I could never find the time to go there and it got overgrown. It would be lovely to have a garden. We go back inside, and I follow Archie upstairs.

'I really can't afford this,' I say as we reach the bathroom. A cream coloured bathroom suite greets us. It's shiny and new.

'No dual flush or remote,' says Archie.

'It's still out of my price range,' I repeat.

Maybe Moira is right, and Archie is a bit deaf.

'How much is the flat you looked at?' he asks.

'Seven hundred and fifty a month but that includes the bills,' I say. 'I can't afford more than that and this place, well it is lovely, but it needs furnishing too and I didn't want to spend all my money on furniture.'

He waves a hand dismissively.

'Oh, furniture is nothing.'

It might not be for Archie.

'It's nice of you to show me around and I'm very grateful but it's way out of my price range. I just know it is.'

Surely he has heard me now?

'It's four hundred a month,' he says. 'That's cheaper than the other flat.'

I stare at him open-mouthed. Now, maybe I'm stupid and I don't think I am, but that doesn't sound right to me.

'You can buy second-hand furniture,' he adds.

He then shifts uncomfortably on his feet.

When Archie Met Rosie

'It's my house. I bought it last year. It's a little investment. I've got a few of them now. I was going to rent it out but as you're looking for a place and ...'

How insulting. I've stood on my own two feet all my life and certainly don't need pity. I feel like crying. I know I'm hard up and can't afford a lovely house. He doesn't have to rub it in by bringing me to one and hammering it home that I could never afford it on my own. Well sod that for a game of soldiers. I've never needed anyone's help before and I'm not going to start now. I pull the straps of my bag over my shoulder and say angrily,

'I don't need your charity Archie Bolton. I've always made my own way in life and I can carry on doing so.'

I march angrily down the stairs with Archie behind me.

'Hold up Rosie,' he says.

'No, I won't,' I say.

'Let's talk about it.'

'No,' I say while fighting back my shame. 'I'll be getting the bus back to work.'

Pride before a fall, isn't that what they say? I've got no idea where the bus stop is. I'll no doubt have to walk miles and then I will be late for work. Sod it. Sod everything. I fumble with my boots. My hands are shaking with anger.

'Please wait Rosie,' pleads Archie.

I pull the door open and storm from the house. I turn left without a clue as to where I'm going. I feel so stupid. If only Frank were here. At least Frank never looked down on me.

I realise I'm heading towards a dead end and curse.

'Rosie,' calls Archie running after me in his socks. He looks a right plonker hobbling along in holey ones.

'Which is the way out?' I snap.

'I don't know why you're so upset,' he says bewildered.

'How dare you offer me charity?'

'Charity? If I was offering you charity I'd let you stay there for free, you silly cow.'

I gasp.

'How dare you call me a silly cow?'

'I just dared. Look Rosie. The house is going to be for rent. I don't need the money. I bought it because it's the best way to invest money. I'd rather rent it out to someone I know than to someone I don't who might well trash the place. You're doing me a favour too, you know. I know the place will be well looked after if you're in it.'

I look at his feet.

'You should put your shoes on,' I say. 'You'll get something in your foot.'

'You didn't give me time. You tore out of there like you had a firework up your arse.'

'Archie,' I admonish.

'It's Alfred I'll have you know.'

'What is?'

'My name.'

'Oh,' I say.

'Don't go anywhere,' he says. 'I can't keep running after you. Not with my dodgy knee. I'll just get my shoes.'

I feel stupid now. He waves from the front door and I walk shamefaced back to meet him.

'I didn't mean to offend you,' he says. 'That's the last thing I wanted to do. I'd rather have someone that I know renting the place that's all.'

'Well ...' I hesitate.

'If it makes you happier you can pay me the seven hundred and fifty. But if you don't mind me saying, I think you would be a silly cow to agree to that.'

'Archie,' I warn.

'It's Alfred but I don't know why I keep telling you.'

'Can I think about it?'

'Yeah, course. Add it to the Paris break that you're thinking about.'

He smiles, and I smile back.

'Come on,' he says, hooking my arm through his. 'Let's get a celebratory drink to you thinking about it and then I'll drop you back at your car.'

Can you believe it? Me living in a spanking new two-up two-down. It doesn't seem possible. I can even park my little car on the drive. I won't know I'm born. I really won't. Paris though, I mean I can't really, can I? Sam will be expecting me over Christmas.

Oh, what to do? Who thought, me, Rosie Foster, would have such dilemmas.

Chapter Thirty-Five
Harry

Steph stroked Harry's chest and leant over to kiss him. Her hand slowly travelled down his torso.

'I'm on my lunch break,' he said. 'I've got to get back.'

'It won't take long,' she whispered huskily.

'I don't think I've got it in me,' he laughed.

'Harry Bolton, you're useless,' Steph said playfully. 'I don't know what I'm doing with you.'

She kissed him on the cheek and slid from the bed. Harry admired her naked body and then yawned.

'Do you want a coffee before you go?' Steph asked, slipping into a silky wrap. The heating was up high. She always made sure the place was warm as toast when Harry visited. It was a small flat and Steph worried that Harry would find it cramped after his own semi, but he seemed happy and relaxed when he came.

'No, I'd better get going,' he said sitting up and pulling on his trousers.

'When will I see you?' she asked trying to keep her voice light.

Harry switched on his phone. It bleeped several times. He looked at the screen and sighed.

'Oh no.'

'What is it?' she asked.

'Moira's been trying to get hold of me.'

'Doesn't she ever leave you alone?' said Steph, irritated.

'It must be important. She's going to the office.'

He grabbed his tie and jacket.

'I'll phone you,' he said, opening the door.

'Blimey, Harry, don't I even get a kiss goodbye?'

Harry looked down at the message on his phone.

I don't know why I can't reach you. I'll pop to the office. It was sent forty-five minutes ago. She's probably there already.

Steph twisted him around and planted a kiss on his lips. She felt his resistance and sighed.

'Honestly,' she said angrily. 'I don't mind telling you this is starting to get on my nerves.'

'Not now Steph,' he said, pulling on his shoes.

'It's always *not now Steph*', she mimicked.

He ignored her and opened the door.

'We still haven't talked about the Christmas holidays.'

'We will. I've got to go.'

'Bloody go then,' she said angrily pushing him out of the door and slamming it behind him. He sighed and hurried down the stairs. What on earth was up with Moira that she needed to see him so urgently?

Lynda Renham

Chapter Thirty-Six
Moira

Moira paced up and down the foyer, searching the street outside for a sign of Harry. Carol the secretary was continually on the phone. Moira felt sure she was deliberately staying on it so that Moira wouldn't have a chance to ask her again about Harry. How long a lunch break did Harry have for goodness' sake?

'He shouldn't be much longer,' Carol said as she finally came off the phone. Moira glanced at the clock on the wall.

The door burst open, and Harry hurried in.

'Sorry,' Harry said, kissing Moira on the cheek. 'Come into the office. I only just saw your text. I had a meeting and I turned my phone off.'

Carol looked at her monitor. There was no meeting scheduled in his diary. She rolled her eyes and answered the ringing telephone.

'Is everything okay?' Harry asked when they were alone in his office.

Moira looked around and shook her head. The desk was a muddle of papers and empty cups. Harry's computer could do with a good clean.

'That keyboard is covered in bacteria,' she said, pulling a face.

Harry pulled off his jacket and sat behind his desk.

'Your tie's all askew,' said Moira.

He fiddled with the tie and said,

'So what's the matter?'

'It's your dad.'

'Is he alright?' Harry asked anxiously.

When Archie Met Rosie

'No,' she said shaking her head. 'I think he's losing his mind.'

Harry looked perplexed.

'He's only knocking about with his cleaner.'

'You what?' said Harry widening his eyes.

Moira paced the room.

'Rosie's her name. She works at Waitrose and lives on that horrible Tradmore Estate in Dagenham. She's got her foot in the door and if we're not careful ...'

'Hold on Moira,' said Harry, trying to take everything in. 'How do you know all this?'

'Celia, Alfred's neighbour, saw her there cooking dinner. What a liberty Harry. What is she up to? Celia said she was right at home too.'

'I don't believe it,' said Harry shaking his head.

'Oh I do. Women like that prey on well-off widowers. She no doubt saw her opportunity the first time she went there to clean.'

'I'm sure it's not what you're thinking,' said Harry.

Is this what he raced back for? He fought back a sigh.

'Martha Sell's husband remarried within six months of her dying, so Celia says. No doubt she's a gold-digger too.'

'Who's Martha Sell?' asked Harry, confused.

'It doesn't matter,' snapped Moira irritably. 'The point is, if your dad remarries, everything will be left to some flipping cleaner. Can you imagine? Holly's inheritance down the drain and his house ... Oh, it doesn't bear thinking about.'

She slumped into the chair at Harry's desk.

'I think you're getting a bit carried away,' said Harry.

'You need to talk to him Harry.'

'What am I supposed to say? I can't tell him he can't have women friends.'

'Then I'll do it.'

'I don't think that's a good idea Moira,' he warned.

'Honestly Harry, I don't know where your brain is these days. That play is taking you over.'

'I don't think …'

She stood up.

'Well, I'm not letting you lose your inheritance to some lower-class scum. It's madness. He's lost his mind.'

'Moira …'

'Don't be late tonight. We've got Sylvia and John from across the road coming for drinks.'

Harry looked confused and Moira sighed heavily.

'I don't know why I talk to you.'

She flounced from the room and Harry rubbed his eyes. He felt certain she hadn't mentioned Sylvia and John coming for drinks. He struggled to remember who Sylvia and John were. This was getting too much. He ought to call a halt to this thing with Steph. It was messing with his head. He couldn't really handle it. The guilt punched him every time he was with Moira. But life was fun with Steph. He got to let go a bit. Throw his tie wherever he wanted. It was relaxed and cosy at Steph's and the sex was great, he couldn't deny that. Sex with Moira was non-existent these days. She said it was the menopause, but surely she was too young to be starting that? Maybe she'd just gone off him. That was what he thought. He only wished she wasn't so obsessed with Dad and that house of his. Honestly, as if Dad would have another woman. It was laughable.

Chapter Thirty-Seven
Rosie

All I can think about is Archie's little house. I try to imagine me living there. It's like a dream.

'Lilian's off,' Brian greets me as I walk into the staff room. 'We've also got two on holiday.'

'Oh,' I say.

'It's going to be mad. What with Christmas,' he moans.

'Christmas is weeks away,' I say. 'People won't be buying Christmas food yet.'

'That's what you'd think,' he says with a wink. 'But I know Waitrose shoppers.'

'Right,' I say.

You can't argue with our manager Brian. I don't have the energy anyway, even if I wanted to.

'You'll be on the till for the whole shift,' he says.

I don't mind being on the till. At least I get to sit down. Mind you, you do get pins and needles in your bum after a while. I glance slyly at the holiday chart. Brian sees me, and a look of horror crosses his face.

'You're not thinking this side of Christmas?' he says.

His cheek begins to twitch.

'More like Christmas week,' I say.

'What!' he explodes 'You should have booked that months ago.'

'I ...'

'It's not possible,' he says, a tone of finality in his voice.

'I only want ...'

'No, you've left it too late.'

This is worse than being at school.

'It's just ...'

'It can't be entertained. If you take time off it will have to be unpaid. I'll need to get cover.'

He looks at his watch.

'Shouldn't you be on the shop floor?'

That went well didn't it? I told Archie it would be difficult to get time off over Christmas especially at this short notice.

'I can't afford to lose my job,' I'd told him.

'They can't sack you if you're off sick,' he'd said.

'Archie, I can't lie.'

But it's very tempting. Paris at Christmas ... The only thing that had stopped me from booking it was the thought of going on my own. I didn't fancy that much. I could go sick, couldn't I? People do it all the time don't they? I bet Lilian isn't really sick. I know she wanted to go to the Christmas market in Bath. I bet that's where she is right now. Living it up in Bath while a knackered me tries to cover her shift as well as my own. I hope she brings me back something nice from Bath. I bet she doesn't. I'd like to go to Bath.

I settle myself behind the till and smile at the next customer. You have to keep a smile pasted on your face. They insist on that. It can be hard sometimes, especially when you get the stroppy cows who talk like they have a plum in their mouth. You often can't see their nose because it's so high in the air,

When Archie Met Rosie

'How's your day today?' I ask the blonde, harassed mum. I'd like to know how she can afford to shop here. You'd never get me shopping here, not even if I had pots of money. You can get the same stuff in Lidl for half the price. Why pay more? I don't care about the smiling cashier. They can throw the stuff at me if they like. As long as it's cheap I couldn't care less.

'Bloody awful,' says the blonde. 'If I'd known what I know now I'd never have had kids.'

She's not your standard Waitrose customer, and then I see, behind her in the queue, another, so not standard Waitrose customer. Matt Fisher. I can't believe my eyes. He's looking at me over his packet of black peppered mackerel fillets.

'Conor, come away from there,' screeches the blonde.

I can't have a run in with Matt Fisher, not in Waitrose.

'Do you want to go to the next till,' Delia says, approaching him.

She's got the worst job, has Delia. Standing around and directing people to tills. I pray Matt Fisher will go to the other till but of course he doesn't. It's me he wants and not black peppered mackerel. The mackerel is just a ploy.

'I'm 'appy 'ere thanks very much,' says Matt, winking at me. It doesn't reassure me in the least.

'Thanks,' says the blonde before screeching to Conor.

Matt Fisher approaches and slaps his mackerel on to the counter.

'Alright?' he asks.

I scan the mackerel and hand it back.

'Four pounds twenty,' I say in my best cheerful Waitrose voice. He hands me a five-pound note and then leans forward.

'You and me have got some unfinished business,' he hisses.

'Anything else I can help you with? Stamps for your Christmas cards, perhaps?' I say.

'You owe me a fair bit of dosh.'

'Nothing else then,' I say, wishing he'd push off.

'What time do you knock off 'ere? I don't want to be waiting outside your flat all evening, now do I?'

I gasp. It's not the thought of Matt Fisher waiting outside my flat all evening but more the sight of Moira, Archie's daughter-in-law. She's fidgeting angrily behind Matt Fisher. She looks about to explode.

'Would you like to go to the next till,' offers Delia.

'No, I would not,' snaps Moira.

Delia keeps the smile pasted on her face. I don't mind telling you I'm having trouble with mine. The tedious Christmas music we've had to listen to for the past few weeks isn't helping much either.

'I'm on a late shift,' I say.

'That tells me bugger all,' retorts Matt Fisher.

'Have you finished?' butts in Moira.

'No, we've got some unfinished business, haven't we?' he says looking at me.

'I …'

I see Karen, the supervisor squeezing her way through the queue.

'Everything okay here, Rosie?' she asks.

'Oh yes,' I say.

Can you believe this? Five thousand, that's all I won. It's not even newsworthy is it? I tell you, I'm beginning to think if I could give it back, I would. I blame Frank. What sensible bugger walks in front of a Domino's Pizza van? If he hadn't, I wouldn't be having this aggro three weeks before Christmas with Matt Fisher, or Moira, come to that. I'm shattered, and it is hours before I get a tea break.

Matt wags his finger in front of my face.

When Archie Met Rosie

'We'll discuss this later,' he says, before walking away. I let out a sigh. I don't think we will. I'll go round to our Sam's. I'll have a bit of tea there and then get Sam to take me home. I only wish I could kill Frank. It might make me feel a bit better. As it is he took the easy way out, the coward that he was. It wouldn't surprise me if he deliberately walked in front of that van.

'Hello,' I say, forcing a smile for Moira.

Crikey, she doesn't look too happy either. This isn't my day is it?

'What do you think you're up to?' she hisses, plonking a packet of pork pies onto the counter.

I never had Moira down for the pork pie kind. It just goes to show doesn't it?

'I'm sorry?' I say.

'Don't play the innocent with me. I know all about your type.'

'Everything okay?' smiles Karen.

'Oh yes,' I say.

Everything is far from okay.

'Anything else madam?' I ask.

'You're after his money, aren't you?'

If Moira only knew how much I don't want money. It's a curse. It really is.

'Please come to the other till,' pleads Delia to the customers behind Moira.

'Whose money are we talking about?'

'Alfred's, of course, who do you think we're talking about? You're just his cleaner. You should know your place.'

Karen is glaring at me. I pull my eyes from hers and turn back to Moira.

Lynda Renham

'I really can't discuss this with you now. I'm at work and ...'

'You need to back off. You're way out of your league. He's not interested in you. I know your type, preying on lonely widowers. Well, you hadn't bargained on me, had you?'

She wags her finger in my face. I wish she'd keep her voice down.

'I'll be getting another cleaner for Dad so ...'

'Now hang on ...' I begin.

'Is everything alright madam?' asks Karen approaching us. She's smiling warmly. 'Anything I can help with?'

'It's a personal matter,' snaps Moira.

'Right, I see,' says Karen in a very irritating 'I understand' kind of voice. Of course, she doesn't understand at all.

'Shall I get someone to take over?' Karen asks, looking at me.

'No, really ...'

'I've said all I've got to say. We won't need you to come next week. I'll let the agency know,' says Moira before striding briskly from the store.

'Sod it,' I mutter.

'Not in front of the customers please,' reprimands Karen.

'Sorry.'

'Yes, right. We can discuss this later.'

'Yes of course. I'm sorry. I didn't know she was coming in.'

'Right, let's get on then, shall we. Would you like to come to the till,' she says gesturing to the customers.

I just want to cry. How could Moira be so patronising? Just because I clean houses and work in Waitrose doesn't mean I'm nothing. She spoke to me like I was just a piece of dirt she'd found on her shoe. Archie would have been appalled. I can't tell Archie. It's too embarrassing. What gives people the right? I know I don't have much and I live on the Tradmore Estate, but I still have feelings. How could she think that of me? That the only reason I'm working for Archie is because I hope to gain his confidence and get his money? I couldn't tell her we liked to discuss books and things. She probably thinks I can't even read, let alone enjoy Thomas Hardy. I bet she doesn't read classics. Sod them, sod all of them. Let her find a cleaner. I can't imagine Archie liking that much. Still it's not my business. All the same, I will miss working for Archie. I scan the next customer's shopping, apologise for the delay and carry on as normal. Well, that's life isn't it? You can't shut up shop every time someone is rude to you, can you? But life does suck sometimes.

Chapter Thirty-Eight
Alfred

Matt Fisher thinks he's something these days.

'Meet me at the Greek place in Romford,' he'd said on the phone. It wasn't difficult to get his number. I just put the word around that I needed a loan and the next thing I knew I had Matt Fisher's details.

I hate Romford any time of year but right now, with Christmas just around the corner it's bedlam. At least I can park the car for free. That helps doesn't it? Except there's a mile-long tailback where everyone else is trying to get into the same car park. Christmas, who'd have it? It's just people spending money they don't have on presents nobody wants. Moira and Harry love it. They're big on Christmas. That's when the whole shoebox thing comes into its own. I don't get it. I really don't. Still it makes Harry and Moira feel better and they can eat their huge Christmas dinner without any guilt.

'We sent off our shoeboxes,' they'd say in that condescending manner they have.

Finally I'm driving into the car park. A parking attendant waves me forward and points to the lane he wants me to go into. Anyone would think I was blind. I know how to get into a car park. I've done it plenty of times without his help. I don't understand why we have to have someone guide us into car parks at Christmas time. The council no doubt thinks we lose all sense at Christmas after spending all that money, and if we don't have guidance we'd drive into walls. He's wearing a silly Christmas hat too. What self-respecting man wears a Christmas hat in public? I won't even wear a paper hat on Christmas Day, no matter how much I'm nagged. The guy motions for me to go into the right-hand lane so I deliberately go into the left hand one. I know how to get into a car park. He'll be getting my ticket for me next. Cath used to say I was too intolerant. She was probably right.

There's Christmas music playing everywhere and more silly people in stupid hats or wearing reindeer antlers. They shake charity boxes and wish me a Merry Christmas. If I want to give to a charity, I'll phone them, get an address and then send a cheque. I'm not going to drop a few bob into a tin for a charity I've never heard of. What's the point of that?

I finally make it to the street where Fisher had said the Greek restaurant was. I hope that's not crowded too. I open the door, grateful for the warmth.

'Have you booked sir?' asked a flustered waiter looking at a clipboard. 'Only we ...'

'I'm meeting someone.'

'Over 'ere,' yells a voice.

I turn to see Fisher. He's lording it up at the table by the window. He lifts a wine glass in salute.

He's sitting with some puny-looking bloke who has a serviette tucked into the top of his shirt. He looks a right plonker.

'Alright Alf?' says Fisher. 'Take a seat. I ain't seen you in a while. I 'eard about your wife. I was sorry to 'ear that.'

'It's Alfred to you,' I say firmly, sitting down.

Puny dribbles humus down his chin and I grimace.

'Is this your sidekick?' I ask, removing my scarf. 'Or are you babysitting?'

'This is Rick,' says Matt.

'Alright?' says Rick.

'No I'm not. I'm cold. It's sodding Christmas and I hate Christmas shoppers. So the last place I want to be is here.'

'Don't be a bah humbug,' says Matt. 'Have some food. These mezes are the business.'

'No ta,' I say. 'I've had my dinner.'

No doubt the food's got garlic in it and that always plays havoc with my stomach.

'So, what can we do for you, Alf?'

I snap my head up.

'Alfred,' he corrects.

'I never thought you could stoop so low as to bully women.'

'Calling yourself an old woman?' laughs Puny, spitting out bits of lamb kofta. He's disgusting, he really is.

Matt opens his mouth to speak.

'I've not finished,' I say. 'Now if grown men are stupid enough to take out a loan with you, then that's up to them. I wouldn't do it. I wouldn't give bullies like you the pleasure of having me by the balls ...'

'Now, 'old on Alf.'

'Alfred,' I bark. 'Can't you get someone's name right? Your mother brought you up better than this.'

'Who is this daft old colossal wank weasel?' asks Rick.

I'll give him colossal wank weasel. The Greek music is getting on my nerves. If I want Greek music I'll go to Greece.

'I'm not as daft as you look,' I say to Rick.

This throws him, and he mulls over the words while eating his meze.

'Can I have a Coca-Cola?' I ask the waiter.

'Have a decent drink,' says Matt, holding up the wine.

'I'm driving. There are some of us who abide by the law.'

Matt wipes his mouth on a serviette.

'So what's your gripe *Alfred*,' he says, emphasising my name.

'I remember you when you were a young lad. You were a bully then. I told your mum you'd come to no good.'

He laughs, his even white teeth sparkling. They've been polished. No one has teeth like that. No one would want teeth like that. What an arse 'ole.

'I've done alright as it 'appens,' he says.

'I don't call what you do, successful.'

'Why don't you take a long walk off a short plank,' sidekick Rick snarls, suddenly jumping up. 'In fact, why don't I help you?'

'Is he a joke?' I ask Matt. 'He's good entertainment. I'll give you that.'

'Sit down Rick,' says Matt, looking embarrassed.

'Rosie Foster,' I say, pushing Rick back into his seat.

Matt has the decency to lower his head.

'Her cockwomble husband …' begins Rick.

'Can't you just stuff humus in your mouth,' I say irritably. 'I hope this dipstick here didn't speak to Rosie using that colourful language.'

'Frank owed me five thousand,' says Matt. 'It's on the grapevine that she had a big win at the bingo …'

'Ten thousand or more,' adds Rick.

'So everyone's entitled to it are they?' I say downing the Cola. 'As it happens it was a small win. Ever heard of Chinese whispers? That's what happened to Rosie's win. It's been whispered about so much that no one even knows now what she won.'

'He owed me five grand,' says Matt stubbornly.

'Without interest, how much did he owe you?'

Matt hesitates.

'Two grand.'

I puff out my cheeks.

'It's criminal what you do. I'll give you the two grand. You don't go near Rosie again.'

Matt sniggers.

'No way. I need my interest and ...'

'Fine,' I say standing up. 'Let's go round to your mum and get what she owes me. I'll give it to you out of that.'

I pull on my overcoat.

'Alright, alright,' says Matt. 'Don't be so hasty. I don't want my mum bothered.'

'And I don't want Rosie Foster bothered.'

Matt takes a toothpick and pokes at his shiny teeth.

'Okay,' he says finally.

I hold out my hand.

'Shake on it.'

'You can't let this cockwomble ...' begins Rick.

'Shut the fuck up,' says Matt, putting his hand in mine.

'Great,' I say. 'Enjoy your meze. Mind you don't choke on your own tongue,' I say to Rick and leave the restaurant.

Chapter Thirty-Nine
Rosie

Sam peeks into the cupboards.

'You've got good storage space,' he says.

'Do you think I should take it,' I say lowering my voice. 'Only if I don't say soon, they'll offer it to someone else.'

'As long as you're sure you can afford it.'

After the debacle with Moira in Waitrose I'd felt sure I wouldn't be able to afford it. But Becky had called, and I had felt much better.

'Stupid cow,' she'd fumed down the phone. 'She wanted me to send someone else to Alfie. I said I didn't have anyone else. That you were perfect for that job, and so you are. She went on and on about how it wasn't professional for cleaners to fraternise with the clients ...'

'I didn't fraternise,' I'd argued.

'I know. Anyway, she threatened to cancel her contract with me. I'm so sorry, Rosie. I don't think Alf will be too pleased though when someone else turns up on Friday, but that's not our problem is it?'

'I only made him a shepherd's pie,' I'd said.

'Don't worry about it, Rosie. Anyway, I've got a new client in Hornchurch. They want three hours so it's more work for you anyway. Alf was only two.'

I hadn't liked to say that more hours were far from what I needed. But at least I still have a cleaning job and the murders when they come up. My supervisor, Karen, was very nice about the fracas with Moira and said that customers do get a little obnoxious around Christmas time and that Karen felt I had handled it very well. Of course, I won't be going to Paris now, so I told Brian I wouldn't be needing time off after all and that cheered him up. So it seems I can afford the flat if I want it. It does worry me that I still have one of Archie's books. I really ought to return it. I'll pop it in the post. That's the best thing. I really don't want Moira getting all arsy with me again. I feel really sad about Archie. I really enjoyed our little chats, especially when we talked about books. I feel myself getting tearful and force myself to stop thinking about Archie. But I really liked him. Not in a sexual way, you understand, but as a friend. It was someone to share my interests with. I've never had that before. Shirl and Doris are good friends and I don't know what I'd do without them, but they're not interested in books and travelling. Archie lit my life up I suppose. I know it was daft, but I bought him some socks from Marks and Spencer. I thought he would appreciate a decent pair. I couldn't have given him Primark socks, could I? Although there's nothing wrong with Primark but Marks would last longer. I'll give them to Sam instead. He'll appreciate them.

'You'll feel safer here,' Sam says breaking into my reverie.

I nod.

The day that Matt Fisher had come into the store had been a bit unsettling and I'd gone to Sam's that night for tea. He said I could have stayed at theirs, but I didn't want to be a burden. Besides I had to go back to my flat sometime. Sam had taken me home but there had been no sign of Matt Fisher or that puny bloke. I'd locked all the doors and taken the bread knife to bed with me. I'm not sure why. I don't think I could stab anyone if my life depended on it. That's not strictly true is it? I mean, surely I would, if my life depended on it. I'd be a stupid cow if I didn't. There's not been much noise from the neighbours. I hope Matt hasn't murdered them. I don't like to knock.

'I have got other people interested,' says the estate agent.

'She's taking it, aren't you Mum?' says Sam.

'Yes,' I say decisively.

'Wonderful,' she smiles. 'If you'd like to come back to the office, we can complete the paperwork.'

Sam nods at me.

'Afterwards we can go to the Harvester,' he says.

I wish our Sam would find a nice girl; someone decent and kind. He deserves that.

'Can you spare the time?' I ask.

'Yeah, I've left Joe in charge. I can take a few hours off.'

I look around the flat and feel a little flutter of excitement in my stomach. I'll need some couches. Doris says she knows this place in Stratford that does second-hand furniture.

'Decent stuff,' she'd assured me.

The estate agent closes the front door and I stand looking at what will be my new home.

'I'll meet you at the office,' she says, shaking my hand.

I can't believe it. I'm getting off Tradmore Estate. It will be a struggle to begin with, but I'm used to struggling. Still, in a few years I'll get my pension and I'll have my bereavement allowance too and if I keep on working for the next few years then I should be okay. I'd rather work than sit at home all day anyway.

*

'I haven't been to Harvester for years,' I say.

'Nor have I,' smiles Sam.

We give the waitress our orders and celebrate my new home with a glass of orange juice.

'Have you heard anything from Matt Fisher?' Sam asks.

I shake my head.

'No. I don't know why.'

'He knows he shouldn't harass women. It's not the thing to do. Dad was an idiot.'

'He didn't have a lot of sense,' I agree.

'How are the murders going?'

I raise my eyebrows.

'Keep your voice down,' I say. 'Or I'll have the police knocking on the door. They're going okay. It's only occasionally. Just as well really.'

'I should hope so,' he laughs.

Sam's eyes light up as the waitress brings our roast chicken.

'It's on me,' I say.

'Don't be daft. I'll pay for my own.'

'You won't,' I say firmly.

I hesitate and then say quietly,

'I lost one of my cleaning jobs though. Archie, the bloke I told you about. His daughter-in-law got it into her head that I was after his money.'

Sam looks surprised.

'You lost the job?'

I nod.

'She phoned Becky and said I was taking liberties …'

'What a cheek,' he says angrily.

'I only made him a shepherd's pie, but I've been borrowing books from him and he invited me round to share the shepherd's pie …'

Sam cocks his head.

'Nothing happened,' I say. 'Anyway, the daughter-in-law came into Waitrose, her nose in the air and told me not to go back. Becky has got me something else but …'

'What a cheek, accusing you of being after his money. I'm not having that.'

When Archie Met Rosie

'Don't go starting trouble Sam.'

'It's a cheek,' he says.

He's right of course. She had a nerve. I expect she'll accuse me of stealing Archie's book. I'll post it later.

'I do miss going there. He's a nice bloke and, well ... I do miss company.'

He squeezes my hand.

'You can always come to us, you know that.'

'I know. But I don't want to be a burden. Anyway, I've got my little jobs.'

'You shouldn't overdo it though, Mum. You've got a little bit of money now and your bereavement allowance. Take it easy. You don't need those murders, not really. You can always have dinner with us a couple of nights a week. That will save a bit on food.'

'Thanks, love, and I probably will. In the meantime, let's enjoy this.'

'Let me and Michael know when you're moving in and we'll get a van.'

'That'll be great Sam.'

Everything is working out for once, except for my job with Archie, of course. I'm really sad about that. I'll put the book in the post. I won't put a Christmas card in with it as I'd planned. Moira might think I'm trying to get in with Archie again and I couldn't cope with another run in with her. It felt funny not going to Archie's house. I wonder what Becky told him. He'll think he's upset me. I could text him. No, on second thoughts, best not. I'll no doubt just get myself into more trouble. I can't believe how much trouble has come my way since Frank died. I never realised how peaceful life was before that.

Chapter Forty
Alfred

I click the kettle on and take two plates from the kitchen dresser. Rosie should be here soon. Cleo purrs around my legs. At that moment the doorbell goes, and Cleo and I stroll to the front door together.

'Here she is,' I say. 'She'll have your treats, I'm sure.'

I open the door.

'Good morning Rosie …' I begin and stop.

Becky stands there with a woman I've never seen before.

'Morning Alf,' says Becky cheerfully, but there's a worried frown across her forehead.

'Where's Rosie?' I say, looking behind them.

If that Matt Fisher has …

'Rosie can't come any more,' says Becky. 'A few personal issues, you know how it is …'

The words sound rehearsed.

'No, I don't know how it is,' I say brusquely. 'Is she alright?'

'Yes, oh yes, she's fine. Don't worry.'

Becky flushes.

'This is Margaret. She'll be doing your cleaning now. I'll show her around, shall I?'

I stand in the doorway, the stubborn mule that I am.

'It's not like Rosie not to tell me,' I say, feeling hurt.

Cleo turns her back on Margaret and skulks into the kitchen.

'I really can't divulge much Alf,' says Becky unhelpfully. 'It's confidential.'

'She's alright though, isn't she? Nothing's happened?'

'Oh yes,' says Becky quickly. 'Don't worry, Rosie is absolutely fine.'

'But, she doesn't want to clean for me any more?'

Becky shrugs uncomfortably and pulls a face.

'Right, well that's that then. Come in Margaret,' I say opening the door wider.

It just goes to show, you really don't know people, do you? Obviously, when I'd shown her my little house, I'd upset her more than she'd let on. Or perhaps she finds me too friendly, the idiot that I am. Well, that's that. I'm not giving any more thought to it. If she doesn't want to come and clean, then she doesn't. I'm not going begging to her.

'I'll show Margaret round,' says Becky.

'Yeah,' I say, picking up the newspaper.

*

Becky had been dreading telling Alf that Rosie wouldn't be coming any more. Moira had been quite clear that her phone call to Becky should be confidential.

'My father-in-law doesn't need to know that his previous cleaner was dishonest. I'd like you to get the key from her please.'

'Rosie isn't dishonest,' Becky had responded, struggling to keep her temper.

'She took liberties. I hope very much you impress it upon the new cleaner that she is there to clean. I prefer them not to have keys.'

'Of course,' said Becky.

It was bad enough telling Rosie that Moira had cancelled her.

'The thing is,' she'd told Rosie. 'There's nothing I can do. It was Moira who hired us in the first place.'

'It's okay,' Rosie had said but Becky could tell she was upset and now Alf looked right fed up and he was usually a cheery soul. Bloody Moira, thought Becky. If anyone was after Alf's money it was her.

Alf buried his head in his paper and Becky fought back the desire to tell him the truth. What was the worst that could happen? Moira would put the word around that Becky's agency hired untrustworthy staff, that's the worst and Becky couldn't afford for that to happen. She'd got loads of clients through Moira; all her church and counsellor friends. It would be a big blow if she lost those. She sighed heavily.

'Right I'm going for a walk,' Alf said suddenly.

'Okay Alf,' said Becky.

'There's angel cake if you want it. Help yourself. What's not eaten will only go in the bin.'

'Thanks Alf, we will.'

The front door slammed, and Becky cursed.

'Everything alright,' asked Margaret.

'Yeah fine,' said Becky. 'I just think I might be cleaning up after one of my own murders.'

Chapter Forty-One
Moira

Moira tried the key in the ignition again. There was a clicking sound and she sighed. She'd no doubt flooded the engine. At least it had spluttered a bit before. She checked the time on the dashboard clock. She'd have to phone. She would never make the parish council meeting now. She stepped from the car and watched as a blue Mini pulled up and parked across the driveway.

'Typical,' she mumbled, striding towards it.

She stopped as a well-built man climbed from the car. He reminded her of the character in a drama she and Holly had been watching on Netflix. He had the same rugged good looks. He studied her critically and Moira felt herself turning hot.

'You'll have to move that,' she said, pointing at the Mini. 'You're blocking my drive.'

He looked at the Mini.

'So I am,' he said flippantly. 'Are you Moira Bolton?'

He had a rough way of talking but there was an undertone of softness to his voice. Although, right now, his brown flecked eyes were flashing angrily her way.

'Yes I am,' she said, folding her arms across her chest. 'Can I help you?'

He cocked his head towards her Range Rover.

'That's leaking oil,' he said.

She followed his gaze to a large black puddle.

'Damn,' she muttered. Why hadn't she noticed that?

She wasn't what Sam had been expecting. She was younger than he thought she would be. Middle forties he guessed, and she wasn't bad looking either.

'You'll have to move your car,' she said dismissively. 'I'll need to call the AA.'

Their house was big like he imagined, and she spoke in velvet tones, exactly as he thought she would. She needed bringing down a peg or two. How dare she insult his mother?

'I'm not moving it until you and I have had words,' he said brusquely.

'Excuse me?' she said, taken aback.

'I've come to talk to you about my mum,' he said, sliding his hands into his jeans pocket.

Moira found him disconcerting in more ways than one. There was something about his manner and way of speaking that unsettled her. He had a confident way about him that Harry lacked and an air of certainty. He wasn't afraid of anyone, she felt sure of that.

'I don't believe I know your mother,' she said turning back to the house.

His hand touched her arm and it tingled all the way to her fingers.

'I'm still talking to you,' he said evenly.

Her legs trembled under his touch.

'I'm Sam Foster. Rosie Foster is my mum.'

'Oh,' she said, letting out a little gasp.

'Is that all you can say?'

Moira brushed the hair back from her face. She could smell the soap he'd used. It had a warm musky fragrance.

'I ...' she began.

'You called her a gold-digger, said she was after your father-in-law's money.'

'Well ... I ...'

'That's a lie,' he said leaning closer to her. Moira grasped the car door handle.

'Wasn't it?' he insisted.

Moira's phone trilled, and she recognised the ring tone. It was Holly's school.

'My daughter's school,' she said, pulling the phone from her bag.

'Mrs Bolton?' said the headteacher.

Moira's stomach did a little somersault.

'Could you collect Holly? She fainted. She seems fine now, but I think it best if she goes home. There's a lot of flu going around this time of year.'

'Oh dear,' said Moira flustered. 'I'll need to get a cab. My car has broken down. I'll be there as soon as possible.'

'I'm sorry I have to go,' said Moira turning to the front door.

'I'll give you a lift,' said Sam.

'What?' said Moira surprised.

Sam couldn't for the life of him think what made him offer. Moira looked at him and for the first time since he climbed from the Mini, their eyes met. She had heavy-lidded hazel eyes, he saw now. Her lashes were dark and long. She fiddled with her hair for a moment.

'My car not good enough for you?' he said harshly.

'No, it's just I don't know you.'

He shrugged.

'Your choice, after all you can afford the cab. I'll be back though. We still haven't talked about my mum.'

He turned and strode to the Mini.

'Okay, thank you, a lift would be great,' she said.

She waited for him to open the passenger door, but he strode round to the driver's side and got in.

The passenger door was stiff, and she had to tug at it to get it to open.

'You'll have to direct me,' he said starting the engine. 'It's a bit noisy. I've got to change the exhaust.'

The car roared down the road and Moira fidgeted in the seat. The car was very small compared to hers and no matter how hard she tried she couldn't stop her knee from brushing his. The car smelt of his musky soap. It was clean inside. She was expecting a mess. She glanced down at his hands as they changed gears. They were very hairy, hairier than Harry's hands.

'Which way at the roundabout?' he asked.

'The first exit,' she replied.

She hoped Holly wasn't coming down with something. Not this close to Christmas.

'My mum isn't a gold-digger,' he said.

'It's just ... my father-in-law is very vulnerable and I ...'

'Want his money,' he said sharply.

Moira gasped.

'That's not quite true ...'

'Mum said Alf told her you're into the God stuff.'

'The God stuff?' she repeated.

'Is that how God people carry on, accusing others of being gold-diggers?'

'You need to take the next right.'

His hand brushed her thigh as he changed gears and she moved it slightly.

'I'm sorry perhaps I spoke out of turn about your mum.'

'There's no perhaps about it.'

'That's the school.' Moira pointed.

'I'll get Holly,' she said as they pulled into the car park.

Sam watched her walk to the school entrance. She had a nice bum, he thought. She's up her own arse alright, Mum was right about that, but Sam could see another side to her. She's too clammed up, that's Moira's problem. Still, that was her old man's problem not his. He'd said his piece. That's what he came to do.

Chapter Forty-Two
Rosie

'Crikey,' says Doris. 'This is lovely. I never imagined it would look like this.'

'It's nice and modern,' says Shirl.

'Better than Tradmore Estate,' agrees Doris.

'I know,' I say.

I'm like the cat that got the cream.

'Are you using your bingo money for this, then?' asks Doris.

I shake my head.

'Just for the deposit as I want to save the rest.'

'For Paris,' says Shirl.

'Maybe next year,' I say.

Doris opens the cupboard doors.

'It's quiet here isn't it? Not a bit like your place in Tradmore.'

'Matt Fisher doesn't know you're moving, does he?' asks Shirl.

'Of course he does. Rosie sent him one of those 'here's my new address cards'. What do you think Shirl?' snaps Doris.

'Blimey, I only asked.'

'And we're not to go telling anyone her new address either.'

'I won't tell anyone,' says Shirl. 'When do you move in?'

'At the weekend, Sam and Michael are helping me.'

'We'll pop over with some bubbly,' says Doris.

'It's all happened for you since your Frank walked into that pizza van,' says Shirl.

Doris makes a loud tutting noise.

'Honestly Shirl, the things that come out of your mouth. You'll be accusing her of having him knocked off next.'

'What would be the point of that?' asked Shirl. 'Frank never had anything worth knocking him off for.'

'I don't know about that,' says Doris. 'He spent enough on that ...'

Shirl nudges Doris in the ribs.

'What was that Doris?' I ask.

Doris blushes.

'I heard at the Co-op that Frank had rented a little place for that brassy bit of his, furnished it and everything.'

'When did you hear that?' I say. 'You never told me.'

'The neighbours,' warns Shirl, 'you don't want them thinking that riff-raff are moving in.'

'I'm telling you now. I only heard yesterday,' explains Doris.

'Well, it's a shit hole he rented,' I say scathingly. 'I went there.'

'You did?' says Doris surprised.

'Frank bought her an engagement ring.'

'You what?' gasps Shirl.

'I took it off her and sold it.'

Doris's eyes widen.

'Well done,' says Shirl.

'What a pig,' says Doris, finally.

'Best not to talk about him,' says Shirl.

'I've got better things to talk about,' I say.

I collected Frank's ashes. I didn't flush them down the loo like I threatened I would. Instead they are sitting on the loo windowsill. Best place for them if you ask me. I've got the week planned. Today I'm going Christmas shopping with Doris and Shirl. I'm going to get something special for our Sam and Michael because they deserve it. There's a computer game that Michael has been on about so I'm buying him that and I've decided to get our Sam a Fitbit. He's always running or down the gym. He'll like one of those. I'm going to have them to my new place for Christmas dinner too. I've got time to get it looking Christmassy.

'Right,' says Doris, 'Let's do some shopping. That will cheer us all up.'

I lock the front door and look admiringly at the outside of my new home.

'Let's go,' says Shirl. 'I've got tons to get. You can look at your house as much as you like once you move in.'

We're getting the underground to Oxford Street. It was Doris's idea. It's been years since I've been up West and I'm looking forward to seeing the Christmas lights. I wonder what Archie is doing over Christmas. I suppose he'll still go to Paris. It was stupid of me to have thought I could have gone with him. I'm getting ideas above my station since winning that money at the bingo. I expect he's forgotten all about me. Becky said he has a new cleaner now named Margaret. I wonder if she likes reading.

'Crabbers asked about you,' says Shirl as we get on the train.

'He's alright is Crabbers,' says Doris. 'You could do a lot worse. Get in with him and you'll get all your bed linen dead cheap. It'll be nice to have new stuff for your place won't it?'

'I'm not going out with Crabbers just to get bed linen and towels,' I say sharply.

Honestly what do they think I'm like?

'I don't mean a romance, you silly mare,' laughs Doris. 'Just a friend, you know; someone to go out with. Life can be lonely on your own.'

She's quite right. Life is lonely on your own. I can't spend every night at our Sam's. Still I figure once I get into my new place, I'll have so much to do there won't be time to be lonely.

'I'm not lonely,' I lie.

'Women do a lot worse to get bed linen,' says Shirl.

'She's not interested in Crabbers,' says Doris.

'I'm not interested in men, period,' I say. 'And I don't need bed linen.'

'Right, so let's shut up about men then,' Doris sighs. 'I'd much rather chat about Christmas. Where are we going first?'

Lynda Renham

Chapter Forty-Three
Sam and Moira

Holly was as white as a sheet. She looked small and vulnerable sitting behind the headteacher's huge desk.

'Are you alright, love?' Moira asked, feeling Holly's forehead.

'I'm okay, Mum. Don't fuss,' said Holly, pulling her head away.

'Oh good, you're here,' said the headteacher coming into the room. 'I hope you didn't mind us phoning you. She'd be far better at home. It's probably the flu. We've got a lot of pupils off with it.'

'It's the time of year,' said Moira smiling.

'I'm feeling a bit better,' said Holly with a weak smile.

'Let's get you home,' said Moira helping Holly on with her coat.

'I'm alright. I don't need help,' said Holly irritably.

Moira forced a smile for the headteacher and followed Holly outside.

'It's cold,' said Moira. 'Where's your scarf?'

'I don't know. Don't nag me,' retorted Holly looking around for the Range Rover.

'Where's the car?' she asked, clutching her stomach. 'I feel sick.'

Moira pointed to Sam's Mini. Sam was lounging against it, tapping into his phone. Moira wondered what he did for a job, if he had a job, of course. Most likely he lived off benefits. That's typical, she thought, anger building within her. How dare he come to her house demanding all sorts when he was most likely living off her and Harry's taxes? What a nerve.

'The car wouldn't start, so I got a lift,' she said pointing to Sam's Mini.

'Who's he?' asked Holly suspiciously.

'Oh, he's just someone I know.'

'From counselling?'

'Yes, kind of,' lied Moira.

'I feel sick,' groaned Holly again.

Moira hoped she wouldn't throw up in Sam Foster's car. That was all she needed. Sam lifted his head at the sound of them approaching.

'Holly feels sick,' said Moira bluntly.

If she warned him, then he couldn't very well say anything if Holly threw up in his car.

'There's a carrier bag in the back,' said Sam casually. 'She can throw up into that.'

Holly fell onto the back seat and closed her eyes. Moira debated where she should sit and finally decided to get into the passenger seat. Sam drove them home in silence. Moira tried to think of something to say but nothing would come to her. Sam pulled up outside the house and Holly who thankfully hadn't thrown up, climbed out wearily.

'Here's the key,' said Moira handing it to her.

She turned to Sam.

'Thank you very much for the lift.'

'Yeah sure,' he said casually. 'You should get that seen to.'

He pointed to the oil stain.

'Yes, I will.'

'Do you want me to have a quick look?'

'You?' she asked, surprised.

'I am a mechanic,' he said brushing past her.

She watched him disappear under the car. Minutes later he emerged.

'The AA won't be able to fix it. You'll need to take it to the garage.'

'Oh right.'

He nodded and climbed into the Mini. He gave a nod and then drove off. Moira watched the car disappear around the corner and then walked into the house. Holly had gone upstairs to her room.

'Do you want a cup of tea?' Moira called.

'No, I'm going to have a sleep.'

Moira walked into the kitchen. She ought to phone the AA and get the car sorted but she couldn't seem to get her thoughts clear. She never imagined Rosie having a son. He was certainly angry. She shook her head and made a pot of tea. She should forget about him. He won't be back. Alf had a new cleaner now. It was all for the best, she felt sure of that. Cleaners shouldn't be overfamiliar, everyone knew that.

She sat down at the kitchen table with her tea and pulled her mobile from her bag and phoned the AA. Of course they could fix it. What was he talking about?

*

Holly threw up again and then fell against the bathroom wall. This was bad. She knew that much. What was she going to do? There was no one she could talk to. She buried her head in her hands and cried. How would she ever tell her mum? She'd have a heart attack and then she'd go on about God, no doubt, and the shame and what the parish council would say. Like Holly cared about the parish council.

If only she would stop being sick. She could think more clearly if she wasn't throwing up all the time. She heard her mum at the front door and wandered back to her room to look out of the window. It was an AA van. She wondered who the man was in the Mini. He seemed nice enough. She laid her head against the window pane and watched her mum talk to the mechanic.

*

'I'm afraid there's nothing I can do. I don't carry the part you need on my van. It will need to go to the garage.'

Moira sighed. She should have phoned the garage first.

'Is there nothing you can do?'

'I would if I could,' he smiled.

'Can I drive it?'

He grimaced.

'You can but it wouldn't be sensible. You'd flooded it, that's why it wouldn't start. You'll have to keep topping up the oil. You'd be sensible to get it fixed as soon as you can.'

Damn it, she cursed.

The garage tried to be helpful, but they had no space until the end of the week and all their courtesy cars were out. She booked it in for the end of the week and then went upstairs to check on Holly. She was asleep on her bed. Moira closed the door quietly and went back downstairs to look for local car hire firms.

*

'We've got nothing until next week.'

It was the same over and over again. What was wrong with these garages? Moira thought with a sigh. She drank the last of her cold coffee and was about to call up to Holly again when she walked into the kitchen.

'I'm going to my friends.'

'Dinner will be in a few hours.'

'Okay,' said Holly meekly.

She looked rough and Moira didn't really think she should be going out.

'It's really cold out and you look terrible.'

'I'm alright. The fresh air will do me good.'

Lynda Renham

Moira was too tired to argue.

'I'll make dinner for six.'

Holly nodded, grabbed her coat and was gone.

Moira scanned the garages on Google again. She bit her lip and then searched for *Sam Foster, garage, Essex.* She was surprised to get a result, but there it was in black and white, 'Fosters Garage' in Dagenham Heath. She stared at the name for a second and then made a note of the address. It wasn't the best part of Essex but if he could fix her car … After all, that's all that mattered. A busy person like her couldn't be without a car too long. She grabbed the car keys and left the house. She couldn't admit to herself that she wanted to see Sam Foster again.

Chapter Forty-Four
Rosie

I approach the flats cautiously. Coming home is beginning to resemble a horror movie for me. I'm scared shitless walking to the entrance and any relief I feel at not seeing Matt Fisher is replaced by another fear that he will be waiting outside my flat.

The kids from number eighty are sitting on the wall. I feel their negativity a hundred yards away.

'Why aren't you at school?' I ask.

'Because we ain't,' says one defiantly. 'What are you going to do about it?'

Nothing as it happens. Their father has already been done twice for grievous bodily harm to interfering neighbours and I don't want to be next on the list, thank you very much. It comes to something when you're scared to answer back to ten-year-olds.

There's no sign of Matt Fisher. There's just a girl sitting on the steps of the entrance. Most likely she's shut herself out. I nod as I walk towards the doors and she jumps up.

'Rosie,' she says.

I turn. It's Holly, Archie's granddaughter. What is she doing here?

'I asked someone on the estate where your flat was,' she says.

Her face is red and blotchy. She's clearly been crying. This is all I need. I really don't want trouble with 'up her own arse' Moira. Not as I'm just about to move into my new flat.

'Holly?' I question, just to be sure. She bursts into floods of tears and rushes towards me.

'Oh Rosie, I didn't know where to go.'

Oh dear, this doesn't bode well, does it? A sobbing teenager sitting on the steps of your home nearly always spells trouble doesn't it? I've got enough trouble on my doorstep with Frank's legacy. I don't need any more, thank you very much. Talking of Frank, I really ought to get a headstone. I've not mentioned it to Doris or Shirl because they'll only tell me I can get a cheap one on eBay. That's a thought, though isn't it? I wonder if you can get cheap headstones on the internet. For all I know there could be a *Tombs R Us*. After all, it's not something you look for every day is it, so how would you know? Maybe they do reconditioned ones. I don't mind one of those. Frank's a popular name. There's a good chance that there are a lot of Frank headstones that went wrong. Frank was dyslexic anyway, so he wouldn't care if the spelling wasn't right and who's going to be looking at it? I certainly shan't bother. Sam might, but he's a man and most likely won't notice if the spelling is wrong. I'll look on Google. I don't want to be spending hundreds on a tombstone for that two-timing whatsit do I?

'Whatever is wrong?' I ask Holly.

She looks around and whispers, 'Can we go to your flat?'

'I'm not sure that's a good idea. Your mum ...'

'Is going to kill me,' she blurts out and promptly burst into tears again.

'Now, come on. You can't keep crying like this. It's ridiculous. You can come up for a cup of tea but then you must go home.'

'Thanks Rosie.'

I can almost hear Frank's voice. 'You're daft you are, Rosie.' I was daft alright. Fancy not realising your husband is playing away. Only a dimwit like me wouldn't realise. I only hope that Matt Fisher isn't outside my flat. If Holly has a run in with him, Moira will have my guts for garters. By the time she's finished I'll be lucky to have a job sweeping the streets.

Holly heads straight for the lift.

'I don't normally use that,' I say.

'Why not, what floor are you on?'

'The sixth but it doesn't take long to go up the stairs.'

'I can't do that,' pouts Holly. 'I've been sick.'

I look to the kids sitting on the wall. I wouldn't put it past them to muck around with the buttons.

'Come on,' says Holly getting in.

It stinks of urine. Holly puts her hand over her nose.

'Disgusting,' she mutters. 'Destiny's lift isn't this bad.'

Lucky Destiny, she's obviously in the best part of the Tradmore Estate.

The lift door opens and we both take a deep breath. There's no Matt Fisher or his puny little sidekick. What a relief. But I don't understand it. That day in Waitrose he made it clear he was coming after me for his money, so where is he? Not that I'm keen to see him, you understand.

I wasn't expecting company, so the place isn't as tidy as usual. I drop my shopping bags onto the couch. It was a relief not having to drag those up six flights. Holly doesn't seem to notice the mess and hurries straight to the loo where I hear her throwing up. My eyes land on the copy of *Wuthering Heights* that I'm reading and with a jolt I remember Archie's book. I'd forgotten to post it.

'Are you okay Holly?' I call.

'Yeah, I think so.'

I fill the kettle and wait for her to come out. She looks awful when she finally does emerge.

'You've got someone's ashes in your loo,' she says.

'Yes. They're my husband's.'

'Why are they in the loo?'

'Because it's the best place for them,' I say honestly.

'I'm pregnant,' she says.

Talk about drop a clanger. My heart sinks.

'I didn't know who else to turn to. Then I thought of you. Will you help me get rid of it?'

'What?' I gasp.

'I thought you'd know where to go.'

'Why would I know where to go?'

'I don't know, I just thought …'

'You just thought that because I live on the Tradmore Estate I'd know all about abortions.'

She fell onto the couch and dropped her head into her hands.

'I can't go to the doctor. They'll tell my mum, won't they?'

'I don't know, probably not as you're over sixteen. Are you absolutely sure you're pregnant?'

'I bought a pregnancy test from the pharmacy.'

I sigh.

'You will help me won't you Rosie?'

It never rains but it pours.

Chapter Forty-Five
Alfred

I scoop up the Saga holiday brochures and sling them into the recycle bin. I've got no interest in Paris now. It's no fun travelling on your own. Margaret walks in with her basket of cleaning materials.

'I've only done one hour,' she says accusingly. 'I'm booked to do two. But I can't make work where there isn't any.'

'No, I'm sorry about that,' I say.

I don't know why I'm apologising for being clean.

'I'll have to speak to Becky. One hour is no good to me,' she says briskly.

'Fine,' I say dismissively. I don't like her anyway. She's got the personality of a flea. Cleo doesn't like her either. She dives under the duvet as soon as Margaret arrives.

'I'll be off then.'

'Okay,' I say.

No angel cake for this one. She's far from an angel. The door slams and I sigh with relief. I'm just about to make a cup of tea when there's a knock.

'Who is it?' I ask.

I'm not in the mood for people peddling stuff at the door.

'It's me, Holly.'

'Hold on love,' I say unlocking the door. I swing it back to see a tearful Holly and standing at the side of her is Rosie.

'Rosie,' I say surprised.

'I wouldn't have bothered you Archie but ...' she says nervously.

She's embarrassed and so she should be. If she hadn't wanted my house, all she had to do was say so.

'It's no bother, come in both of you,' I say, although I'm feeling far from gracious.

Holly sniffs and wipes her eyes.

'What's up with you?' I ask.

'Rosie will tell you,' she says and hurries into the living room.

I look at Rosie. It's good to see her, although I can't help feeling cross. She hands me a book.

'I didn't get to give you this back.'

I don't understand what on earth is going on.

'I'd like to know why you stopped coming,' I say bluntly. 'Out of the blue, no explanation, honestly Rosie, I expected more from you.'

No point beating about the bush. It was hurtful what she did, and I want her to know it.

'Can we talk about Holly first?' she asks, blushing.

She looks harassed and anxious. If Matt Fisher has been to see her, I'll have him.

'Matt Fisher hasn't been harassing you, has he?'

She shakes her head.

'Grandad,' calls Holly.

Rosie walks into the living room and I follow.

'What's going on Holly?' I ask.

'I didn't want to tell you, but Rosie said I had to. She said she wouldn't help me unless you knew.'

'Knew what?' I say angrily.

'I'm pregnant Grandad.'

'You're what?'

Surely I misheard. Of course I did. My hearing isn't all it used to be. Maybe I should get some hearing aids after all.

'Sit down, Archie,' says Rosie. 'I'll make a cuppa.'

'I'm having a baby,' says Holly, ramming it home.

'How the hell did you get pregnant?' I ask shocked and let me tell you, it takes a lot to shock me.

'The usual way,' says Rosie calmly, walking into the kitchen.

'Does your mother know?'

The minute I ask I realise what a stupid question that is. I'd have heard the ruckus all the way from Gidea Park if Moira knew.

'I can't tell Mum,' says Holly tears rolling down her cheeks.

'You silly mare,' I say before thinking. 'Why didn't you go on the pill? Who is he?'

'Archie,' says Rosie, coming in with a pot of tea. 'She's really in a state.'

'I don't care if she's in a state. What were you doing worrying Rosie with this?' I say.

I can feel my blood pressure rising.

'I didn't know who else to go to. I thought Rosie would be able to help.'

'Why would you think that?'

'Archie,' says Rosie.

'You're sounding like my Cath,' I say, turning to Rosie.

'Sorry.'

'Why did you think Rosie would be able to help?'

'Because … because …'

'I live on the Tradmore Estate,' says Rosie, in a matter-of-fact tone.

'Holly, what's wrong with you?' I say crossly.

'I don't know what I'm going to do.'

I look to Rosie. She shrugs.

'Don't look at me. I'm not Vera Drake. I don't do backstreet abortions. I suggest she tells her mum and gets it over and done with.'

I sit down and take the teacup from Rosie.

'Why did you stop coming. Becky won't tell me anything. She treats me like some old codger who doesn't know his arse from his elbow.'

Rosie smiles and it lightens the atmosphere.

'Moira thought I was after your money and told me I wasn't needed any more,' she says flatly.

'You what?' I thunder.

I don't believe I'm hearing this.

'After my money?' I echo. 'Do they think I'm stupid?'

'Apparently I shouldn't fraternise with the clients and I did have shepherd's pie with you.'

'What a load of old bollocks.'

'Grandad,' scolds Holly.

'You've no right telling me off, not the predicament you're in.'

Rosie hands Holly a cup of tea and she takes it gratefully.

'What are we going to do?' Holly asks.

'Firstly, Rosie, you're coming back as my cleaner and secondly, we're going to have all this out with your mother, Holly.'

Rosie sighs and sits down.

'Oh dear,' she says

Holly wipes her eyes.

'I think that's a bad idea.'

'I don't have any others,' I say.

Lynda Renham

Chapter Forty-Six
Sam and Moira

Sam was still thinking about Moira. For some reason he couldn't get her out of his head. She was a stuck-up little madam that's for sure, more strung out than an elastic band. They had a nice house too. He couldn't imagine why she was getting so uptight about her father-in-law's money. It's not like she hadn't got any of her own. As if his mum would be after someone's money. He worried about his mum. Maybe this new little flat would make a difference; as long as that Matt Fisher didn't come after her. Honestly, what had been wrong with his old man, getting involved with people like that? You needed your head examined borrowing money from loan sharks. He'd heard what Matt Fisher did to people. He ought to phone the police, but Mum would go spare if he did that. He wished he had a bigger house. She'd be able to come and live with him and Mike. When he'd made the last payment on the garage perhaps he'd look at houses. The garage would be his in a year. Mum could sell her little flat and move in with him and Michael then. Anyway, he decided, if Matt Fisher bothered her again then they'd phone the police and that's that, whether Mum liked it or not.

'I'm making a brew,' said Joe, breaking into his thoughts. 'You want one?'

'Sure,' said Sam sliding beneath a shiny new Audi.

It was late night shopping tonight. Maybe he'd pop to Lakeside. He ought to get some presents. They needed decorations for the tree too. Christmas was looming. Snow was forecast. He sighed. As if the garage wasn't cold enough.

Joe slid a mug of steaming tea under the car.

'That should warm you up.'

'Thanks mate.'

He was so busy working on the Audi and singing along with the radio that he didn't really notice the clicking of heels in the workshop. It was only when he turned and saw a shiny black pair of heels at the side of him that he realised she was in the garage. He looked up at the slim legs and heard a voice say,

'Is that Sam Foster?'

There was a slight tremble to her voice. He recognised it immediately. Well I never, he thought. He slid out from under the car and forced his eyes from her legs. Moira stepped back and looked shyly at him.

'Hello,' he said, grabbing a rag to wipe his hands. He looked beyond her to the Range Rover outside.

'The garage couldn't look at it until the end of the week and they didn't have a courtesy car so ...' the words came out in a rush.

'You thought of me?'

'I just wondered if ...'

'It's a long way to come from Upminster.'

She flushed. She looked more vulnerable when she blushed, Sam thought.

'Well, if you can't do it,' she said turning.

'I never said I couldn't do it.'

She stopped.

'How urgently do you need it?' he asked.

'As soon as possible,' she said.

She was back to her old uppity self and Sam smiled.

'Yeah, well, that probably won't be possible.'

'You're not being very helpful,' she snapped.

'Well, there are other garages,' he said dismissively, bending back to the Audi.

'Alright,' she said, changing her tone. 'Can you just take a look at it for me?'

'Right now?'

'If you don't mind?'

'Take a seat in the office. I'll look at it in a bit.'

'Oh but ...'

'Take it or leave it,' he said sharply.

She took a step back at his firmness.

'Okay,' she said meekly strolling into the office.

'Do you have the keys?' he asked, stopping her.

'Oh, yes of course,' she said handing them over.

Her hand touched his and he was amazed at the sensations that produced. She blushed again and hurried into the office.

'You want me to bring in the Range Rover?' asked Joe.

'No, I'll do it,' said Sam.

The inside of the car smelt of Moira's perfume and he wondered what it was; an expensive one, no doubt. She certainly had expensive tastes. He drove it into the garage and slid underneath to investigate the oil leak. Odd she'd come here. There were plenty of garages in Gidea Park. He wondered why she hadn't gone to one of them.

*

Moira watched him through the doorway of the office. She was still shaking. How ridiculous. She'd started trembling as she got near the garage and hadn't stopped since. This was madness. She watched him slide his firm body out from under the Range Rover. He strolled confidently into the office and nodded at her.

'I can do it for you. It'll take about an hour. You can bring it back tomorrow or wait and I'll do it in a bit.'

She thought of Harry and dinner and checked the time on her phone.

'What time do you think it will be ready?'

'I don't know. Sometime after six I imagine.'

'Oh, I ...'

'Bring it back tomorrow then. Joe can look at it in the morning.'

'I'd rather you look at it,' she said.

'I've got other jobs on tomorrow,' he said pulling off his top.

She was unprepared and didn't have time to turn her face away. Moira couldn't take her eyes off his toned body. He pulled on a clean top and faced her.

'What do you want to do?' he asked.

'What?'

'What do you want to do about your car?'

'I'll wait,' she said decisively.

'Right, there's a kettle over there and some mugs. Feel free to make yourself a cup of tea.'

Chapter Forty-Seven
Rosie

I hurry to the pub. I'd forgotten I'd agreed to meet Doris and Shirl for a Christmas dinner. It's started to snow, and my fingers are frozen. The smell of beer and chips greet me at the door of the pub. I'm feeling much happier. It will be nice cleaning for Archie again. What a muddle though. I don't know what to do about the flat now. I didn't like to ask Archie about his house. Not with all that Holly malarkey going on. I'm really glad I won't be around when they tell Moira that Holly is up the duff. That's going to be a shock, not to mention the bollocking Archie will no doubt give her. I wouldn't like to be in Moira's shoes.

Doris and Shirl are all dolled up.

'Oh,' I say. 'I didn't know we were tarting ourselves up.'

'We're not really,' says Shirl.

Not much. I could smell her Estee Lauder *Youth Dew* perfume the minute I opened the doors.

'Becky is coming, and Crabbers,' says Doris, avoiding my eyes.

'Crabbers?' I repeat.

'Sorry,' apologises Shirl. 'Bill is bringing him. It didn't seem right you being the odd one out without a bloke.'

'I don't want a bloke,' I say hotly.

'They should be here soon,' says Doris. 'Bert just texted me.'

'Let's get you a drink,' says Shirl, hitching up her bra. 'That'll loosen you up.'

I don't need loosening up. Honestly, these two. It'll be good to see Becky anyway. I can tell her about Archie. She'll be pleased. Perhaps

Margaret and I could just swap jobs. I make my way to the bar with Shirl, who's wearing a dress so tight you can see the outline of her bum.

'That dress is far too tight,' I say.

'I know. I need to go to one of those slimming clubs. I'll go after Christmas. It's pointless going before, isn't it?'

'I suppose so.'

'Are you going to your Sam's for Christmas?'

'Yes, I expect so.'

'What happened to your Frank's ashes?' she asks, taking me by surprise.

'They're on the toilet windowsill.'

'You what?'

'I didn't know where else to put them. It's a bit depressing having ashes in the house ...'

'Crikey, remind me not to have a pee at yours. I don't fancy your Frank watching.'

'I don't know where I'm going to put them in the new place.'

'What's wrong with that loo?'

'I don't want it ruined with Frank's ashes, do I?'

We look at each other and then laugh until tears roll down our cheeks.

'What are you like?' she says wiping her eyes.

'I've got to get a tombstone,' I say.

Shirl throws back her vodka and orange.

'Doris knows someone who does them cheap.'

I'm not surprised.

'It's just I'm still so cross with Frank. What with the debts and Peroxide Blonde Pat and …'

'Forget about her, she's nothing.'

I see Crabbers enter the pub. He's looking smart in a white shirt and tie. He waves and hobbles to the bar.

'I'll get these,' he says whipping out a twenty-pound note. 'I hear you're getting a new place Rosie. You'll be needing bed linen, won't you?'

'I already have bed linen but thanks all the same.'

'Won't you want new stuff?' asks Shirl. 'After all you can afford it after your win.'

'Please don't mention my winnings Shirl,' I hiss.

'Ooh sorry,' she says. 'I'll have a vodka and orange,' she tells Crabbers.

I take a white wine from the bar and follow her back to the table. Becky has arrived, and I sidle up to her.

'I saw Archie,' I say.

'Who?' she says.

'Did you get menus Shirl?' asks Doris.

Bert kisses me on the cheek.

'You're looking perkier,' he smiles.

'Thanks Bert.'

I turn back to Becky.

'Archie Bolton,' I say.

'Oh Alfred. Where did you see him?'

'At his house. It's a long story but he wanted to know why I'd stopped cleaning, so I had to tell him. Anyway, he wants me back. He's going to have a word with Moira.'

Becky pulls a face.

'I hope this doesn't affect my business with her. I'm not being difficult, Rosie but she does get me a lot of clients.'

'Oh I know,' I say quickly. 'I mentioned that to Archie and he said it won't affect you at all.'

'Oh good,' she says with a relieved sigh.

I take the menu from Crabbers and try to relax. Matt Fisher won't come after me in a crowded pub, surely.

'How are you feeling now?' asks Crabbers.

'Feeling, how do you mean?'

'About Frank, it must be hard.'

'I'm alright.'

'She's fine, aren't you Rosie. She's got her mates,' smiles Doris.

That's right. I have my mates and now I have my job back with Archie and a new place to live. The only fly in my ointment is Matt Fisher and I just don't understand what he's up to.

Lynda Renham

Chapter Forty-Eight
Moira

Moira checked the time on her phone. It was nearly six. Harry would be home. From the corner of her eye she saw Sam slide out from beneath the Range Rover. The other mechanic had already gone home. She typed a text to Harry.

I'm getting the car repaired. It's got an oil leak and I need it tomorrow for the counsellor's monthly meeting.

It was delivered, and Harry answered immediately.

I'm still at work. A late meeting. Dad phoned. He wants to speak to us both. I said tomorrow would be best. I'm going straight on to the rehearsal. Holly is eating at Dad's. I'll see you later.

Not another late night, thought Moira. This was getting ridiculous. She threw the phone back into her bag and wondered what it was that Dad wanted to talk to them about. Had he finally seen sense about the house? He's probably finding it too much on his own. She had warned him. It would be much better for him to live there with them. She'd talk to Harry about these late nights. It seemed to be all the time these days. She only saw him a couple of evenings a week now. Maybe things would be better when the play finished. It was too much for him. Working late and then going on to the rehearsals. They needed to get ready for Christmas too. She couldn't do everything on her own. She'd talk to him tonight. They'd have a lot to do if Dad had changed his mind about the house.

'It's done.'

Moira jumps. She hadn't heard Sam come into the office.

'Great,' she said, standing up. 'What do I owe you?'

'I'll write you out a bill. It's eighty-five pounds for the part. I haven't charged you for the labour.'

'Oh, that's good of you,' she said rummaging in her bag for the money. He wiped his hands and then grabbed a pad from the desk.

'But I really should pay for the labour.'

'Nah,' he said without looking at her.

A mobile on the desk bleeped and he glanced down at it.

Moira held out a credit card.

'You do take cards, don't you?'

'Yeah, we're in the twenty-first century, like everyone else.'

He seemed to growl at her and she struggled to think of what to say that might put things right about his mum. He took the card and slipped it into the machine on the desk. She hovered close to punch in her pin and found herself looking at the text on his phone.

Dad, we're all going for a curry. It's Tony's birthday. I won't be late.

She glanced up at him. He had a son? He didn't look like the father type somehow. So, he had a wife. Moira wondered what she looked like. Had he told her he was working late too?

He handed her the card.

'I'll drive the car out for you.'

She followed him through to the garage. It was cold there and smelt of oil and his soap. He climbed into the Range Rover and drove it out of the garage. It was snowing outside, and Moira wrapped a scarf around her neck.

'Thanks so much,' she said walking out into the cold.

'No worries. Sorry it took so long. Your family will be wondering where you are.'

She bit her lip and then said,

'My husband is working late, and my daughter has gone to her grandad for dinner.'

She had no idea why she was telling him this. He simply nodded.

'I expect your wife is wondering where you are too,' she smiled.

'I doubt it. She walked out over a year ago.'

He looked at the snow.

'Maybe we'll have a white Christmas.'

She nodded and went to climb into her car.

'Is there a fish and chip shop nearby?' she asked impulsively.

'Fish and chip shop?' he repeated.

'I need to get something to eat. I'm not going to cook just for me.'

Oh goodness, what must he think of her?

He stroked his chin and then pulled keys from his pocket.

'There's a pub around the corner. They do good food. There isn't a local chippy. I'm going to the pub if you wanted to come along,' he said casually.

Her heart fluttered. It was exactly what she had been hoping he would say.

'Well …' she began, now unsure of herself.

What on earth was she doing? She was a married woman. This is what happens when your husband keeps working late. She must talk to Harry. This is Rosie Foster's son. Heaven knows where he lives. In some run-down house on a council estate, no doubt. What an idiot she was being.

'I really should be getting back,' she heard herself say.

He shrugged.

'Whatever. Drive carefully.'

He turned from her and walked back into the garage. She looked after him for a few seconds and then hurried to the car. She sat in it for a few minutes, trying to warm her hands. She thought he might come out, but he didn't, and she knew she couldn't sit there much longer without it looking a bit strange. She realised her hands were trembling and her face when she looked at it in the mirror was flushed. She put the car into gear and headed home. She passed a pub on the corner and wondered if that was the one that Sam was going to. Perhaps she'd stop at the Chinese near home and get herself something. She fancied she could smell Sam's soap in the car. How ridiculous. Of course she couldn't.

What a strange day it had been.

Chapter Forty-Nine
Alfred

Moira opens the door and smiles at me. She thinks I've come to talk to them about my house. She's going to get a shock.

'I've made a lasagne,' she says.

I try not to groan. There'll be garlic in that. It's no good telling her that garlic doesn't agree with me. Harry walks from the living room. I try not to look at his slippers in disgust. He takes my overcoat and hangs it neatly in the hall cupboard.

'You look cold,' he says.

'It's snowing. It's bitter out there.'

'Will you be alright driving back?' he asks worriedly. 'Only they say the temperature is going to drop. It could get icy.'

'I've driven in snow before,' I say dismissively. 'I'm a man not a mouse.'

Maybe he doesn't like driving in a little bit of snow, but it doesn't bother me.

'Yes, of course,' he says.

He turns to Moira.

'Shall we have dinner?'

I'm still feeling angry. It probably shows. Cath said I get a look on my face when I'm angry. Harry is probably wondering what's wrong. What is it with your kids? It seems as soon as you hit a certain age they start treating you like you're an imbecile. It's insulting. Moira starts rattling on about Christmas while Harry lays the table. I wonder where our Holly is. She'd better be here. I'm not making any announcements on my own.

'You're coming to us for Christmas, aren't you Dad?' asks Moira.

I shrug.

'You always do,' says Harry, pushing a bowl of salad towards me.

'I'll call Holly,' says Moira.

Harry slices into the lasagne. I want to ask him what he's up to, because I know he's up to something. I can't believe he could be so stupid. I know Moira is difficult, but another woman isn't the answer.

'How's that play?' I ask.

He nods enthusiastically.

'Yes, very good, you're coming to see it aren't you?'

'Yeah, of course.'

'Good, I'll get you a ticket.'

'I'll have two tickets,' I say.

Harry's head snaps up.

'Two tickets,' he repeats.

Don't they think I have friends?

'Yes, that's right,' I say, helping myself to salad.

Holly and Moira walk in and I give Holly a wink.

'Alright love?' I ask.

She nods and gives a weak smile.

'Try and eat something,' Moira tells her.

'How's your tummy today?' asks Harry.

Holly shifts in her seat.

'It's okay.'

They're going to find out there's a lot more going on in her tummy than they at first thought. Moira takes my plate and heaps lasagne onto it.

'So what do you want to talk to us about Dad?' asks Harry.

'Rosie Foster,' I say bluntly.

There's silence. The only noise that can be heard is my cutlery hitting the plate. It's deafening in the silence. I'm the only one eating it seems.

'Who?' says Harry, but I can see from his expression that he knows who I'm talking about.

Moira lays down her fork.

'What about Rosie Foster, Dad?' she asks.

'You tell me Moira,' I say crossly.

I'd better stop eating. Her lasagne gives me indigestion at the best of times.

She lifts her head proudly.

'I had your interests at heart Dad,' she says.

'Huh,' I scoff loudly. 'Your interests you mean.'

'Moira, did you ...?' begins Harry.

'Yes she did,' I say pushing my plate away. 'You've got no right to interfere in my life. It's not your place to tell a cleaner she can or can't come.'

Holly grips her stomach.

'What's the matter?' asks Moira anxiously.

'I don't fancy it,' says Holly.

'I don't know what happened, Dad,' says Harry, picking up the lasagne. 'I'll pop this in the microwave. I think we should eat later when everyone is less upset.'

'Moira went to see Rosie at her job in Waitrose, that's what happened. She then embarrassed her by calling her a gold-digger. If that wasn't enough she then phoned Becky and told her to send a different cleaner. What a cheek Moira. I'm not having it; do you hear me?'

'I just thought …'

'I know what you thought, Moira, and you couldn't be more wrong.'

'I know,' she says, bowing her head

'I like Rosie,' says Holly.

Moira sighs.

'She's not our kind of person, Holly,' says Moira softly.

'Well she's my kind of person, I'll tell you that much,' I say loudly.

Harry looks horrified.

'You don't mean you're …'

'What?' I snap.

'You know,' he says avoiding my eyes.

'Don't be disrespectful to your mother,' I say standing up.

Harry flaps about. Honestly, I didn't bring my son up to be such a wally.

'I'm … I'm sorry, I just …'

'Am I not allowed to have friends?'

'Of course … I … It's just …'

'Now, you both listen to me. I will have whoever I want to clean my house and I'll have whoever I want round for dinner too. It's my life. It's my house and it's my money. You're my son, who else am I going to leave it to? But I get a bit lonely and Rosie's alright. I'm letting her rent one of my houses. I might as well tell you now as have you find out from someone like Celia. Nosy old cow she is. I won't take in any more of her parcels.'

'And I'm pregnant,' says Holly.

I stare at her. Blimey, she chooses her moments.

Harry's mouth drops open.

'What did you say?'

Moira has turned ashen and sways in her chair.

'No,' she says firmly. 'No, Holly.'

'I'm having a baby,' says Holly. 'Grandad came round to give me moral support.'

'What?' Harry gasps.

Moira turns on me.

'You have the gall to come here and have a go at me when all the time you've been keeping secret the fact that our daughter is pregnant. How dare you …'

'Now hold on Moira,' I say sharply.

'I went to see Rosie and …' begins Holly.

'You went to that woman?' screeches Moira.

I think she's in danger of having a heart attack. Her blood pressure must have gone through the roof. She's leaning over Holly, her face contorted with anger.

'Why did you go to her?'

'I … I …' begins Holly and then starts to cry. 'I didn't know what else to do and she took me to Grandad and they said I had to tell you.'

Moira slumps in her seat.

'Best to make her a cup of tea,' I say to Harry and then realise he's in a bigger state of shock than Moira.

'Where's that Bell's whisky?' I ask.

Harry looks around the kitchen.

'Top cupboard.'

'Right,' I say getting up. 'Holly, get some glasses. Your parents have had a shock.'

'How far gone are you?' Moira asks in a strained voice.

'I'm nearly six weeks. There's time to get rid of it.'

Moira claps a hand to her heart.

'If God hears you,' she mutters.

'Unfortunately, God can't get rid of it can he?' I say.

'I didn't have to tell you,' says Holly placing the glasses on the table.

'Who is he?' snarls Harry suddenly, jumping up.

It took him a bit of time to realise there was a man involved.

'Did he rape you?' asks Moira.

I sigh and pour whisky into the glasses.

'No, I wanted to do it.'

'Oh, Holly, please,' cries Moira.

'He'll have to marry you,' says Harry, frowning. 'I'll go round and see the family. We'll need to get things organised before you start showing a bump.'

I gape at him.

'Have you lost your marbles? She's only seventeen. She's got her education to think of and …'

'I'm on the parish council,' butts in Moira. 'I'm a councillor. I can't have my daughter having an abortion.'

I take a swig of the whisky. It's rough but it does the trick.

'This isn't about you, Moira,' I say crossly.

'How dare you,' she bites back hotly. 'This is none of your business.'

'Okay, Moira,' stammers Harry.

'I don't want to marry him. He's a dick,' exclaims Holly.

'Holly!'

Harry falls back into his chair.

'What will people say?' Moira says, throwing back the whisky and shuddering.

'It's nothing to do with other people,' I say. 'They don't have to know anything about it.'

'That Rosie will probably tell all and sundry,' says Moira tearfully.

'Rosie is discreet. She won't tell anyone.'

'We need to think about all this,' says Harry. 'Does the boy know?'

'No and I'm not telling him. I made a mistake. I won't make another one. I'll go on the pill and …'

'Lord help us,' groans Moira.

'Right, well I'm off,' I say walking into the hall.

'But you've not had any dinner,' protests Harry.

'I haven't got an appetite now. I think Moira should apologise to Rosie when she gets a chance.'

Moira sniffs.

'I've got a lot on my plate.'

'Haven't we all. I'll see myself out.'

I pull my overcoat from the cupboard. Holly follows me out.

'Thank you Grandad,' she says hugging me. 'It was easier with you here.'

'Don't you be bulldozed into marrying that clown?'

'I won't.'

I kiss her on the cheek. I'll be glad to get home to my lovely warm house. It's freezing in Harry and Moira's. It's below zero, what's wrong with them? Economising I suppose. Maybe I'll get some fish and chips on the way home. I'm starving and anything is better than Moira's cooking.

Chapter Fifty
Rosie

'Come on, you two,' calls Doris. 'We'll miss the coach.'

We're off to Leigh-on-Sea. I'm going to scatter Frank's ashes there, although quite honestly, I have no idea where exactly in Leigh-on-Sea I'm going to scatter them. Doris suggested Southend Pier as Frank used to like it there. I think he would have liked them scattered at Millwall, but no one fancied a day trip to a football pitch.

'Anyway, you don't want loads of people treading all over your Frank,' Doris had said.

'Huh,' Shirl had muttered. 'They did it all his life so what difference does it make.'

She wasn't wrong. But I decided to take them to Leigh-on-Sea in the end. After all, Millwall got plenty of money out of Frank. I don't see why they should get his body too.

There's a few of us. I asked Sam if he wanted to come but he said no.

'I said goodbye at the funeral. That was enough for me,' he'd said.

We're going to have a short ceremony and then I'm going to scatter them. Pete has written a little something. After that, Doris suggested we get some whelks and play on the amusements. It's a bit too chilly to walk along the front but I didn't want to wait until the summer. That would mean I'd have the ashes in my new place, and quite honestly, I didn't want a new start with Frank, dead or alive. I want to put the past behind me and that includes Frank, his peroxide blonde bit on the side and the Tradmore Estate. I got five hundred for Peroxide Blonde's ring, so God knows what Frank paid for it and there's me wearing a second-hand wedding ring. If he was going to buy anyone a ring it should have been me. Anyway, that paid John at the off-licence. I've been looking at learning a language too, I'm thinking I might learn to speak French. I haven't told Doris or any of that lot. They'll think I'm getting ideas above my station. But I want to better myself and there's nothing wrong with that is there? I still haven't heard anything from Matt Fisher. That's suspicious that, isn't it? One minute he's harassing me in Waitrose and then suddenly he disappears. Still, I suppose I should be grateful. I think I've paid all Frank's debts now, apart from Matt Fisher's, of course. I can't afford to pay that one. I'll be flat broke if I do and I don't suppose Matt Fisher takes instalments. It's not like the tally man is it? I'm hanging onto the rest of my winnings and that's that. I'm going to make sure my twilight years are lived out in peace and comfort.

Bert helps Crabbers onto the coach and he sits next to me.

'I've got some nice pillow shams for you,' he says. 'Remind me to give them to you when we get back.'

'That's nice of you,' says Doris. 'Isn't that nice of Crabbers?' she adds turning to me from the seat in front.

'Very nice, thank you,' I say.

'I thought it would cheer you up after, well, you know.'

'That's thoughtful,' says Shirl.

I wish they'd shut up.

I'm feeling much happier. I cleaned for Archie yesterday and it was so nice. We had a chat about books and then he told me that Holly's parents knew about the pregnancy.

'I bet they were upset,' I'd said.

'Moira looked about to have a heart attack. I plied her with whisky and she seemed alright after that,' he'd smiled. 'They want her to marry the lad, can you believe it?'

I'd been appalled. After all, that was what happened to me. I was a bit older, granted but a mistake like that can ruin your life. Just look at mine.

'She can't do that,' I'd said without thinking.

'I agree. An abortion is the best thing.'

Archie wants me to move into his little house. I did say it would be difficult now as I'd signed all the paperwork for the flat, but he said his solicitor can sort that out. I should tell Sam. He was going to help me move in. I'd even booked time off work. Brian wasn't happy. That's an understatement actually. I thought he was going to have a seizure when I told him.

'I thought you weren't having time off over Christmas,' he'd said accusingly.

'I wasn't but I'll be moving, and I'll need a few days to get myself sorted.'

'Unpaid,' he'd practically shouted. 'You'll have to take it unpaid.'

'Okay,' I'd said reluctantly. 'I am owed five days though.'

'Can't be entertained,' he'd said briskly.

Sometimes I think the whole world is against me getting off the Tradmore Estate. The rocking of the coach makes me sleepy and the next thing I know I've dozed off. I'm woken my Crabbers shaking me.

'We're here,' says Shirl.

'Aw look at those Christmas lights,' says Doris.

We climb from the coach and I smell fish and chips and seafood. The sea looks a bit rough though.

'I could do with a pint,' says Bert.

'Yes, let's have some lunch,' says Shirl.

Pete clambers from the coach clutching the ashes. I need to keep an eye on those. After a few beers who knows where they might end up; left on a dodgem if I'm not careful.

'I'll take those, shall I?' I say to Pete.

'Oh, yeah, right. I don't feel comfortable with them anyway, if I'm honest,' says Pete.

He hands me the Co-op carrier bag. I know, I should have found something better to carry them in, but a Co-op bag is as good as anything. Frank always liked the Co-op. I prefer Lidl, so I suppose when my time comes I'll be carried in a Lidl bag. As long as they don't put me in a Waitrose bag, that would be too uppity for me.

'Don't lose them,' says Doris.

We trundle along the seafront, the cold sea air whipping at our cheeks.

'Not the best day for it,' shivers Shirl.

'There's never a good day for it,' says Bert.

'Let's go to Osbourne Bros. They do the best cockles,' says Crabbers.

'I think we should have the ceremony first,' I say.

I don't really want to be clutching Frank's ashes all around Southend, do I? I only need to accidentally drop them. That would be my kind of luck wouldn't it, scrambling around on my hands and knees picking up bits of Frank.

'I guess she's right,' says Doris. 'Shall we go to the pier first?'

'It's a bit cold,' groans Shirl.

'It's got to be done,' says Bert. 'He needs a send-off.'

Everyone nods in agreement and we head to the pier. It's nippy here, I can tell you. We all stand on the pier, the biting wind taking our breath away. I hang onto the ashes for dear life, while Doris fights to get a scarf on her head. I look to Bert who pulls his phone from his pocket. He fiddles with it for a few seconds and then says.

'You say when.'

Everyone looks at me. I take a deep breath. I don't think I'll ever be ready, so best to just get it over with.

'Okay,' I say.

He clicks into his phone and *Fuck You,* by Lily Allen plays loudly through the tinny speaker. I gasp.

'What's that?' asks Shirl. 'Surely that's not ...'

'Wrong song,' says Bert, hastily clicking into his phone.

I fight back a sigh.

We wait for what seems like forever before Prince begins to sing *Purple Rain*. It was a song Frank used to sing when he was drunk. Doris wipes a tear from her eye. I look to Pete and nod. He steps forward and clears his throat. I take the urn from the Co-op carrier. We all look at Pete and wait. He straightens his tie, pulls a scrap of paper from his pocket and reads hesitantly.

'For Frank. If I die before I wake. I left a pasta bake in the fridge. And if I say so myself. It was to die for'.

He folds the piece of paper and pushes it back into his pocket. There's silence. The only sound is the crooning of Prince and the wind howling around us. I swallow and finally say,

'What was that?'

Pete coughs.

'I know. It didn't work. It should have been pizza but that didn't rhyme. I wanted something fitting, you see.'

'And that's it?' I croak.

'Blimey,' mumbles Doris.

'Yeah,' says Pete. 'I got it off the internet.'

I don't believe this. I knew I shouldn't have left it to Pete.

'The music will finish soon,' says Bert, anxiously.

I rub my eyes. Crabbers limps forward. We all look at him in surprise. He lifts his head and says,

'We thank the universe for giving us Frank. He lit up our lives and things won't be the same now he's gone. Let's remember Frank for the fun-loving person he was as we now scatter his ashes to the wind.'

'Aw,' says Shirl.

'That was nice,' says Bert.

Nice, but not strictly true. I don't think Frank lit up anyone's life but best not to say anything. At least he said something that didn't have pizza or pasta bake in it. I'm really fed up. I don't mind telling you. How could Pete have come with such a crappy poem?

'Thanks Crabbers,' I say.

'I'll play the music again,' says Bert fiddling with his phone.

We wait for the music to start again and I remove the lid from the urn.

'Throw them over your shoulder,' advises Shirl. 'They won't come back and slap you in the face then.'

Yes, that would be Frank alright, wouldn't it, coming back to slap me in the face. I take her advice and throw the contents over my shoulder. Everyone spins round. After all, no one wants a fistful of ashes in their face, do they?

'Bye Frank,' says Bert emotionally.

I don't say anything. I'm not a hypocrite. Clearly I turn back too soon for at that moment a gust of wind blows in from the sea.

'Aw, don't get upset,' says Doris, putting an arm around me and handing me a tissue.

I don't like to tell her that a bit of Frank just blew into my eye.

'I'm okay,' I say.

'Let's get a drink,' says Bert.

'Thanks Crabbers,' I say.

'It was nothing,' he says, limping alongside me. 'Don't let me forget those pillow shams.'

Chapter Fifty-One
Moira

Holly felt sick. Now they were actually here, she wasn't so sure she wanted to go through with it. Moira's hand shook as she took Holly's.

'Are you alright, Holly?' she asked.

'I won't die, will I?' said Holly, her face white.

'Die? Of course not, but if you've changed your mind …'

'No, let's go,' said Holly pulling Moira through the hospital entrance doors. Moira sighed and struggled to control her trembling body. She was torn. Half of her knew this was the best thing but the other half was consumed with guilt. The counselling had been very helpful. Although Moira had no idea what had been said to Holly during her own counselling, but Moira's session had been excellent. All the same, the guilt now overwhelmed her. *You can't let her throw her life away,* Alf had said. He'd really laid into Moira about the Rosie business. He'd been way over the top, Moira thought. All she'd tried to do was protect him. She'd spent her life trying to protect her family and for what? So they could all turn on her, that's what. First Alfred and then Holly, it was too unbearable. Maybe she had been selfish about the house, but no one could blame her for trying to protect it.

The nurse greeted them and put Holly at ease.

'You're going to be just fine,' she smiled.

Moira was relieved to sit down. She didn't think her trembling legs would hold her up for much longer.

'I'll get you a cup of tea,' said the nurse.

'Oh no, don't worry,' said Moira. 'I'll pop down to the café in a bit.'

She didn't want to wait here with this awful sterile smell around her.

'Are you going to be okay Holly?' she asked.

She felt like she was sending her daughter to her execution.

'Yes, I will be,' said Holly giving a weak smile.

'She'll be absolutely fine,' said the nurse cheerily.

You'd never think this was an abortion clinic, thought Moira.

Holly disappeared from view and Moira had to fight back tears. She must be strong for Holly. Moira daren't think about that awful boy that put Holly in the family way. She couldn't understand what was wrong with Harry. Why didn't he go around to the boy's house and have it out with the family? Harry was too involved with work lately. She needed to talk to him about all those late nights. If he was so busy why wasn't he bringing home more money? And that play, that stupid play. It was driving her mad. She'd be glad when the thing was over. Still, Christmas would be here soon, and all this would be behind them. Her only nagging fear was that Alfred would want to bring that Rosie woman to them for Christmas. Surely she would be going to her son's for Christmas? At the thought of Rosie's son, Moira felt that little flutter in her stomach. She found herself wondering what he would have done if Holly had been his daughter. She imagined he wouldn't have hesitated going around to the family and having it out with the dad.

She watched Holly disappear from sight and then pulled herself out of the chair. A cup of tea would help. She followed the signs to the cafeteria, shrugging out of her coat as she walked. Why was it always so hot in hospitals? She pulled off the coat and turned the corridor corner, only to walk into Sam Foster.

'Oh,' she said, surprised.

For a moment he looked confused and then he seemed to recognise her. Moira saw that his hand was bandaged.

'Hello,' he said. 'It's amazing who you see here.'

She frantically thought of an excuse for why she was there. She couldn't possibly tell him her daughter was having an abortion. The shame of it all made her blush profusely.

'What happened to your hand?' she asked.

He looked down at the bandage.

'Oh, it was stupid. I grabbed an exhaust and it had a sharp edge. I should have been wearing gloves.'

She didn't know what to say so simply nodded to the cafeteria.

'I was going to get a coffee.'

'Ah, so what brings you here?'

She couldn't turn any redder if she tried.

'My daughter is seeing a consultant. I'm waiting for her.'

'Is she better now?'

'Better?' queried Moira.

'She'd been sick when I saw you last.'

'Oh,' said Moira flustered. 'She's much better.'

'That's good to hear. Anyway I'd better get on.'

She nodded and watched him walk along the corridor. Yes, she thought, he would most certainly have gone around to confront the boy's father. What was wrong with Harry? She should text him. Let him know Holly had gone in. She felt tears welling up again and hurried to the cafeteria. A cup of tea, that's what she needed.

Chapter Fifty-Two
Rosie

'This is Archie,' I say.

Sam looks at Archie curiously.

'Nice to meet you,' says Sam, shaking Archie's hand.

'What have you done there?' asks Archie pointing to the bandage.

Sam looks down at his hand.

'I had an argument with an exhaust pipe.'

'It looks like the exhaust pipe won. You could have waited until after I'd moved,' I joke.

'Mrs Foster,' calls a voice.

I look over the bannister.

'Hello, Mr Singh,' I say.

I've known Mr Singh for five years and I still don't know his first name. I don't think he knows mine either.

'Do you need some help?' he asks in his sing-song voice.

'That would be lovely,' I say.

'I'll come up.'

'That's another pair of hands,' smiles Archie.

I'm moving into Archie's house today and I still can't believe my luck. I'm finally getting off Tradmore Estate. It feels like a dream. I truly believed I'd be carried out feet first from this flat.

'A happy day, Mrs Foster,' says Mr Singh coming up the stairs.

He's right there. It's one of the happiest days of my life. Life's funny isn't it? My life changed with a win on the bingo. If I hadn't have won the bingo and Frank hadn't walked in front of the pizza van I wouldn't have met Archie. I never go to the pub with the girls normally; once a fortnight to the bingo was my outing. We never had money for me to go anywhere exotic or glamourous. Not that Frank would have gone anyway. He thought the café at the dogs was fancy. Frank had no class. Of course, if I'd known that Frank was spending all our hard-earned cash on furs and rings for his bit on the side then I'd have … Well, I don't know what I would have done, quite honestly. I still can't believe it. They say the wife is the last to know, don't they? Let's face it if a pizza van hadn't have killed him, I probably still wouldn't know. When I think what we could have done with that money.

'I was sorry to hear about Mr Foster,' Mr Singh says, as though reading my mind.

I bet he isn't sorry really. Frank used to call him Nappy Head. How insulting was that? He would say it to his face too. He was insensitive was Frank.

'He's probably taken my job,' Frank used to say.

'Which one?' I'd argue. 'You've had that many.'

How ridiculous. Frank couldn't hold a job down for five minutes. The only job he kept longer than three months was the one down at the dog stadium and most of those earnings went back into the dogs, so to speak. When you hear people say, *'It's all gone to the dogs,'* that was us. It really did all go to the dogs in more ways than one. I like Mr Singh. I always have. He's been a good neighbour. I can't say that about the rest of them in our block. I'm glad to be getting out. After all I'm sixty now. A pensioner by all accounts and it won't be long before one of the buggers around here tries to steal my pension. It will be no good telling them that the government haven't given it to me yet.

'Yes, it was unfortunate.'

'I heard he was knocked down by the Indian takeaway, Deliveroo,' says Mr Singh.

He probably thinks that was fitting for Frank. I feel bad telling him it wasn't the Indian takeaway that killed him.

'Actually it was a Domino's Pizza van,' I say.

'Oh,' he smiles. 'I knew it was something to do with fast food.'

I sigh and look back into the flat. It's sad saying goodbye isn't it? Even if you hate the place, it's still hard. Still, it will be lovely walking out of my own front door without having to face six flights of stairs. I can't wait for Christmas. It'll be lovely in the new house. I wonder if I should ask Archie over for Christmas. Not Christmas Day, obviously. He'll be spending that at Moira's. I could invite him over for Boxing Day. I'll see what Sam thinks.

'Grab the end of that couch, Mr Singh?' says Archie.

'You can't carry that down six flights,' I argue.

I don't want Archie having a stroke before I've even moved in. Moira has enough on her plate without that. Although why I'm thinking of Moira, I'll never know.

'I'll be alright,' says Archie stubbornly.

'I'm really not happy ...'

'Don't fuss.'

'I'll go backwards,' says Mr Singh.

'I'll be helping Archie,' smiles Sam.

'We've come to help out,' calls a voice.

'It's Doris,' I say.

I hear her panting up the stairs.

'I won't be sorry to see the back of these,' she sighs on reaching us.

'Bert got the afternoon off. I tell you, those stairs are a killer. It's a good job you're moving out, Rosie. They'll be the death of you.'

'You see, everything works out,' says Archie, winking at me.

Doris looks at him and raises her eyebrows.

'Hello,' she says. 'We haven't met, have we?'

'This is Archie,' I say.

The lift opens, and Crabbers steps out. He's laden down with pillow shams and bedcovers.

'Oh,' I say on seeing him.

'Crabbers offered to help. He's got the van so he can take a few bits. He's brought you some lovely things.'

'I couldn't do them stairs,' he says handing me a pile of sheets.

'There are pillow shams, duvet covers, sheets and some towels there,' he smiles. 'House warming.'

'Isn't that nice,' gushes Doris.

I'm recently widowed. What's wrong with her and Shirl, trying to palm me off onto Crabbers?

'This is Archie,' I say.

I suppose I should say that I clean for him. I suppose I also should say that it's his house I'm moving into but instead I say, 'Archie's my friend.'

Three little words but they convey so much don't they? Doris is silent for a moment and not much silences Doris. Crabbers nods before saying.

'Hello Archie.'

'Alright Johnnie,' says Archie, remembering Crabber's name.

'Yeah, not bad, you?'

'Right,' says Sam. 'Shall we get this couch down the stairs?'

Bert came at that moment and thankfully Archie didn't have to lift anything. I may have had a toad for a husband, but I've got good friends.

When Archie Met Rosie

'Can't wait to see the house,' says Doris nudging me. 'He's lovely, Archie, isn't he?'

'He's just a friend,' I whisper following the men downstairs.

Moira would never allow us to be anything else, let's be honest.

*

It's almost eight by the time everyone leaves. I've enjoyed showing them the new house. Sam went and got everyone fish and chips. I couldn't eat anything I was that excited.

'How about we go out for a meal,' Archie suggests after everyone has left.

'That would be nice,' I say. 'But I insist on paying my half.'

'I can't let you do that,' says Archie. 'You'd insult me. Anyway, I'm starving and I miss going out for dinner so let me pay, it'll give me pleasure.'

I couldn't really say no. Archie has done so much for me.

I lock my new front door and sit in Archie's car looking at it for a few minutes before we set off. It feels lovely knowing I won't be going back to the Tradmore Estate.

The restaurant is in Gidea Park. I don't go to restaurants, so I don't know it, but Archie insists it is a good one. We park the car and Archie offers me his arm. I can't believe any of this. I feel like I must be dreaming. We turn the corner and walk straight into Matt Fisher and his sidekick Puny and suddenly my dream turns into a nightmare.

'Well, look who it is,' he says, his eyes narrowing.

Chapter Fifty-Three
Harry

Harry watched Steph as she pushed her arms into her jumper. Her pert nipples disappeared inside. He felt less stressed now. Being with Steph had eased the strain. There's nothing like a good sex session to release the tension, he thought.

He checked the time on his watch. He ought to get back to the office. He'd had far too long a lunch break.

'I'll see you tonight then,' said Steph reaching on tiptoe to kiss him.

'Yep, the last rehearsal.'

'You'll come back to mine after, won't you?'

'I can't Steph. I've got all this business with Holly. I need to be with Moira. I've been with you this afternoon.'

'Not for long,' she said, pulling out of his arms.

'It's our lunch break and we've been gone far too long,' said Harry.

'I think it's time you decided who you want to be with, Harry. You can't have two women on the go forever.'

He sighed.

'It's a difficult time, that's all.'

She turned away and pulled on her leggings. He didn't really have time to argue with her. Not now. He'd talk to her after the rehearsal.

'We'll talk later,' he said.

'I know we will,' she said softly but something in her tone unnerved him.

*

Moira

Holly forced down the toast that Moira had placed in front of her.

'I don't have clients today,' said Moira. 'Do you want to do something special as you're off school? Shall we do some Christmas shopping and then go somewhere nice for lunch.'

Holly nodded.

'Can we go to Grandad's first? He might like to come for lunch.'

Moira nodded.

'Okay, we'll see if he wants us to pick him up after shopping.'

Moira waited for Holly to finish the last of the toast. At least she wasn't as pale as yesterday. Moira had phoned the school. She'd told them Holly had had a little procedure to help her periods. She rationalised that it wasn't quite a lie. Soon it would be Christmas and they'd have a lovely family time and in the New Year this would all be behind them. She'd agreed to go with Holly to the doctor and have her put on the pill; although Holly said she never ever wanted to do that with a boy again. Moira knew that would change and she couldn't bear this to happen again. Moira felt that she had let Holly down. Perhaps if she had been a better Christian mother then Holly would have stronger Christian morals. She still felt disappointed with Harry too. Maybe she'd have a word with Alf. She felt sure he would understand her wanting Harry to go and see the boy's father. Maybe he could make Harry understand.

'I don't see the point,' Harry had said when she'd broached the subject. 'It's a bit late to be making a fuss now isn't it?'

Harry had been quite upset that Moira had agreed to an abortion.

'It's not right,' he'd said.

But Moira could see Alf's point. It would be awful to ruin Holly's life. She had her whole future ahead of her.

Snow had been forecast so it was a good idea to get the final Christmas shopping done. Moira hated driving in bad weather. She'd check what Alfred wanted to do for Christmas. Hopefully he'd come to them. She couldn't very well leave him in that huge house all alone over the whole of Christmas. What would people say?

'Okay?' she asked Holly.

Holly wrapped a thick scarf around her neck and nodded.

'Yes, I'm looking forward to it. I feel lots better.'

'Good,' said Moira.

They'd managed to avoid the word abortion and baby. Much better that way, thought Moira.

Holly huddled in the front seat until the car heater had warmed up.

'We'll have a cup of tea at Grandad's,' Moira said.

'Do you think he'll come shopping with us?' asked Holly.

'I doubt it. But we'll pick him up afterwards and take him for lunch.'

They reached Alf's and Moira parked across Alf's car.

'He's home anyway,' she said.

They climbed out and walked to the front door. Holly rang the bell and waited.

'Try the knocker,' said Moira. 'He doesn't always hear the doorbell.'

Holly rapped hard on the knocker. They waited for a while but still Alf didn't answer the door.

'Perhaps he's popped out for a newspaper.'

'Don't you think we should check in case,' said Holly, looking worried.

'I don't know Holly. You know how funny he gets when we use the key.'

'But if he's fallen over or had a stroke or …'

'Okay,' said Moira, fumbling in her bag for Alfred's key.

'Let's knock again though. He could be in the loo.'

'All this time?' replied Holly.

'Well yes, when people get older ...'

Holly peeked through the letterbox and called to Alf. They waited patiently.

'Right,' said Moira pushing the key into the lock.

She hoped very much they wouldn't find Alfred on the floor. It would be too much.

'Dad,' she called. 'Where are you?'

'I'll check upstairs,' said Holly.

Moira walked into the living room but there was no sign of him. The house was tidy and smelt of polish. At least the house was clean these days.

'He's not upstairs,' said Holly. 'His bed's made.'

'He's probably popped to the corner shop.'

All the same, thought Moira. It was odd there was no sign of his breakfast.

'Let's go. We'll pop back later and get him for lunch.'

*

Doris

'She must have gone out,' said Shirl.

'She's not at work,' said Doris. 'She took today off. Where would she go?'

'She's probably got tons of things to get for the house.'

Doris looked thoughtful and scrambled around in her bag.

'I did text to say we were coming.'

She finally found the phone and after rubbing some spilt blusher from it she studied her messages.

'It's been delivered. So she must have read it.'

'Shall we wait?' asked Shirl.

'I'll give her a bell,' said Doris tapping into her phone.

They waited as Doris listened to the ringing tone. Finally it clicked into Rosie's voicemail.

'Huh,' said Doris. 'She's obviously out with that Archie and doesn't want to be disturbed.'

'I'm pleased for her,' said Shirl.

'Yes,' said Doris but she felt uneasy. It wasn't like Rosie not to respond to messages. Maybe they'd come back later just to be on the safe side.

Chapter Fifty-Four
Moira and Harry

'I can't work with him,' cried Louise, holding her hands up. 'He's impossible. He emphasises all the wrong words at all the wrong times. It's ridiculous.'

Steph sighed. She'd be glad when this play was over.

'Let's try again,' said Harry.

It was so close to opening night. The last thing he needed was for Louise, the leading lady, to walk out.

'I'm not sure what I'm doing wrong,' said Eric, perplexed.

'Everything. You're doing every-bloody-thing wrong,' Louise snapped.

Harry looked at his watch. He was knackered and just wanted to get home.

'I've got to get home soon,' said Michael. 'I'm taking Rita out for her birthday.'

'It's the last rehearsal before our dress rehearsal,' said Harry. 'We want to be sure everything is right.'

'I've reached a stage where I don't care,' said Louise, checking her phone.

'And it's so cold in here,' complained Marsha. 'My hands are like ice.'

'For goodness' sake,' muttered Steph. 'Don't they ever stop complaining?'

Louise threw her phone into her bag and turned to Harry.

'If you want the truth,' she said, putting her hands on her hips. 'I think you're a lousy director. If you two stopped eyeing each other up, we might get something done.'

Steph gasped.

'A bit below the belt,' said Michael.

'Right, tea break,' said Harry.

'We've just had one,' said Steph.

'I've got to go soon,' said Eric.

'For goodness' sake, is anyone apart from me serious about this play?' complained Harry.

'It is Christmas,' said Michael. 'We've all got families.'

'You shouldn't be doing this then,' said Harry angrily.

There was silence. Finally Louise said, 'I'll stay for another half an hour.'

'Thank you,' said Harry.

It was all getting too much for him, what with Holly. What a worry that was. Supposing people found out? What would everyone here think? Surely they hadn't realised about him and Steph. That's all he needed. He ought to bring it to an end before it got out of hand.

'Harry,' said Steph, nudging him. 'Everyone's waiting.'

Harry shook his head and said 'Right, let's go from the top.'

*

Moira pulled up outside Alf's. His car was there. But that had been there when they'd popped in at lunchtime. It was a quarter to six now. They'd had a good day shopping, but it had been tiring and now all Moira wanted was to collect Alf and get home. She'd left a lamb stew cooking in the slow cooker. Harry had texted to say he would be home about seven. Maybe she'd decorate the tree tonight. She'd also make sure that she and Harry had a good talk. They need to sort out the food for the opening night party.

'Give Grandad a knock,' she said. 'I'll wait here.'

Holly climbed wearily from the car. The shopping expedition had taken it out of her too. She'd be her old self soon. In a week, they'd said at the hospital.

'It's more an emotional thing,' the nurse had told them.

Moira checked her reflection in the car mirror. She looked tired. Things were getting on top of her, that's what it was. She looked up at Alf's house and again thought how selfish he was to hang onto such a huge house just for himself. He didn't need all those bedrooms. It really was ridiculous. She looked to Holly who shrugged her shoulders and walked back to the car.

'He's still not there,' she said.

Moira checked the time.

'Where can he be then?'

Rosie's, thought Moira. That's most likely where he is.

'You do think he's okay, don't you?' asked Holly.

Moira glanced at the house and felt a small pang of anxiety. Where could he be? He didn't like being out in the evenings much. It was getting very cold too.

'I'll phone his mobile,' said Moira.

The mobile rang for ages and eventually cut off.

'I wish he'd set his voicemail,' said Moira irritably.

'I'm worried,' said Holly. 'Grandad is nearly always home. I think we should try Rosie's.'

'I'm not going to the Tradmore Estate,' said Moira firmly.

'We need to find Grandad though.'

'He's not a child,' said Moira starting the engine.

'Oh alright, I'll get the bus,' said Holly haughtily, getting out of the car.

'Don't be stupid,' said Moira. 'You've not been well.'

'I'm not an invalid.'

'Alright, we'll drive there but then I need to get home to check on dinner.'

She put the car into gear and drove reluctantly to the Tradmore Estate.

'If we get mugged you can tell your father this was all your idea.'

*

'You can drive in, you know,' said Holly as they got close to the Tradmore Estate. Moira had parked the car in the road outside the high-rise flats. A ball bounced against her window. Moira jumped.

'Sorry,' yelled a boy, grabbing the ball.

Moira glanced at the entrance of the flats. A woman wearing rollers strolled to the dustbins and threw in a carrier bag.

'I'm not parking my car in there,' said Moira, horrified.

'We'll look uppity parking here,' said Holly and pointed to a space in the car park.

'Let's park there,' she said.

'I'm happy here,' said Moira, feeling far from happy. She got out of the car, locked the doors and checked again just to make sure.

'I don't know why I'm bothering,' she muttered. 'They'll just smash the windows.'

'Honestly,' sighed Holly, walking ahead.

Moira hurried after her. It was icy and twice she nearly slipped.

'Watch yourself darling,' someone shouted.

She didn't turn. Best not to give them attention, she thought.

'Don't look at them,' she told Holly.

'Honestly, Mum, they're not lepers.'

They reached a block of flats and Holly said 'This is where Rosie lives. She's on the sixth floor.'

'The sixth floor?' repeated Moira.

Holly made for the lift where the woman in rollers was waiting.

'It takes an age,' she said smiling.

Moira didn't respond.

Someone was banging at some drums. Moira rubbed at her temples. How can people live in places like this, she wondered? What on earth was Alf doing coming here? Harry really ought to talk to him. What was wrong with Harry these days? Maybe he was going through the male menopause. He was about the right age.

'We're going to see Rosie,' said Holly. 'Do you know her?'

'Rosie Foster? Yeah, I know her but she don't live here no more.'

Moira tutted. All this effort for nothing and heaven knows what was left of the car. She only hoped they still had tyres to drive away with. This will teach Harry for not talking to his dad.

'Holly, let's go,' she said, grabbing Holly's arm.

'Do you know where she lives now?' asked Holly.

'Nah, she never told no one.'

Holly allowed Moira to pull her away.

'Your grandad mentioned letting her have one of his little houses,' said Moira. 'I never for one moment thought he was serious.'

'That's nice of Grandad,' said Holly. 'Shall we go there?'

'I don't think so.'

'We should just check.'

Moira had no desire whatsoever to see Rosie Foster again. She'd caused far too much trouble as it was. She checked the time on her phone. It was getting late and dinner would be ruined.

'I don't think it's a good idea, Holly.'

'Please, I'm worried.'

Moira sighed. Why did she have to get lumbered with this?

'Okay, but that's it. What Grandad does is really up to him.'

Holly kissed her warmly on the cheek.

'Thanks, Mum.'

Much to Moira's surprise the car was still in one piece.

'Let's go,' she said accelerating away from the estate. The more distance they put between themselves and the Tradmore Estate, the happier she would be.

*

Doris, Shirl and Crabbers

'I don't understand it,' said Doris. 'She should surely have been back by now.'

'It's her new place, you'd think she'd want to be here making it look nice,' agreed Shirl.

'It's sodding freezing,' said Doris, pushing her cold hands into the pockets of her coat. 'Where could she have gone in this weather?'

Crabbers peeked through the window.

'What are you doing?' hissed Doris. 'People will think we're trying to break in.'

'Just checking everything looks normal. It doesn't look like it's been trashed,' he said, forming an arch with his hands and peering into the living room.

'Trashed?' said Shirl. 'Who's going to trash it?'

'Matt Fisher,' said Crabbers dryly, straightening up. There was silence as Doris and Shirl took in his words.

'Oh God,' muttered Doris finally. 'I'd forgotten all about him.'

'Hell's bells, you don't think,' whispered Shirl as Crabbers limped away from the window.

'She wouldn't be the first person that owed Matt Fisher money and suddenly went missing. Joey Smith disappeared for five days and was found ...'

'Shut up,' snapped Shirl. 'I don't want to hear about Joey Fisher. Oh, poor Rosie, she's been through so much. What an end if she's ...'

'Oh do stop it Shirl,' said Doris harshly. 'This isn't *The Essex Boys.*'

'No, it's far worse. Matt Fisher is ...' said Crabbers.

'Crabbers,' exclaimed Doris. 'You're frightening Shirl.'

She punched into her phone.

'I'll try her again,' she said. 'She must have seen my missed calls and messages by now.'

But still there was no reply.

'It's not like her, is it?' said Shirl worriedly.

'I think we should call the police,' said Crabbers.

At that moment a Range Rover pulled up outside the house.

'This doesn't look good,' said Doris, her voice shaking.

*

Moira slowed down. There was a group of people standing outside Rosie's house.

'Who are they?' asked Holly.

'I don't know,' said Moira. 'But we should be careful.'

'For goodness sake' Mum, I think you're neurotic.'

The women turned to look at the car. Holly recognised Crabbers. He was the man that had been with Rosie that Friday night.

'I know him. He's got a handicap,' said Holly.

Moira removed her driving glasses and then she too recognised Crabbers. Holly dived from the car before Moira could stop her.

'Hello,' she said. 'Do you know if Rosie Foster lives here?'

The women looked at each other and then Doris said.

'Yeah, she does. She's not home though.'

'I'm Holly and this is my mum,' Holly said nodding towards her mum.

'I know you,' said Crabbers.

'We've met, yes,' said Moira.

'We're looking for my grandad,' said Holly. 'I'm a bit worried. We can't seem to get hold of him. Do you know if he's with Rosie?'

'Oh God,' groaned one of the women.

'This is Doris and Shirl,' said Crabbers. 'We've been trying to get hold of Rosie too but she's not answering her phone.'

Moira's heart began to beat a little faster.

'How long have you been trying to get hold of her?' she asked.

'All day,' said Doris.

'We think Matt Fisher may be involved in her disappearance,' said Crabbers.

'Disappearance?' repeated Moira.

'It's not like Rosie,' he said.

'Or my grandad,' said Holly who seemed to be enjoying the excitement.

'Who's Matt Fisher?' asked Moira.

She didn't really want to know. She should have known Alf's relationship with Rosie Foster would be trouble. This will serve Harry right.

'He's a loan shark,' said Doris.

The words seem to drip with fear as she spoke them.

'A loan shark?' repeated Moira again.

Crabbers nodded.

'They lend you money and …'

'I know what a loan shark is,' said Moira.

Crabbers fidgeted on his feet. He didn't like Moira very much. She'd been rude to Rosie the last time he'd seen her.

'Other people have disappeared when they owed him money. Joey Smith was found …'

'Crabbers,' interrupted Shirl.

'Oh,' groaned Moira. 'Do you really think …?'

'She's most likely fine,' assured Doris.

'I doubt it,' said Crabbers pessimistically.

'We need to phone your father,' said Moira.

Holly pulled her phone from her pocket with shaking hands.

'Will there be a ransom note?' asked Moira dramatically.

'Oh no,' said Crabbers. 'He doesn't bother with those.'

Moira felt faint and had to sit on the wall.

'You look really pale, love,' said Shirl.

'I don't believe this is happening,' said Moira. 'Things like this never happen in Gidea Park.'

'I'm sure they don't,' agreed Doris.

'Dad's phone is off,' said Holly.

Moira rolled her eyes. She'd throttle Harry.

'We should phone the police,' said Crabbers again. 'Only the longer we leave it …'

'You don't think they've just gone out for the day?' asked Moira.

'Where would you go all day in this weather?' questioned Doris. Moira nodded in agreement.

'Alf doesn't like the cold.'

'I don't think we should panic,' said Shirl.

'We need to tell Dad,' said Holly.

'I've got dinner cooking,' said Moira.

'You can drop me home and then go and get Dad,' said Holly sensibly.

'I can give you my number,' said Doris. 'If Rosie and your dad turn up you can give me a ring. I should take your number, so I can let you know if they turn up here.'

'He's my father-in-law,' said Moira.

'Well, same thing,' said Shirl with a laugh.

Moira gave Doris her phone number and then she and Holly climbed back into the car.

'Don't worry, love,' called Doris.

But Moira was already worrying.

Chapter Fifty-Five
Harry

'I really must go, Steph.'

'Harry, we haven't sorted things out,' said Steph, her voice rising.

He really didn't want to have this conversation with Steph. Not while they were in the church hall.

'People will wonder what we're still doing here,' he said.

'I don't care.'

'Keep your voice down Steph. I promise we'll talk about this, but not now.'

'I thought you were coming back to my place,' she said, blocking his way. 'You usually do.'

'I know, but I have this thing with Holly. She's not well.'

'What's wrong with her?' she demanded.

He didn't like Steph when she was in one of these moods. He didn't want to tell her about Holly. It was best if they kept it as quiet as possible. The last thing they needed was for it to be broadcast all around Gidea Park.

'She's not well.'

'I don't think you love me any more,' she said sullenly.

'Don't be silly.'

He could end it now, he thought. She was giving him the opportunity. All he had to do was say that he didn't love her at all. He couldn't face the confrontation though, so instead he said,

'I'll come round at the weekend.'

She draped her arms around him seductively.

'Do you promise?'

'Of course,' he said trying to disentangle himself.

'Kiss me.'

'Steph, anyone could walk in.'

'But they won't will they?' she argued.

He leaned forward. She pulled him close and his mouth touched hers. She clung to him and hungrily devoured his lips. A high-pitched shriek pulled them apart.

'Harry!'

He turned sharply, his foot stamping on Steph's.

'Ouch,' she gasped, jumping back in pain.

Harry stared in shock at Moira who stood in the doorway of the church hall. Her mouth gaped open and she blinked several times. He saw tears glistening on her cheeks.

'Moira,' he said, his mind racing with excuses but none seemed plausible. 'What ... what ...?'

'Harry,' she repeated but more quietly this time. 'How could you?'

She broke into a little sob. Her face was bright red. Harry's eyes met hers and he started to walk towards her, but she turned on her heel and rushed from the room.

'Shit, shit,' Harry muttered.

'Just as well,' said Steph, rubbing her foot. 'You had to tell her some time.'

He turned to her.

'It's over Steph.'

'What?' she said surprised. 'What do you mean? She'll get over it.'

'I have to go after her.'

'Oh for goodness' sake,' sighed Steph. 'I don't know why I bother with you.'

Harry ignored her and hurried from the hall, but Moira was already driving away.

'Oh no,' he groaned walking to his car. He had left his lights on.

'Shit,' he yelled, slapping his thigh. The battery was bound to be dead.

*

Moira could barely see the road ahead. Tears were blurring her vision. She'd taken her driving glasses off so that didn't help either.

'How could he?' she repeated over and over. 'How could he do this to us?'

She couldn't go home. Not yet. How would she explain being so distressed to Holly? Poor Holly. It wasn't her fault her father was a dick.

'Bastard,' she yelled, thumping the steering wheel.

With that stupid bimbo too, what was wrong with him? She recognised her. She worked in human resources at Harry's office. She remembered her from last year's works party. She couldn't be more than twenty-five.

'I can't stand it,' she groaned. What had become of them? First Holly and now Harry. It was shameful. She braked sharply as the car in front of her slowed down. A pedestrian waved angrily at her. She was going too fast. She really should slow down. She turned the car onto the A13 and headed towards Dagenham East. Her phone bleeped. It must be Harry. He'd have to wait until she stopped. She ought to tell him about his dad disappearing. That was surely more important than their marriage problems.

'Oh, how could you Harry?' she moaned.

She hadn't fully realised where she was heading but she suddenly found herself outside Sam Foster's garage. The lights were on. She checked her face in the car mirror. It was blotchy from her tears. She sighed heavily and looked down at her phone.

There were two missed calls from Harry and a text.

Moira, please. We need to talk about this. I'm stuck here. The car won't start. The AA are on their way. Please call me.

Moira stared at the message for a moment and then typed a reply.

I need time to think. I came to tell you that your dad seems to have gone missing. I can't get hold of him. I will see you later. How could you Harry? I've gone to see Rosie's son. No one has seen her all day either.

She wiped away the tears that just didn't seem to stop flowing and sent a text to Holly.

I'm going to see Rosie's son. Dad has a flat battery but will be home soon. Keep the dinner warm.

Although Moira had no idea how she would face going home. The tears started to flow again and she sniffed. Why weren't there tissues in her bag when she needed them? She was fumbling for a tissue when there was a tap on her window. She looked up, for a moment forgetting her tear-streaked face and puffy eyes. Sam Foster was peering at her.

'Oh,' she said flustered and quickly patted at her hair.

She wound down the window.

'You're blocking my entrance ...' he began and stopped on seeing her face. She went to speak but just found herself in floods of tears again. Sam looked uncomfortable. He opened the car door and offered his hand.

'You can't stay in your car,' he smiled. 'You'll drown.'

'I'll ... I'll move it,' she hiccupped.

'Don't worry. It's only me wanting to get out. Come and have a cup of tea.'

His voice was matter-of-fact. There was no softness in it. Just as well, thought Moira. I'll probably start blubbering all over again if he shows me any sympathy. She didn't even want to imagine what she looked like. She followed him into the garage and through to the tiny office. It still smelt of his soap.

'I'll put the kettle on,' he said.

Moira blew her nose and wiped her eyes. Sam made the tea silently and Moira waited.

'I've put three sugars in it,' he said placing a mug of strong tea in front of her.

'My husband's having an affair,' she said, feeling the tears run down her cheeks again. 'I just went to the church hall. He's putting on a Christmas play. They were kissing and … She works in human resources. I think she types up the scripts and … and … Oh, how can this be happening?'

Sam bit his lip.

'I'm sorry.'

She lifted her head.

'You probably think I deserve it.'

He raised his eyebrows.

'No. I don't think anyone deserves that. I've been there so I wouldn't wish it on anyone.'

'You think I'm uppity,' she said, sipping from her tea.

'You're up your own arse a bit,' he said handing her a tissue.

Her lips quivered.

'I didn't think Harry … Well I never imagined he had it in him. She's only about twenty-five. It's made me feel old and ugly.'

'You're not ugly,' he said softly. 'And you're certainly not old.'

Moira sniffed.

'She's got legs up to her armpits and shiny blonde hair. I'm forty-three and going through the menopause and what's more my daughter has just had an abortion.'

Sam's expression didn't change.

'What you need is a Custard Cream,' he said, standing up.

'Can I use your loo?' she asked.

'It's a mess but yeah, it's through there,' he said pointing to a door.

Moira grabbed her bag and made her way to the loo. She stared at her face in the cracked mirror and sighed. Oh, she looked terrible. Her hair was all over the place and her eyes were red and sore. Her face was flushed. She looked like an old hag. No wonder Harry was knocking off a 25-year-old. It was her fault. Sam Foster was right. She'd always been too much up her own arse. She pulled a hairbrush through her hair, felt the tears prick her eyelids and quickly walked from the toilet.

Sam had placed some Custard Creams onto a plate.

'Thank you,' she smiled.

'Feeling better?' he asked.

'A bit, thank you. You're right though, I am up my own arse.'

He nodded.

'I can't blame Harry really,' she said thoughtfully.

He put his hand on her arm.

'Don't be too hard on yourself.'

Her arm tingled under his hand and she waited for him to remove it, but he didn't.

'You're alright,' he smiled.

'Really?' she asked.

'Yeah, I'd give you a second glance if you weren't married.'

Her stomach fluttered.

'But I am married.'

He shrugged.

'This is true.'

She realised that her breathing had quickened and blushed. He removed his hand and said briskly,

'Anyway, I'm sure you never came to discuss your husband.'

'Oh,' she said, remembering, 'We can't get hold of Alfred and ...'

'Alfred?' he queried.

'Your mum cleans for him.'

'Archie,' he said.

'They both seem to have gone missing. Rosie's friends are worried and I thought I should tell you. Apparently, Matt Fisher the loan shark was after your mum and ...'

'They've gone missing?' he repeats.

'It seems so. I've been trying Alf all day and your mum's friends have been trying your mum all day. Apparently, they're not the first people to owe money to Matt Fisher and go missing.'

Sam stood up.

'Let's go,' he said, pulling her up.

'Where to?'

'Doris's first and then the police. Maybe I'll go and see Matt Fisher.'

'Oh no, he sounds very dangerous.'

'I'm not scared of him.'

Moira rummaged in her bag for a hairbrush.

'I look awful, my hair is a mess.'

'You look okay, Moira. You need to relax more.'

She wobbled on her feet and he helped steady her.

'Let's go,' he said.

Shakily, she followed him.

Chapter Fifty-Six
Moira and Sam

They strolled towards the police station. Doris had donned the fur coat she'd bought down Petticoat Lane the day before. She'd been dying to show Rosie. She wiped away tears at the thought that she may now never show her anything again.

'I can't believe it,' sniffed Shirl. 'I mean she's been through enough with her Frank.'

'Finally got herself a nice house too,' agreed Doris.

'I reckon they're at the bottom of the Thames,' said Crabbers thoughtlessly.

Shirl slapped him.

'What?' he asked.

'You'll upset Sam,' said Shirl.

Sam took Moira's arm and escorted her into the police station. Doris nudged Shirl and nodded towards Sam and Moira.

'What's going on there?' she whispered.

'No, never,' gasped Shirl.

A weary-looking policeman glanced up.

'Well, what have we got here then?'

'My friend's gone missing and her bloke too …' said Doris.

'Alfred's not her bloke,' corrected Moira.

'They were in a bit of trouble …' began Shirl.

'Alfred wasn't in any trouble,' said Moira.

'We think they're … you know,' said Crabbers.

Sam sighed and said.

'My mum and her friend Alfred seem to have gone missing. We've all tried to contact them today and they're not answering their phones, and neither of them has come home. It's unlike both of them. My mum's sixty and Archie is in his seventies so they're not out clubbing.'

'Rosie owed Matt Fisher some money,' added Crabbers.

'No she didn't,' argued Doris. 'Her old man owed the money. I'm not having rumours put about especially if she's …' Doris trailed off.

'Who's Matt Fisher?' asked the policeman.

'He's a loan shark,' said Sam.

'Okay. Let me get a few things clear, who's related to whom?'

'We're just friends,' said Shirl.

'Rosie Foster is my mother and Alfred Bolton is Moira's father-in-law. My dad owed money to a loan shark named Matt Fisher. My dad died a few weeks ago and Matt Fisher has been chasing my mum for the money.'

'Which she hasn't got,' piped up Doris.

'Although she did have a win on the bingo,' said Crabbers.

'But it wasn't much,' said Shirl.

'Ten thousand,' said Crabbers.

'Five thousand,' said Sam. 'It was only five thousand.'

The policeman stroked his chin.

'So, they've both gone very quiet and you think Matt Fisher has …'

'Done away with them,' finished Crabbers.

Shirl bursts into tears.

'Right,' said the police officer. 'I think I need to take some statements.'

'Aren't you going to put out a search for them?' asked Doris.

'Not quite yet. But we will speak to Matt Fisher. Now, if you'd all like to come this way.'

*

Sam paid for the fish and chips and walked back to the car where Moira was waiting. He climbed in beside her and opened the fish and chip wrapping.

'Help yourself,' he said offering her a plastic fork.

'I ought to get back soon.'

'You've messaged Harry?'

She nodded and stabbed some chips with her fork. She was starving.

'I may have put too much salt on,' smiled Sam.

'It's not good for you,' she said.

'Yeah, Mum is always telling me that.'

He glanced at the clock on the dashboard.

'We'll have these and then I'll drop you back to your car. I need to get back to Michael. He's got some mates round. They're having a Chinese. I can't imagine what the place looks like.'

'They will find them, won't they?' said Moira suddenly. 'Harry is very worried.'

'I'm sure there's a good explanation.'

Moira nodded but she couldn't think of any explanation for why they hadn't been in touch.

The policeman had been very kind and said they would visit Matt Fisher. He seemed confident that Rosie and Alfred would make contact soon.

They ate their fish and chips in silence and then Sam started the car. The exhaust roared loudly.

Lynda Renham

'I must get that fixed,' he mumbled.

Moira sighed. The thought of facing Harry filled her with dread.

'Here we are,' said Sam.

Moira looked out of the window. They were at the garage already.

'I'll be in touch,' he said. 'Hopefully we'll hear something soon.'

'Yes,' she said softly. 'Thank you, Sam.'

She hesitated for a second and then leaned over and kissed him quickly on the cheek.

He tapped her knee and said, 'You've always got a friend here.'

She nodded and climbed from the car. She had to go home. It was time to face Harry. He must be distraught about his mum. She should be with him.

*

Harry

'That's Mum's car,' said Holly jumping up.

Harry's heart banged in his chest and he glanced out of the window to see Moira climbing from the Range Rover. Then he heard her key in the lock and then she was standing in front of him.

'What's the news Mum?' asked Holly anxiously.

Moira pulled off her coat. It was lovely and warm in the house. She could smell the lamb casserole.

'Have you eaten?' she asked.

Harry couldn't meet her eyes.

'Not much,' said Holly.

'What did the police say?' asked Harry. 'I've been trying Dad but still no reply.'

'I went to his house before I came home,' said Moira wearily. 'He's still not home. The police are going to see Matt Fisher.'

Holly began to cry.

'It's okay,' said Moira, hugging her.

'The loan shark,' said Harry. 'Holly told me. How could that Rosie woman have been so stupid?'

'We're all stupid at times Harry,' said Moira, trying to keep her voice even.

Harry avoided her eyes.

'I hate Matt Fisher,' sobbed Holly.

'I need a drink,' said Harry. 'Do you want one?'

Moira nodded.

'Why don't you have a lie down, Holly,' she suggested. 'I'll let you know as soon as we hear anything.'

Holly sniffed.

'I think I will.'

Moira waited until Holly's bedroom door had closed before following Harry into the living room.

'Is gin alright?' he asked, his back to her.

'How could you Harry?' she asked softly. 'I know I can be difficult but ...'

He turned with the drinks in his hand.

'I ...' he struggled. 'I ... I think I felt unappreciated. She made me ... I don't know,' he broke off.

Moira took the glass and downed the contents in one go.

'I need to be on my own for a while, Harry. It's a lot to think through. I'd prefer it if you slept in the spare bedroom. But please be discreet. I don't want Holly upset.'

'Moira …,' he pleaded walking towards her.

She turned and walked from the room. In the kitchen she turned off the slow cooker and looked out of the window where heavy snowflakes were now falling. What if Dad was out in the cold, stuck somewhere strange? Tears rolled unbidden down her cheeks. Sam Foster was quite right, of course. She was up her own arse most of the time. It was easier for her to be that way. It wasn't sensible to make yourself vulnerable. But he was right. She did think she was better than everyone else. Thought she knew what was best for everyone. Maybe Rosie Foster was the best thing for Dad. Moira had been wrong to interfere.

'Oh Dad, I'm so sorry,' she whispered.

She always worried what other people thought. That had been her problem. She wanted people to think good of her. That was the only reason she'd wanted to move into Dad's house. People would think how well they were doing. She laughed quietly to herself. How well they were doing? That was a laugh. They couldn't be doing any worse if they tried. Karma had well and truly bitten her in the bum. Her daughter was pregnant at seventeen and her husband was screwing a 25-year-old. What would people think of that? She let out a heavy sigh and closed her eyes. Sam had broken down her barriers and brought her down a peg or two. She wiped her tears away only to have more fall.

'I'm such an idiot,' she muttered. 'I put things before people. Oh, Dad, please be alright.'

It was her fault Harry had strayed. She knew that. If she'd given him more time and attention he wouldn't have been so flattered by another woman's attention. She laid her head against the French doors and felt the coolness against her forehead. The snow was falling heavily now and had started to settle on the ground. She then remembered that she was going to put the tree up this evening. She wiped the tears away again and made her way slowly upstairs. The living room light was off now. Harry had already gone up. She didn't think she'd get much sleep tonight, but it would be good to rest her aching head. She'd pray for Dad. Surely God would answer her.

Lynda Renham

Chapter Fifty-Seven
Sam

Sam decided he wasn't going to wait for the police to visit Matt Fisher. This was his mum after all. Michael still had his mates round. The place was a mess, but the state of the house was the last thing on Sam's mind.

'I've got to pop out,' he told Michael.

'You've only just come in,' said Michael.

'And you can stop being so cheeky, young man. I want this mess cleared up when I get back.'

Michael had pulled a face, but Sam had just ignored him. It was best not to mention about his Nan yet. Hopefully there would be nothing to tell him.

The noise from the exhaust annoyed him. He really should fix it but there never seemed to be time. He was always working. If he didn't have to pay Maureen every month he might have enough to save. His mind travelled back to Moira. What a strange thing that was. He wouldn't have considered her his type. It just goes to show. Anyway, nothing would come of it. He didn't mess with married women. She'd sort it out with her husband. If she didn't … well that was a whole other ball game. The weather was terrible. The snow was heavy now. He had to admit that it wasn't like his mum to be out in weather like this, especially not now that she had that nice new house of hers. He ought to swing by there, just to make sure. Who knows, she could be sitting all nice and cosy in her new living room. But the house was in darkness and he knew it was pointless knocking.

He parked the car outside the pool club where he'd heard Matt Fisher hung out and strode confidently through the doors. It was warm inside. Some men were playing pool while others were drinking at the bar. He ordered himself a beer and when the barman handed it to him, he asked,

'Is Matt Fisher around?'

'Matt, yeah, over there,' said the barman pointing to a pool table.

Sam nodded and glanced over at the three men playing. He guessed the burly one with the heavy gold necklace around his neck to be Matt Fisher. He took his beer and walked over.

'Fisher?' he asked.

The men looked up.

'Who's asking?' said a puny-looking bloke.

'Sam Foster.'

The burly man grinned.

'Rosie's son?' he questioned.

'That's me,' said Sam.

'You look like her,' said Matt laying down his cue.

Sam sipped his beer and said bluntly,

'Have the police been to see you yet?'

'What's your problem, mush,' snarled the puny bloke pushing his face close to Sam's. Garlic wafted up Sam's nose and he grimaced.

'At this present moment, you're my problem,' said Sam, pushing the puny bloke to one side.

'Don't mind Rick,' said Matt Fisher. ''e's got no manners. Now, I ain't seen no police but …'

Before he could finish Sam had grabbed him by the shirt and bent him over the pool table.

'My mum's gone missing and I think you know something about it,' he hissed into Matt's ear.

Rick grabbed a cue and was about to attack Sam with it when Matt yelled, 'Don't be a dick, Rick.'

Sam almost laughed at the poetry of it. If he hadn't have had the worry of his mum, he probably would have done.

'Get off 'im,' yelled Rick. But Sam wasn't letting go of Matt Fisher until he found out where his mum was.

'Hey, come on,' yelled the barman. 'That's enough.'

'Your mum's in Paris,' croaked Matt, struggling under Sam's hold.

'You what?' exclaimed Sam.

'Let me up will yer? Your mum's alright.'

Sam released his grip and yanked Matt Fisher upright.

'Blimey,' groaned Matt. 'You ain't a bit like your dad are yer? Alf and your mum are in Paris. I sold them the air tickets.'

'You sold them the air tickets?' Sam repeated.

'Yeah, dirt cheap. I offered as a joke really. Never thought they'd take me up on them. I was joking about them having a dirty weekend away, you know ...'

'No, I don't know,' said Sam frowning.

Sam felt anger rise in him. Why hadn't his mum phoned him? She could at least have sent a text. What was she thinking of, putting him through all this worry?

Rick's hand was clutching the cue, his eyes fastened on Sam.

'Anyway, I said I got air tickets for Paris going cheap if they wanted a dirty ... a break. Alf took them.'

'You've been after my mum though, for money, haven't you?'

Matt straightened his clothes and nodded to Rick.

'Put that down, you plonker, before you trip over it and do yourself an injury.'

He turned to Sam.

'Alf sorted that out, okay. Put me in me place, so to speak. Now, can I get on with me game?'

Sam cursed under his breath. What was his mother up to? He drained his glass and placed it on the pool table.

'Carry on,' he said. 'Don't let me stop you.'

With that he strolled from the pool club.

Lynda Renham

Chapter Fifty-Eight
Rosie (Two days earlier)

My heart is almost bursting from my chest. I haven't been this close to Matt Fisher since that evening he came to my flat. This is it isn't it? Face the music time. I grasp Archie's arm. Surely Matt Fisher wouldn't hurt a seventy-year-old, would he? Archie's done nothing wrong. Then again, from what I've heard of Matt Fisher, being ninety wouldn't stop him. He looks a granny basher. It wouldn't surprise me if he'd been chasing Frank when he ran into the Domino's Pizza van. So what's another body notched up on his bedpost? No, that's wrong isn't it? It's not dead people you notch up on your bed post is it? I'm a nervous wreck, that's what it is. I always talk out of my backside when I'm nervous. Not that I'm talking much to Matt Fisher. I haven't opened my mouth yet. I'll have to give him my five thousand. I can't possibly have Becky cleaning up after Archie and me. Although, I suppose, if he throws us in the Thames there won't be any clearing up to do, will there? He's grinning at us. I can smell his aftershave and I sneeze. Matt hands me a fragranced hanky which just makes me sneeze even more. My teeth chatter with the cold, or is it fear? I can't tell the difference. It's most likely fear.

'This is Matt Fisher,' I whisper to Archie through my chattering teeth.

'Just our bad luck to bump into you, isn't it?' says Archie to Matt Fisher.

Matt laughs loudly, his white teeth dazzling in the dark.

'Bee-ayve, Alf ... whoops, I mean Alfred,' says Matt loudly.

I turn to Archie.

'Do you know him?'

'Matt and I go back a fair bit don't we lad?' says Archie. 'I know his mum. She still owes me money, isn't that right Matt?'

'We sorted that,' says Matt, buttoning his overcoat. 'Do you like it?' he says nodding at the coat. 'Looking nice costs money. This coat cost me five hundred nicker. Worth it though.'

When Archie Met Rosie

'You wouldn't get me wasting five hundred quid on a coat,' retorts Archie.

Nor me, I want to say but keep my frozen blue lips together.

Puny Rick stamps his feet.

'It's fucking cold, Matt, can we get on.'

His nose is bright pink. I can see a bubble of snot bulging as he breathes. I want to offer him the fragranced hanky, but I don't.

'You've got such a potty mouth,' says Archie crossly. 'Talking like that in front of a lady.'

That's nice of Archie isn't it? I've never been called a lady before and Frank's language used to be a lot more colourful. But Frank's not here any more is he? It is freezing though, I can't disagree with that. I can't feel my fingers or my toes any more.

'Yeah, shut it, Rick,' says Matt tiredly. 'So, are you two an item?'

I feel myself flush.

'It was nice seeing you Matt,' says Archie moving past.

'He'll follow us,' I whisper.

'No he won't. I sorted it about your loan.'

'You did?' I say surprised.

'You two fancy a dirty little break in Paris?' calls Matt.

'What did you say?' asks Archie turning around.

Oh no, just as I thought we were going to get away too.

'Keep your 'air on,' says Matt holding up his hands. 'It's just I got two air tickets for Paris. The flights in a couple of hours and I can't go. They won't change them. I tried. The thing is I've got a fight on later. It's me own boxer, and he's a good little fighter too. I don't want to miss it. So I figured I'd give 'em away.'

'I'll have 'em,' says Rick.

'What are you gonna do with two tickets to Paris?'

'I don't know.'

Matt raises his eyebrows.

'It's 'ard work with this one, I tell yer.'

'Let's see them,' says Archie.

Matt takes off his black leather glove and pulls a wallet from his overcoat. He hands the tickets to Archie.

'I got 'em in exchange for a debt. If you don't 'ave 'em, I'll just throw 'em.'

'What about him?' Archie asks, nodding towards Rick.

Matt laughs.

'What's he going to do in Paris, except complain that everyone speaks a different language?'

'How much?' asks Archie.

'Twenty quid.'

'Done,' says Archie, pulling out his wallet. I watch in amazement as Matt hands over the tickets. He pats Archie on the shoulder and says,

'Don't do anything I wouldn't do.'

'That gives us a lot of scope,' Archie says before taking my arm.

We walk away from Matt Fisher and along the street. I don't mind telling you that I'm in a bit of a daze.

'Right girl,' says Archie. 'Let's get our stuff together and get to the airport. We're off to Paris.'

Me, Rosie Foster, off to Paris, just like that. Who'd have thought it?

*

I barely have time to think. Archie drops me off at the house and I throw things into a suitcase. I charge my mobile up while I'm packing and then take a quick shower. We have an hour to get to Stanstead, and even then, Archie said we'd be late but hopefully we'd catch the flight.

'Where will we stay?' I'd asked.

'That's easy. There'll be plenty of places. It'll be lovely walking along the Champs-Élysées. They'll have the Christmas lights. You're going to love it.'

I'm that excited. Paris at Christmas, it's my dream come true. I'm almost ready when Archie knocks. I remember to phone work and leave a message. I don't say I'm off to Paris, obviously. I feel guilty saying I'm sick when I'm not, but what else am I supposed to do? I'm expected back at work tomorrow, but I have to go to Paris, don't I?

'Let's go,' he says.

The taxi driver takes my case and puts it into the boot.

'Do you have everything?' asks Archie.

'I think so,' I say.

I have myself and that's what counts. Butterflies flutter in my stomach. I'm off to Paris. Just wait until I tell Doris and Shirl. I must get them something when I'm there, something typically French.

We catch our flight in the nick of time and it's only when I go to turn my phone off that I realise it is still charging back home in my little house. Sam is going to kill me.

Chapter Fifty-Nine
Rosie

I must admit to feeling I am in a whirlpool. We had a glass of French wine on the plane, to start off the holiday in style. Before I know it, we are landing at Charles de Gaulle airport, Paris. I'm sure I spend most of the journey to the B&B with my mouth open. I'm amazed to discover that Archie can speak French and he arranges a taxi and books two nights in a guest house. We drive along the Champs-Élysées in the early hours and I feel like I'm in a film. It's beautifully illuminated with Christmas lights. Everywhere is so alive and vibrant. Archie says there is a Christmas market and that we will go and see it tomorrow.

I'm really cross that I left my phone behind. I can't even phone Sam as his number is in my phone. How stupid is that? What a daft brush I am. Frank was always calling me one. Still we're only here for a few days. I doubt anyone will notice we've gone. Archie is as bad as me and didn't even bring his phone.

'Who am I going to call?' he'd asked.

'Won't your son be worried?' I'd said.

'Huh, they're too full of themselves. They won't be thinking about me.'

The taxi pulls up and we trudge our suitcases up the stairs of the guest house. Archie gets us adjoining rooms.

'Here we are,' says Archie as we stand in the hallway. 'Sleep well. I'll give you a knock in the morning at nine. We'll go to the Christmas market.'

'Thank you Archie,' I say. 'This is wonderful.'

He smiles. He's quite handsome when he smiles, is Archie.

'Sleep tight,' he says.

I close the door. I doubt I will sleep at all. I'm in Paris. Who sleeps when they're in Paris? The bedroom is small and compact. I look out of the window onto the brightly lit Champs-Élysées. A small sigh escapes me.

What would Frank think if he could see me now? So much has happened in such a short time. One minute, Matt Fisher is chasing me for money and the next he is paying for my dream to come true and all for twenty quid. I had imagined spending quite a bit of my winnings on a trip to Paris. Who'd have thought it would have been Matt Fisher who would save me money?

I lie on the bed and close my eyes and within seconds I'm asleep.

It's freezing cold in Paris too, but somehow I don't feel it. We have warm croissants and coffee for breakfast at a little café near the guest house. We sit at a small table where I can watch the other customers, and I drink up the atmosphere. There is music playing but this is drowned out by the chatter of the others in the café. The waitress asks Archie something and he replies, but I have no idea what he said. We then go to the Christmas market. It's bustling with people and we jostle our way amongst the stalls. I see so much that I want to buy. Archie insists I try a macaroon and we share a bag between us. He takes photos of me outside the guest house, sitting on the carousel and walking along the Champs-Élysées. He even takes photos of me devouring a pastry from the boulangerie. I'm going to get some croissants when I go home. Lidl sell them. I don't imagine they taste anything like the ones in Paris, but it will bring back memories. I've never been so happy. I nag Archie so much about the Eiffel Tower that eventually we leave the market and walk to it. It is more breathtaking than I even imagined. I could look at it for hours. Archie says we can go up to the top tomorrow.

Archie suggests we go back for a little nap before going to dinner. I say I couldn't possibly nap but of course, I do, because I'm that exhausted. Archie knocks for me about six and we go to a lovely restaurant.

'Here's to us,' says Archie, lifting his wine glass.

Archie had ordered a lovely rosé wine. It tastes wonderful.

'Thank you so much for bringing me,' I say.

'Don't be daft,' he smiles. 'It's been nice coming with you. It's nice having company again.'

I nod. He's quite right. It's no fun being on your own. Frank wasn't a great husband, but he was company and I miss that a lot.

'Yes, I miss the companionship,' I say. 'Although, Frank wasn't great company but having that presence, you know. It made a difference.'

'Don't bother getting a cat,' he laughs. 'They're no flipping company.'

'I love your cat,' I say.

'She loves you too. She always knows when you're coming.'

I pick at my hors d'oeuvre.

'I bet Moira will be cross when she finds out you brought your cleaner to Paris.'

'You're not just my cleaner,' he says, his expression serious. 'You're my lady friend.'

That sounds lovely doesn't it, to be someone's lady friend?

'I'm really pleased to be your lady friend,' I say shyly.

'Here's to us then,' says Archie, touching his glass against mine.

We walk back to the guest house arm in arm, stopping to do some shopping on the way. I buy a lovely candleholder for Doris and a pretty bag for Shirl. Tomorrow I'll choose something for Michael and Sam. I only hope they aren't too cross with me.

We climb the steps to the guest house and I hesitate outside my bedroom.

'Well, goodnight,' says Archie.

I lean forward and kiss him on the cheek.

'Goodnight,' I say.

'See you in the morning,' he smiles giving me a quick peck on the lips. I realise my legs are trembling. How daft is that? I close the door and lean against it. What would Moira make of that, I wonder?

I'm about to turn back the bedcovers when there is a light tap on the door. It's Archie.

'Oh,' I say, smiling.

'Can I have a word?' he asks.

'Of course,' I say opening the door wider.

He steps inside, and I wait patiently. Good heavens, he surely isn't going to make a pass at me, is he? I've no idea what I'll do if he does. The last time a man made a pass at me, I was about seventeen and the boy was drunk.

'The thing is ...' begins Archie.

'Yes,' I say.

I'm quite worried. Supposing he's regretting this whole Paris trip and is now realising he can't possibly keep me as his cleaner? I can't go through all that worry again. Becky will get right fed up with me.

'This is my Cath,' he says, pulling a photo from his pocket.

He hands it to me. It's a fairly recent photo, I imagine. She was attractive and quite elegant. The type of woman I would expect Archie to be with.

'We had a good marriage. Fifty years we were together. I miss her, of course.'

'Of course you do. She was lovely,' I say, handing back the photo.

He slides it back into his pocket and looks at me.

'The thing is life goes on doesn't it? Cath would hate me to be alone and miserable, and you're on your own now that your Frank has gone.'

I don't like to say I was alone long before Frank went.

'So, I see no reason why you and I can't be a couple.'

'Oh,' I say.

He looks closely at me.

'What do you think?'

I blush.

'I'd like that, Archie.'

He exhales.

'Good, we'll take it slowly.'

'Yes,' I agree.

'Just friends for the moment?' he says, with a wink.

Now, I really am blushing.

'Yes.'

'Right,' he says turning to the door. 'I'll leave you in peace. Night, Rosie.'

'Night, Archie.'

The door closes behind him and I stand staring at it. Finally, I wander to the window and look out at the lights of Paris. I feel a little tear drop onto my cheek. It may be a bit late but I'm finally feeling that my life is looking up. They say you're never too old, don't they?

*

Paris is everything I always imagined it would be. Our three days here is nowhere near long enough to see everything.

'We'll come again,' Archie had said.

We walk through the busy Parisian streets. Everyone is excited about Christmas and their excitement is contagious. When we get too cold we stop at one of the street-side cafés where red wine and hot chocolate are in abundance. We sit quietly and watch the street scenes. It's magical. Each time I see the Eiffel Tower I tingle with excitement. The view from the top of is breathtaking. The whole of Paris is laid out before us.

'What do you think?' asks Archie.

I'm speechless. I'd dreamed of this moment, but the reality is far better.

'It's beautiful,' I say breathlessly.

We walk under the Arc de Triomphe and towards the street café we have frequented for breakfast. We have pastries and red wine and sit enjoying the view until it becomes too cold to sit any longer.

'We'll come back in the spring,' says Archie.

I want to see Paris every season. I slide my arm through Archie's as we stroll along the river Seine. I've never been so happy. My dreams have come true. I no longer live on the Tradmore Estate and I have finally been to Paris.

Chapter Sixty
Moira and Sam

Moira opened the door and stepped back in surprise when she saw Sam.

'Oh,' she said.

'Sorry to drop by so late but I was hoping to catch you and your husband.'

'Come in,' Moira said, stepping to one side.

Sam didn't feel at all comfortable in Moira's house. It was too fancy for his liking and he didn't really want to see that idiot husband of hers either, but he had no choice.

'Harry,' called Moira.

Harry walked into the hall. He wasn't at all what Sam had been expecting. He didn't look in the least like Archie. He was tall and slim. There wasn't any muscle on him, Sam noted. He certainly didn't look the type to be screwing with a 25-year-old.

'I came to tell you that Archie and my mum are okay. They're in Paris.'

'Paris?' echoed Harry.

'Matt Fisher gave them air tickets.'

'Matt Fisher? But I thought ...'

Sam grinned.

'Yeah I thought the same thing. It seems your dad had a word with him.'

'Dad had a word with Matt Fisher?' said Moira.

'He'll get himself into trouble one day,' said Harry, his lips tightening.

'I think your dad can handle himself,' said Sam turning to the door. 'Anyway, they're safe, that's the important thing.'

'Thank you, Sam,' said Moira.

He nodded and opened the front door.

'They'll be back in a few days,' said Sam.

'I'll have a few choice words for him when he does,' said Harry. Sam ignored him and walked to his car. What a plonker, he thought.

*

Holly rushed down the stairs.

'Is that Grandad?' she asked breathlessly.

'Grandad is in Paris,' said Harry scathingly. 'He didn't even bother to tell us.'

'Probably because you never listen to him,' said Holly bitterly. 'You always talk down to him.'

'Holly,' reprimanded Moira.

'Well, it's true,' said Holly, storming back upstairs.

The bedroom door slammed behind her, and Moira sighed.

'Moira …' began Harry.

'Not now,' she said walking away.

He touched her arm.

'I felt rejected,' he said.

She turned to look at him. His face was drawn and there were dark rings under his eyes.

'Is it over?' she asked.

'Of course, I don't even understand why I started it.'

She bowed her head.

'I know I can be a bitch at times …'

'That's true,' he smiled.

'I just want the best for us,' she said feeling the tears beginning again.

'We have the best, Moira.'

She nodded.

'I know.'

He hugged her uncertainly.

'It will take time Harry.'

'Yes. Let's just think about Christmas.'

She wiped away her tears and pulled back.

'I'll make tea.'

Perhaps shedl put the tree up later, she thought.

*

'She's in Paris,' said Doris, accepting the lager from Crabbers.

'You what?' said Shirl.

'She's in Paris, with that Archie.'

Crabbers squeezed into the seat beside Shirl.

'I was sure they were at the bottom of the Thames,' he said. 'I would have taken bets on it.'

Christmas music blasted out from the pub's speakers.

'She might have said something,' said Doris. 'Here we were all worried and she's living it up in Paris.'

'I'd like to go to Paris,' said Crabbers.

Doris saw Bert enter the pub and waved.

'Over here,' she called.

'What's this about Rosie in Paris?' he asked.

'She's gone with that Archie bloke.'

'She's a sly one,' grinned Bert.

'A dark horse alright,' said Shirl.

'I hope she brings us back some French perfume,' said Doris.

'I'm relieved,' said Becky joining them. 'For a while I had these horrid visions of cleaning up after her murder.'

Doris laughed.

'Wait till we tell her the goings-on here.'

Chapter Sixty-One
Rosie

Doris clings to my arm as we step through the snow. It has been snowing for over a week now. Archie and I had our flight cancelled because it was so bad. We didn't mind though. It meant we had another day in Paris, and Paris in the snow is magical. Oh, I did have a fabulous time. Of course I had to come back to Brian's outraged face. Crabbers had mentioned to one of his market customers that I was in Paris. It just so happened she works on the meat counter at Waitrose. He wasn't to know. In fact, he was so relieved I wasn't at the bottom of the Thames that he just wanted to tell everyone. So, I couldn't have a go at him. He even gave me three bath towels and a set of flannels to apologise. He's alright is Crabbers.

'You said you were sick,' Brian had said accusingly.

'I know. It was all so sudden and ...'

'If I could swan off to Paris at our busiest time just before Christmas I'd be a happy man.'

'I'll take it unpaid,' I'd offered. After all, I could afford to. I'd been to Paris and still had four thousand pounds in the bank. How lucky is that?

My fingers sting from the cold. Even the gloves I'm wearing aren't helping. I stop and look around the cemetery.

'It should be here somewhere,' I say.

Doris strains her neck.

'That one looks new,' she says pointing.

We step through the untouched snow, feeling it crunch beneath us, until finally we reach the headstone.

'It's your Frank alright,' says Doris, bowing her head.

I look warily at the headstone. I so hope there aren't any big errors on it. It was relatively cheap. Not dirt cheap or anything. I wouldn't get Frank a dirt-cheap tombstone, but it was reasonable. To be honest with you, Frank's greyhound paid for it. Well, the back part of it. I sold it. What good is the backside of a greyhound to me?

Frank Foster
1953 - 2018
Sadly Missed

'Not a lot of words,' remarks Doris. 'Still, you don't need many do you?'

'I didn't want to say things that weren't true,' I say.

'That's right,' nods Doris.

I feel like we should stay a bit. Although it is freezing, and my cheeks are stinging something awful.

'We don't have to linger,' says Doris, as if reading my mind. 'Frank wouldn't want you to catch pneumonia.'

'Yes,' I agree. 'Thanks for coming Doris.'

'Oh, my pleasure. Well, not a pleasure, obviously. It's no pleasure seeing Frank's headstone.'

I place the flowers I had bought onto the grave and then take Doris's arm.

'Let's go. It's too cold to be in a cemetery.'

'It's too cold to be any-flipping-where except home by the fire,' shivers Doris.

I hang a Christmas bauble over the headstone and we make our way back.

'Five days before Christmas,' says Doris. 'It's going to be a white one.'

'Yes,' I say.

'Who'd have thought you'd be having Christmas in a posh house in Emerson Park. It just goes to show, you never know what's going to happen from one day to the next.'

When Archie Met Rosie

She's quite right. If someone had told me six months ago that by Christmas I would have money in the bank, gone to Paris and have a lovely man friend in my life, I'd have laughed in their face. It's funny, life, isn't it? We're only here for a short time and all most of us do is moan. We moan about the weather, about other people. In fact, we moan about everything. It's stupid really. I've always tried to count my blessings, even when I didn't have many. I've got a lot now. I'm only hoping Christmas will be okay. Archie is insistent that everyone comes to him. Well, not everyone, obviously; just me, Sam and Michael, and of course, Moira and Harry with Holly. It will be strange. But it's only one day. All the same, I'm dead nervous. Sam's met them already. It seems our little jaunt to Paris caused a real uproar. So, at least it won't be too uncomfortable on Christmas Day. I'm glad Archie suggested his place. I don't want Moira coming to mine to have a nose, although I bet she is dying to.

'What you dreaming about?' asks Doris.

'Oh nothing. You're all still coming to me on Christmas Eve, aren't you?'

'Try and keep us away,' she laughs. 'It'll be lovely. At least I won't have to hide behind the couch.'

We laugh at the memory and then hurry to the bus stop.

Chapter Sixty-Two
Sam

Christmas Day

Sam tucked his shirt into his jeans and grabbed his jacket.

'You ready Mike?' he called up the stairs.

'Not quite.'

Sam sighed and checked the time on his watch.

'I'll wait for you in the car,' he said, opening the front door.

The last person he expected to see standing on the step was Maureen.

'Oh, hello,' he said surprised. She was clutching a large carrier bag. Sam raised his eyebrows.

'I thought you were in Spain.'

'Ray is. I … I didn't go.'

Sam nodded. She looked tired, he noted. Her hair was neatly pulled back, but she wasn't wearing the usual make-up he was used to seeing on her.

'We're off to Mum's friend for Christmas,' he said.

Her eyes widened.

'Has your mum got a bloke already?'

'He's a friend really. Not exactly her bloke.'

She nodded.

'I bought Michael's presents. I thought as I was home and that ...' she trailed off.

'So, is it over with him, then?'

She nodded tearfully.

'We're around tomorrow,' he said as he heard Michael's footsteps on the stairs.

'Hello Mum,' said Michael looking at the carrier bag.

'I brought your presents.'

Michael looked at Sam.

'We're going to Nan's friend for dinner.'

'We're late too,' said Sam closing the front door. 'Why don't you bring those tomorrow? We're having dinner about one. You're welcome.'

'Thanks Sam,' she said quietly.

Michael walked to the car.

'It's for him,' said Sam. 'No other reason.'

She nodded.

He climbed into the car and started the engine.

'When are you getting the exhaust fixed?' asked Michael. 'It's embarrassing.'

Sam watched Maureen through the rear-view mirror and sighed. Life sure is full of surprises.

*

Rosie

'I wish you'd calm down,' says Archie, slicing into the turkey. I glance at the clock on the wall. It's nearly one. They should be here soon.

'Do we have everything on the table?' I ask.

I can't think clearly. It's like my brain has seized up. My stomach won't stop churning and I've been in and out of the loo more times than I'd like to count. Well, I have counted, actually. I've been about four times.

'If we've forgotten something, then it's not the end of the world,' he smiles. 'Try and calm down.'

I wish my stomach would calm down. I fumble in my bag for my Imodium. I always buy Imodium before Christmas. Don't ask me why, I'm a daft brush. I don't know why I think I'll need them at Christmas but not at any other time. Anyway, it's a good job I did. I hope it settles soon. There's nothing worse than leaving a smell in the bathroom is there, and I know how fussy Moira is with her dual flushes. I swallow two capsules and take some deep breaths.

'Have a glass of wine,' suggests Archie.

I can't do that. What would Moira think if I breathed alcohol over her as she walks into the house?

The doorbell rings and my heart jumps into my mouth. Archie strolls to the door and opens it to Sam and Michael.

'I've parked in the driveway,' Sam says. 'Is that alright?'

'Yes, of course,' says Archie, shaking Sam warmly by the hand. 'Merry Christmas.'

'Hello,' says Michael, looking at Archie curiously.

'Hello lad. I'm Archie. Merry Christmas to you.'

Michael smiles shyly and shakes Archie's hand. I pretend to look nonchalantly down the street. There's no sign of Moira. What if she decides not to come? It's the kind of the thing she would do, if you ask me.

'Merry Christmas, Mum,' says Sam, kissing me on the cheek and handing me a carrier bag.

'These are our presents. I thought they could go under the tree.'

'What a big house,' exclaims Michael.

I nudge him in the ribs. Archie laughs and takes their coats.

'Come into the living room. We've got the fire going. It's bitter out there isn't it?'

My stomach rumbles and Sam raises his eyebrows.

'I've got to go,' I say dropping the carrier bag.

Oh no, this is terrible. I can't pebble-dash the loo a few minutes before Moira arrives. I'll have to take some more Imodium. I may be bunged up for a week but surely anything is better than this.

I can hear Sam laughing. At least he's relaxed. I spray the bathroom with fresh air spray and then check my hair in the mirror. I'm far too flushed. Moira will no doubt think I've been drinking. I hurry downstairs and am about to go into the living room when the doorbell goes. For a second I freeze. Archie will come in a minute. But he doesn't. They obviously didn't hear the bell. I walk nervously to the door and open it. A man stands there laden down with prettily wrapped presents. I can barely see his face.

'Sorry we're late Dad,' he says. 'Moira's getting the rest from the car.'

'Hello,' I say.

He peeks around the presents to look at me.

'Oh, hello, sorry I thought you were Dad. I mean, I couldn't see.'

'That's okay,' I say, forcing a smile.

'I'll get Archie,' I say.

'Archie?' questions Harry.

'Rosie calls Grandad, Archie,' says Holly, hurrying in.

'Archie,' I call. 'Your son is here.'

I hear the tremble in my voice. If only I could disappear for a few hours.

'They're getting logs,' says Michael.

Of all the times to get logs.

'I'll help them,' says Harry, dropping the presents onto the hall table.

'Hello,' Holly says, smiling shyly at Michael. 'I'm Holly.'

'Hello,' says Michael, fidgeting on his feet.

It's getting cold with the front door open. I wish Moira would hurry up.

'They've got a fabulous tree,' says Michael.

'Yes, I know,' says Holly, following him into the living room.

I wait shivering by the front door for Moira to come. I feel like I'm waiting to go to my execution.

Chapter Sixty-Three
Moira

Moira looked at herself in the bedroom mirror. She was sure there were new lines around her eyes. That's what bitterness does to you, she thought. She was nervous. She had no idea what she was going to say to Rosie. She glanced around the perfectly decorated bedroom. She was so lucky. It had taken her a long time to realise it. They were fortunate to have such a lovely house. It was ridiculous of her to crave something bigger. It would only mean more work, more stress.

'We have to go soon,' Harry called.

'I'll be down in a bit.'

Harry had been over-the-top attentive the past week. He was desperate to put things right. The play had gone well but it had been bitter-sweet. Dad had missed it because the flight from Paris was cancelled, and Moira hadn't been able to face it. Harry had assured her that Steph wouldn't be there, but she still couldn't do it. Steph had handed in her notice. At least Moira hoped that was true and that Harry hadn't had her sacked. No, she felt sure he wouldn't do something like that. Her mind travelled to Sam Foster and she felt that little flutter in her stomach that thoughts of him always produced. He'd brought her down to size. She sighed and grabbed her handbag. Everything was going to be all right. Dad was fine. He hadn't been murdered by Matt Fisher as they'd at first thought. It had been such a relief. People were what counted. It had taken her a long time to realise that. It seemed strange not having Christmas Day at theirs, but Dad had wanted to do it with Rosie and it was only fair that they went. Harry was looking forward to it.

'I'm glad Dad's got a friend,' he'd said. 'It will be less of a strain on us.'

Alf had assured them that he and Rosie wouldn't be moving in together.

'We're mates,' he'd said. 'We're taking it slowly, not that we've got much time but ... anyway, it's company.'

She glanced one last time at her reflection and then left the bedroom.

*

Her heart began to race as they got closer to Alf's.

'They're here already,' exclaimed Holly on seeing the car in the driveway. Moira recognised Sam's Mini and her heart beat even faster. Harry parked the car and lifted the presents from the boot.

'I'll bring the chocolates,' said Moira, fiddling in the back seat.

She was putting it off. She knew that. She managed to spend a fair bit of time fumbling about. Harry and Holly had already gone in and she knew she had to do it sometime. Finally she locked the car and walked to the front door where she saw Rosie was waiting. Moira had no idea how long she'd been waiting but she looked frozen.

Moira hurried up the path and walked in.

Chapter Sixty-Four
Rosie

'You'll catch a cold,' Moira says, closing the door.

I step back.

'It is freezing,' I say.

My voice trembles and I could kick myself.

'I bought chocolates,' Moira says, handing over a carrier bag.

'That's kind, thank you,' I say, taking it.

Moira turns her face away and says, 'I owe you an apology. I was rude to you in Waitrose.'

'Oh, we get it all the time,' I say.

'I'm sure you don't.'

'Anyway, that's past,' I say graciously.

Moira nods.

'They're getting logs,' I say, walking into the living room. The men enter through the French doors and I let out a sigh of relief.

'Hello there,' Sam says leaning forward to kiss Moira on the cheek.

'Hello,' she smiles.

Goodness, is she blushing?

'Let's get you all a drink,' says Archie, walking to the drinks cabinet.

'Who'd have thought you'd be at my grandad's for Christmas,' laughs Holly.

'We've you to thank,' says Archie, handing Holly a bottle of cider.

'Me?' she says surprised.

'If you hadn't have got yourself in a bit of trouble that Friday night, Rosie and I would never have met, and we wouldn't all be here now, celebrating Christmas.'

'And if I hadn't gone round to Rosie's that afternoon you two still wouldn't be talking,' says Holly.

Moira bows her head and Harry puts his arm around her.

'That's all in the past,' says Archie.

'Life is a funny thing,' says Harry.

'It certainly is,' smiles Sam.

'Here's to Holly,' says Archie, lifting his glass.

'To Holly,' everyone choruses.

Michael gives Holly an admiring look and I smile. Life is funny all right. I can't disagree with that. I lift my glass and wish a silent Merry Christmas to Frank.

Printed in Great Britain
by Amazon